SPRING CAME ON FOREVER

SPRING
CAME ON FOREVER
by
Bess Streeter Aldrich

A BISON BOOK

UNIVERSITY OF NEBRASKA PRESS
LINCOLN AND LONDON

First Bison Book printing: February 1985
Most recent printing indicated by the first digit below:
3   4   5   6   7   8   9   10

Library of Congress Cataloging in Publication Data
Aldrich, Bess Streeter, 1881–1954.
   Spring came on forever.
   "A Bison book, BB904"—Spine.
   Reprint. Originally published: New York :
D. Appleton-Century, 1935.
   I. Title.
PS3501.L378S6 1985   813'.52   84-19671
ISBN 0-8032-5907-7 (pbk.)

The Author and her Publisher wish to acknowledge the
courtesy of Mrs. Vachel Lindsay and The Macmillan Company
in permitting the reprinting of lines from "The Chinese
Nightingale," from the volume entitled *The Chinese
Nightingale and Other Poems,* by Vachel Lindsay, and the use
of the line "Spring Came On Forever" as the title for this
novel.

Published by arrangement with E. P. Dutton, Inc.

SPRING CAME ON FOREVER

"Years on years I but half-remember . . .
Man is a torch, then ashes soon,
May and June, then dead December,
Dead December, then again June.
Who shall end my dream's confusion?
Life is a loom, weaving illusion. . .

One thing, I remember:
Spring came on forever,
Spring came on forever,"
Said the Chinese nightingale.

VACHEL LINDSAY

CHAPTER I

IN the telling of a story the narrator takes a bit from life as definitely and completely as one would cut out a paper doll, trimming away all of the flimsy sheet excepting the figure. A section of real life is not so detached and finished, for the causes and consequences of it reach backward and forward and across the world. For that reason no mere story can ever be complete, no family history contain a beginning or an end.

This is the story of two midwestern families and the strange way in which their paths crossed. It begins in Illinois in the year 1866, and ends in Nebraska in the present one, severed from all that went before and all that will continue beyond—a thing of incompleteness.

Matthias Meier was twenty-one in that year of 1866, tall and stalwart of form, with only a healed red furrow across his upper left arm to show for the last day's fighting of his Illinois regiment.

We find him, now, sitting on a high stool before a sloping desk in the office of his uncle. Office, it may have been called, but the word was something of a misnomer, for it was no separate room, merely the end of a dingy salesroom in connection with the foundry of which his relative was sole owner.

The whole place gave an impression of scowling blackness. Iron coffee-pots, flat-irons, long-legged frying-pans and short-handled spiders occupied several shelves; and the larger utensils, huge kettles and boilers, stood on the floor in disarray, with plowshares shouldering them, as well as rough kegs containing nails of various sizes. At the opposite side of the long room, through an opening, one could see into the blacksmith shop with its anvil and multitudinous horseshoes hanging about on spikes as though this were the luckiest place in all Illinois. Iron was everywhere. Iron was king. One felt there was no other metal or substance in the world.

Matthias, now, was going over an old ledger in which accounts had been kept for a dozen years, and not very accurately either, he was deciding. A master-hand at the molding, his uncle was less punctilious about records of purchases and sales than his more mathematical-minded nephew.

Late morning sunshine filtering through a spattered and cobwebby window fell across the yellow pages of the book.

It was March, and apparently it was going to be an advanced one. The maples were feeling the push of the sap against the dark of their bodies. The hickory and oaks of the virgin timber-land not far away were vaguely responding to the stir of life. In the pulpiness of the bog the trailing arbutus would soon be showing its mauve-colored face,—on the hillside a thousand lavender crocuses spring forth to the call of the sun.

If Matthias Meier, too, vaguely felt the call and the push of the springtime, he was quite unaware of it, and merely checked and figured in the thumb-blackened and well-worn pages of the yellow book.

Up to this time, the room had been quiet save for the bumbling of a single advance guard of bottle-green flies and the sound of some one cutting timber far away. But into the stillness now came the creaking sound of wheels in the yard, the pull of horses' feet from the stickiness of mud and the lusty "whoa" of an unseen driver.

Matthias uncoiled his long legs from their crowded posture under the high table and swung himself off the stool. He even walked over to the opened door, although it went through his mind at the time that it was rather an undignified procedure to hurry out as though customers were so few and far between that they needed a committee of welcome.

A large and sandy-bearded man was swinging himself over the lumber-wagon's wheel preparatory to entering. But it was not at the man Matthias looked. For who, indeed, would look elsewhere with such a flower-like face before one as that of the girl in the green silk bonnet? Her full lips were rosy pink, and in their velvet blueness her wide eyes were like cornflowers. The braid of her soft hair, wound round her head and showing just at the edge of the bonnet, was the color of cornsilk before the summer sun has seared it.

Not that Matthias had time or inclination for any poetic rhapsodies. He merely took in the composite whole with a sensing of the girl's dainty perfection, and the fleeting thought that here was a little Dresden shepherdess.

The girl, in turn, may have been not unpleased at the appearance of the young foundryman, for Matthias was strong-featured and very good to look upon. But so intent was he just now upon the loveliness of the girl that he found himself staring a little stupidly at the man coming toward him.

"Good-morning to you, sir."

"Guten morgen."

When he heard the German tongue, Matthias, too, turned to the language of his ancestors for, although English schooled, he could speak it readily. So in the German he asked politely: "What can I do for you?"

"I'm Wilhelm Stoltz," the man answered much more loudly than the short distance between the two demanded. "I want to look at the large kettles."

"Certainly. I'll be glad to show you." Matthias hesitated, and looked toward the pretty occupant of the wagon sitting rather like a little queen on her high and homely throne. "Perhaps the young lady would like to come and see them, too."

She smiled. "I can give help, Father,"—this, too, in the German tongue,—and began gathering her voluminous skirts in a little mittened hand.

"Nein," the father said brusquely. "It does not take two."

Matthias winced at the domineering tone and felt an embarrassment for the girl who in spite of her youth was apparently no child. So it was with relief and perhaps something more which he had not then analyzed that he heard the man call back over a huge shoulder: "Come, then, if you must." But even so, the father stomped his way on down a path toward the first of the pits, leaving the girl to climb over the high wheel as best she might.

At once Matthias sprang to the wagon and gave her his hand. So daintily small was she that a heady feeling of the strength of his masculinity surged over him as he assisted her to alight in a billowing of skirts.

"It is a nice day," he said a bit inanely in the German.

She nodded gayly: "Meadow larks are singing, and I smell spring."

Quite true. He noticed it for the first time. Meadowlarks *were* singing. You *could* smell spring.

He walked behind her into the dingy room, noting the pretty way she carried her shoulders and held her head. A patrician-looking little thing, not solid and big-boned like so many of the German girls thereabout.

Inside, the two customers moved among the pots and kettles, the nails and plowshares, the man stomping about noisily as though he would tell the business world that no one could pull wool over his eyes, the girl daintily holding back the dark cloth of her skirts and the wide fringe of her flowing shawl.

Each time the man asked the prices in the German tongue and was answered in kind by Matthias, he blustered: "Too much," or "The price . . . it is crazy," until Matthias heartily disliked him, so that if it had not been for the girl he would no doubt have lost a sale by some ill-advised retort.

He could read in the girl's heightened color her embarrassment, and so did his best to make her feel at ease. Once while the blustering parent was squeaking in his cowhide boots at the end of the long room, Matthias pointed out to her a special kettle. "This one I made

5

myself," he said to her very low. "Mostly my uncle does the kettle molding."

The kettle was huge and faultless in its rounded symmetry. Matthias had been painstaking to make the wooden pattern absolutely right,—the inside mold called the core and the outside one called the jacket,—had poured molten metal carefully between them and covered the whole thoroughly with sand to keep every particle of air from it while it cooled.

"It is perfect." She glanced up shyly.

Vollkommen, was it? Matthias, looking down on her daintiness, thought she, too, was perfect. "I wish then, that this should be the one you choose. A perfect kettle for . . ." He wanted to say "a perfect little lady," but that would have been too bold, so he finished "for you." But, after all, he knew the words were synonymous.

She looked up again through long lashes. But this time a little twinkle invaded the blueness that lay behind them and a smile just faintly curled at the edge of her lips: "Do not, then, say to him that this is the one to buy," she suggested demurely.

And Matthias, sharing her little secret of filial disloyalty, grinned sympathetically and said: "That I will not."

"How much is this one? . . . and this? . . . and this?" Wilhelm Stoltz was asking.

And then Matthias Meier did a foolish and unaccountable thing. He priced the kettle which was of his own molding at a lower figure than his uncle had put upon it.

Stoltz looked them all over again, craftily, suspiciously,

thumping their sides for the answering sound of the metal, and then said suddenly and loudly, as though Matthias might discover his mistake: "This one I take."

Matthias looked quickly at the girl and she gave him the ghost of a swiftly mischievous and understanding smile, so that he felt the same headiness of spirit and body which he had experienced before. For with no words she was saying: "I am glad it is your kettle." And Matthias was saying: "I made it for you before I had ever seen you." The messages were as plain as spoken language. No one knows how it can be transmitted,—this Esperanto of Youth. It just is so.

Wilhelm Stoltz took out a leather pouch, counted out the money into the palm of Matthias' hand, lifted the huge iron kettle as though he must get away with his bargain before any attempt to rectify a possible mistake had been made, and said loudly: "Come now, Amalia, we must go." He pronounced it A-moll-ea in the German way.

Coughing and wheezing and blustering, he stalked ahead of the two young people out to the wagon. And Matthias, heady and bold, was saying: "Your name, then, is Amalia?" He, too, pronounced it Amollea, letting his voice linger over the liquid syllables.

"Yes."

"It's . . . like . . . like a bit of music."

And when she smiled up at that, he asked quickly while there was time: "Where do you live?"

"Over the Plum Creek road way . . . on the far side of the Big Woods. But . . ."

But what, Amalia? Say it now before you have taken

7

*away with you that which you should not accept. Or
have left behind you that which you should not give.*

But Amalia did not say it. And when Matthias turned
back into the dullness of the room magic gifts had been
exchanged.

And so—such is life—had Wilhelm Stoltz driven up to
Peter McClure's hardware store, or sent to Chicago, or
even to Springfield for an iron kettle, or, for that matter,
had Amalia but finished her sentence, the history of future
lives and of a state might have been different. Some call
it Providence, others Fate. But, Providence or Fate,
"life is a loom weaving illusion."

As it was, Matthias stood looking a little bewildered
now at the remaining kettles and the plowshares and the
spiders, as ugly as ever, but somehow different. How
queer that into so gloomy a place should have come something so shining-winged! He set himself again to the task
of the book-work and, although the same sand-colored
pages of a half-hour before confronted him, they were
now strangely illustrated with shadowy half-pictures of
blue eyes and rosy lips and hair the color of cornsilks
before the summer sun has seared it.

After a time his uncle came in, a quick-moving little
man with a bushy graying beard. "Any one here?"

"The Stoltzes . . . a man and daughter." Matthias
realized that he was making the simple statement with a
certain degree of consciousness.

"Hm! Wilhelm Stoltz, that would be! Up the Plum
Creek way . . . one of the several Lutheran families
scattered about."

Even now "up Plum Creek way," Amalia and her

father in the high wagon were lumbering along toward their farm which was the first one just out of the Big Woods on the timber road.

The journey had taken much of the afternoon, for it lay over prairie and creek-beds, through muddy roads and timber-land, and the horses which they drove were heavy brood mares, their legs large and clumsy and shaggy with hair.

The two said little as they rode. Sometimes the father made a gruff comment on the stickiness of the mud, the amount of the last rainfall, or the slowness of the horses. Always it pertained to the material world and especially that part of it which lay close at hand. And always when he spoke Amalia agreed with him. For adverse opinions from his daughter or any other human were not welcomed. So, riding beside the bulky form of her father, Amalia lived in her own world, not always the material one and most definitely not that part of it which was close at hand.

Once she volunteered: "The young man . . . he was pleasant."

Her father grunted and said gruffly: "You will do well not to let your thoughts linger on strange young men." Immediately after which he turned toward her so abruptly that she jumped from the sheer fright that, having done this very thing, her thoughts were betraying her.

"You are not doing so?"

"*Nein,*" Amalia said demurely.

But thoughts are acrobats, agile and quite often untrustworthy. So now, with impish disregard of the command, they hopped about quite easily. They asked Amalia innocently why the nice young man wanted to know where she lived. They suggested with subtle art the possibility that he would try to find out. And then when the gruff person at her side questioned their activities they urged her quickly to answer *"Nein."*

It was only in the late afternoon when the heavy horses turned into the barnyard of the Stoltz farm, that the exigency of a quick change of dress, the gathering of the eggs, and the planning of the supper brought all the vagrant thoughts into subjection and made them subservient to matters more practical, that Amalia ceased dwelling on the day's experience.

The Stoltz farm-house was modest but as neat and shining as white paint and green blinds could make it. There were no pigs or chickens boldly running about as there were at many of the neighbors'. Pigs were in their pens and chickens in their yards, both conditions of which were made possible by fences formed of small hickory posts for the pigs and of tall willow saplings set close together for the chickens. That the fence of the chicken yard was now putting forth faint green shoots did not detract from its utility. On a sloping cellar door, scrubbed like a bake-board, sat the milk crocks sweetening in the sunshine. Currant bushes and gooseberry bushes nearby, looking ready to burst their tightly closed buds, held countless freshly washed dish-towels. Lilac bushes which were beginning to feel the stir of sap were near the front door, and a rose vine, brown yet from the winter's sleep, trailed over the doorway.

Amalia coming into the kitchen door now, sighed that there were to be changes so soon. Inside the house, thinking of those changes, she looked about her as with the eye of a stranger. She saw the shining blackness of the cook-stove (the neighbor Kratzes still cooked on an open fire), the scrubbed table with its checkered cloth, the tin brush-and-comb holder on the wall with the mirror above, the clean wooden pail of water with its gourd dipper on the shelf, the rag rugs—Oh, it was a pleasant house. The cellar still held many *schinken* from the butchering, stone jars of *äpfel-butter* and *pflaumen-butter*. No old housewife—not even Mrs. Kratz or Mrs. Rhodenbach—had put by more food last fall than she.

There was soon supper. She and her father and her brother Fritz, fifteen years old, sat down together to the *met-wurst* and the *kartoffel pfannkuchen*. They were Fritz's favorites,—those pork-sausages and potato-pancakes.

Wilhelm Stoltz spoke very little while attending to the primary object of eating. When he did it was about the stock, the shoeing of a horse, and the assignment of Fritz's work for the morrow. The purchase of the iron kettle, too, came in for some explanation to Fritz,—the bargain he had made and the fact that the young man must have made a mistake in the price.

This set all the little acrobatic thoughts somersaulting again in Amalia's pretty head. And, later, if they mischievously put on their tumbling act several times during the ensuing week, who was there to say the performance in that year of 1866 could not be transmitted through Youth's own particular short waves down through the damp, dark timber road and across the prairie?

Spring Came On Forever

For on Sunday, Matthias Meier, with clean-shaven face and in his best suit, mounted his uncle's saddle-horse, Trixie, and turned her head toward Plum Creek and the Big Woods.

CHAPTER II

TO Matthias Meier the ride to the Stoltz farm that Sunday was a long one, but pleasant. The road lay through the straggling town, over the river bridge under which the dark waters of the recently melted snows foamed and charged in wrath at the sturdiness of the timbers, on across the level lands where mud and matted grasses clutched but could not hold Trixie's flying hoofs, and then into the darkness of the Big Woods where it wound sinuously among the maples and oaks and hazelnut underbrush, a leaf-soaked and twig-covered track just wide enough for a single wagon, so that one must turn into the spaces between stumps when meeting another.

As he rode, Matthias tried to analyze what peculiar force in his nature had summoned him on this unbidden call,—what emotional upheaval had urged him to plan this trip all week. He was not accustomed to follow up all his uncle's customers, he admitted, and grinned to himself at the thought.

For the first half of the trip through river bottoms, creek-beds, and on open trails, he rode enthusiastically toward his destination. About the third quarter, on more distant meadow land, he grew a bit apprehensive over his impulsive journey. In the last quarter through the Big Woods, his fervor collapsed so perceptibly that he called himself all kinds of a fool for coming. But it was noticeable that he held doggedly to his way.

At a weather-beaten cabin in a clearing he inquired of a young boy how far it was to the Stoltz farm and was told he was nearly there, that he would find it lying just beyond the third bend of the road and that he would know it from the red barn standing where the timber began to thin for the open land. He thanked the voluble informer and rode on slowly, entirely apprehensive now because of the bold thing he was doing.

The woods were thinning,—the maples and the oaks and the walnuts were not quite so close together,—not quite so thick now, the bare hazel-brush and the sumac. He rounded a clump of undergrowth that tangled with a thicket of wild plum trees, and there in a clearing not twenty feet away was the girl herself. Evidently she had heard the sound of Trixie's padding hoofs for she stood facing the trail, her hand at her throat in an attitude of startled expectancy. To-day she was bareheaded, and the sun shining into the clearing turned the braided coronet of her light yellow hair into a pale golden wreath.

She came forward hesitatingly when Matthias slipped off his horse.

"*Guten nach mittag,*" she said shyly,—and then by way of explaining her presence added, as always, in the German: "I was searching for signs of the first blue-bells."

Bridle-rein over his arm and hat off, Matthias approached and held out his hand.

Even while she put her own little hard hand into it, she flushed and said: "You should not be here."

"Why?" Now that he was here and safely over breaking the ice of the meeting, he felt no fear, but a heady boldness instead.

She raised her eyes to his slowly, and Matthias' heart beat quickly at seeing again the deep blueness of them. "Because . . . I should have told you when you asked where I lived . . . but, of course, I could not know by the asking you meant to come."

Then why were you down in the timber road, watching, Amalia?

Her hand still held in his, Matthias asked: "What is it you meant to have told me . . . Amalia?"

She dropped her eyes away from Matthias' searching ones.

"That I am betrothed." And with that Amalia had completed the unfinished sentence.

"You are betrothed?" . . . he repeated slowly. "I . . . I had not thought of that. I have thought of many things . . . but never that. All week I thought only of you . . . and that I would come to-day."

"I, too, shall be truthful now. Something . . . also . . . some queer thing," she spoke shyly in spite of her honesty, "made me wonder if you might."

"If you are . . . as you say, betrothed, . . who . . . who is he?"

"An old friend of my father's. Oh, not old . . ." she added apologetically, "at least not as old as my father. He is a good man. My father and my brother Fritz are very fond of him. My mother is not living."

"I'm sorry . . . perhaps if your mother . . ."

"I should not be here talking to you," she said, when he seemed not intending to finish his thought. "I don't know why I came. It is not right. I have been promised since I was sixteen. I shall be eighteen soon."

15

But the hand of Amalia which had been promised for nearly two years still lay trembling in the hand of Matthias Meier. As though just now discovering that member's perfidy, she withdrew it suddenly.

"Where is he now?" Matthias asked quietly.

"Gone with the men to the Nebraska Territory to find suitable holdings for some of our church people. We are to move as soon as they return for us. It is said that sometime before many years it may be a state, too, even as Illinois."

"Yes, I suppose so." He felt definitely disappointed, vaguely sad that this lovely girl of whom he had thought all week was betrothed. A door that had so recently opened a bit seemed suddenly shut in his face.

"You have come a long way. Perhaps you would like to sit down awhile . . ." she smiled, "beside your kettle."

And almost for the first time Matthias gave heed to the fact that the kettle which he had fashioned with such meticulous care hung on three hickory stakes in the clearing with a mound of ashes underneath.

"Already you have used it?"

"Yes . . . we made the soap, using all of our grease from the butchering so we will have a plentiful supply for the long journey and a whole year after."

But the words recalled this disquieting thing he had heard of her betrothal and going away, and he frowned as he seated himself beside her on a log near the kettle.

"But this man . . . you do not love him?" It was as much a statement as a question. She was a mere child and Matthias felt very old.

Amalia pondered. "I respect him . . . and my father says that is the same thing."

"I don't agree with him," Matthias contended boldly, and in the impulsiveness of youth stood up. "Where is your father? I would like to see him."

But Amalia, alarmed, was saying: "Do not go to the house to see him, I beg of you. I am sorry not to be more hospitable. You saw how domineering he was." *Herrscht* was the word she used. "He should not know you are here. He would only anger and hurt you. Always after Sunday dinner he sleeps. Indeed . . ." and the gay little smile which had so captivated Matthias was there again for a flashing moment; "he begins it in the church service."

Matthias laughed at that and sat down again beside her. "What causes you to think of going to that troubled territory?"

"It is no longer troubled. The Pawnees have long been quieted, and my father thinks all is well now to settle there. We are of the Lutheran faith and here our farms are scattered. My father says that by moving there and keeping together we can retain our customs and our language and our church relations."

"But why . . . ?" Matthias wanted to know. "What advantage is there in the people of one church being so close? I can see how the Pilgrims of England—persecuted as they were— But you're not."

"My father says none but the followers of Luther are right, and it is not well to mingle so much with others. Already two of the young people have married out of the church."

If Matthias held his own opinion on the iniquitous depths of that sin, he did not say so. Indeed, when she was speaking so earnestly he found himself far more interested in watching her long lashes sweep a soft cheek.

"Our farm is already sold to the English Dunbar family. All things are as near ready to go as is possible . . . the wagons are kept always in repair—and the harnesses. Already many barrels are packed. When the men arrive, all the families need is a short time for the last of the baking and the loading of the wagons, and the colony can start. My father says it is like the German army, each knowing his part and obeying orders instantly."

For some time sitting there on the sunken log in the clearing the girl told of the plans for the coming journey. Matthias, listening and commenting, was disturbed at his own disturbance over the moving. Once he ventured again: "This man . . . if you do not love him . . . ?"

She glanced away. "I am promised," she said simply.

Very soon, in spite of nature's heralding of the spring, it grew too cool, and when the sun dipped behind the top of the timber, the chilliness of the air made the girl suddenly shiver.

"You must go in," Matthias was all solicitude, but found himself hinting broadly: "You do not wish me to go?"

"*Nein.* It would be too hard to explain to my father. He could not understand that you were—" she put out her hand, "a new friend."

At that, Matthias forgot the coming journey and the faith of Martin Luther, the domineering father and the affianced who was far off beyond the Big Muddy.

"Meet me here again next Sunday afternoon, Amalia. You'll come? It couldn't be otherwise."

When she hesitated, he said, to test her: "Or I shall come boldly to the house to call on my new friend."

"I'll come," she turned away, anxious and hurried now that she had been here such a long time. "But it will be wrong," she called over her shoulder.

"And beautiful," Matthias grinned back at her impudently so that she, too, was smiling a bit mischievously when she went away.

CHAPTER III

ALL week Amalia went about her housework. She cooked and cleaned and scrubbed in her energetic and immaculate way. Everything was as it had been,—save one. And all week Matthias sold his uncle's iron wares, kept the books, and occasionally shod a horse at the blacksmith end of the shop. And everything was as it had been,—save one.

Sunday was milder. The Big Woods gave forth the pungent odor of bursting buds and warming leaf-mold. At the creek-bed fuzzy pussies scratched insistently inside the branches of the willows. Wild gray geese flew honking across the timber-land and disappeared in the distant north. Swallows darted high in their nuptial flight and a meadow-lark sat on a stake-and-rider fence and sang the prairie's love song to the spring.

Amalia had been in the clearing only a short time when Matthias came riding through the damp dark timber road and into the open. At the sight of the gallant figure that had scarce been out of her mind all week, she stopped, frightened at the import of the moment, her hand at her throat as though she must stifle the call of her heart to him.

With no word Matthias dismounted, threw Trixie's bridle-reins over a scrub oak and with open arms walked toward the girl.

With no word Amalia, trembling, waited for him to

come. It was not until his arms closed around her and he had kissed her—and even for a long moment afterward —that a word was spoken.

"I have thought of you every moment." His voice shook with emotion.

"And I of you."

"You must break your betrothal, Amalia."

"At this moment it is broken, Matthias."

"This . . ." said Matthias after a time, "is what love is."

"Yes," said Amalia, "I know now. All week I have known."

"And when the homesteaders go you will stay with me? My uncle is old. In time I shall be able to buy the foundry from him. It is not my choice of businesses. I have been restless in it, but with you to be there with me, I shall settle down and like it better."

"I will stay, Matthias. I fear for the trouble it will make, but I will stay."

"And you do not think it wicked, then, to marry outside the church?" he teased her. "Do I seem now such a heathen . . . such a monster?" But when he saw how troubled it made her, he drew her to him again with comforting words, calling her his *kleine taube*,—"little dove" in the English.

The afternoon slipped away as they talked of this new-old thing that had come to them.

"Spring! It seems that this spring belongs just to us, and to no other," Amalia said once.

"But they will keep coming, little dove. Think of it. They will *all* be ours. All our lives we'll live them over and over together . . . this same feel in the air . . . the odors of the woods . . . the wild geese honking . . ."

"Even when we grow very old . . ."

Matthias laughed at that. How could youth grow old? "I shall hold you close then, just as I do now, and say: 'It's spring again, Amalia! They keep coming.'"

"And I shall say: 'They will go on . . . forever . . . even though we grow old . . . and after.'"

But there were other things besides these sentimental generalities to discuss, so that they must put an end to their first rapturous moments, sit down on the log and speak of the seriousness of the future. Matthias would have gone immediately to the house but Amalia would not hear of it. "Not to-day—" she begged him. "It is so beautiful. For when that time comes, we shall have anger and harsh words. No, Matthias, give me my perfect day."

And because she would have it so, he did not go in to confront her father, but left her there in the clearing until he should come again.

On the next Sunday there came a dash of warm rain as he rode into the clearing, and at once he saw her in the doorway of the sheep-shelter, a hooded gossamer about her shoulders.

He had brought her a gift,—a little work-box covered with shells,—angel-wings and moon shells, Roman snails, and other fragile fan-like shells of a sea they had never seen. On the under side of the cover a mirror fitted into the blue silk lining and in the various compartments were a needle-ball and a pin-cushion and a tiny silver thimble.

Amalia, to whom gifts were rare, was quite beside herself with joy at the daintiness of the treasure. Almost were the strange queer shells symbolic to her of things to come,—unknown journeys with Matthias to far-off seas, hearing the sound of wind in whipping sails and the call of the gulls on the sand.

But when Matthias would have gone in to see her father, she put him off again. She had meant to break the news, she told him, but always when she was about to speak, her courage had failed her. If he would give her but another week, she would prepare him for the announcement which would so anger him. Of one thing she was certain, it must come first from her own lips.

But on the following Sunday when he arrived there was no question about Matthias interviewing the father this time, for Wilhelm Stoltz was away,—gone to one of the church friend's home many miles up the river. It gave Amalia a delicious sense of freedom so that she was as gay as a child.

She had a wonderful piece of news for him,—she had used the thimble and one of the needles. Already she had started a quilt,—the Tree of Life pattern,—*Baum des Lebens*. Even now two finished blocks were in the shell box.

"Ever since I was a tiny girl I have sewed," she said to him. "It comes very easy to me. Many times I have made things for my hope chest"—*hoffnung kiste*, she called it—"knowing I must some day wed but not knowing who the man would be. When I knew it was but my father's friend Herman . . ."

She sighed, so that Matthias' arms went around her

23

again and he drew her close. "But it will be no Herman now . . ." (*kleine taube*) . . . "little dove."

"No . . . never. And this is so different . . . to think of you as I sew."

But even while she clung to him she told him this: "I wake in the night and think of this which I am doing contrary to my father's wishes. I feel then that I am wicked . . . but when morning comes I know that it is not wicked at all . . . just happiness and right."

And when Matthias said nothing could come between them now, she confessed: "Of that I am sure . . . and yet I am sad to part from my young brother Fritz. That is my greatest sorrow. As for leaving our good people . . . they will all be angry and hurt . . ."

But Matthias turned that away with lover-like speed. "When they know how much we love each, other . . . they will see that it could not be otherwise." Of such are the simple rules of youth.

"But my father has so often said only woe comes to those who marry outside the church."

"Love . . . our kind of love . . . is greater than the teachings of a single church."

And now that the afternoon was waning she was anxious and alert about her father's return.

"What was that, Matthias?" she would say, startled.

"Nothing . . . some little wild thing . . . a chipmunk or a squirrel."

And because of her constant watchfulness on this Sunday, Matthias was firm. "You shall cease your worries," calling her *liebes kind*. "It is not good to fear so. It shall not go on longer. Next Sunday I shall tell him, and we will face the consequences. If he is too angry, I shall take you home with me on Trixie with no baggage. My aunt will take you in and we shall be married at once."

He kissed her again and again, held her close to him, could scarcely bear to leave her. Even when he had mounted Trixie and was riding into the timber road he turned back for the last sight of her.

She stood just in front of an alder thicket, and as he looked, she raised her hand high in farewell.

He carried that picture with him all the way home: Amalia, a little blue and pink and golden figure against the green of the new leaves, as though Spring herself had just stepped out of the alder thicket. His *kleine taube,*— little dove!

CHAPTER IV

THE week dragged for Matthias,—seven days that were weighted down with the iron of horseshoes and kettles, plowshares and skillets. The first part of it was all sunshine and mild showers, but on Thursday night a storm broke. The rains came in torrents. All day Friday they lashed and tore at the woods and the prairies. All night and all day Saturday and all that night they beat in a fierce onslaught. A part of the mill-dam went out and a weakened span of the river bridge could not stand the pounding of the flood waters. On Sunday morning the water was roaring and lashing through all the creek-beds and then spreading less turbulently over the valley, inundating all that which had been pasture lands.

Matthias made every attempt to make the trip to Amalia. All day he worked, hoping to find some means whereby he could get through. Many times he rode back and forth seeking some more narrow place where Trixie could make the crossing. But always it was too wide or too turbulent. He tried getting her into a flat boat but she reared and kicked and was completely beside herself with fear. He knew that even if he had been able to manage a boat through the roaring waters for himself the distance for walking was so great that it would have taken into the night to get there.

When he gave up the attempt, he stood for a long time on the bank as the water swept by. In a mental rage he watched a pigeon fly straight for the Big Woods community. How impotent was man. Only the birds could lift wings and soar high over the flood waters. Amalia was waiting for him over there but he was helpless in the face of nature. A winged thing could fly to its mate. Only man and the beasts must cling to the earth and crawl.

But on the next Sunday he could get through. The river was still high and the creek-beds running full, but man's ingenuity had made the river passable with a temporarily trussed-up bridge span.

He took a lantern with him for he knew he might be well into the night getting back. This was the day he was to confront Amalia's father, possibly the day he was to bring her home with him. He had a feeling that there would be a scene, ending, no doubt, in his taking Amalia away without baggage. If it came to that, he was prepared to do so.

Two weeks not to have seen her! The time had been interminable. But he was on his way at last even though the going was formidable. Sometimes Trixie sank in mud so deep she nearly floundered. Sometimes he had to dismount to clear fallen branches away from the wet timber road. Then he would mount and ride on with the air of a conqueror glorying in this journey which was to end by his claiming that which was his own,—the girl who had been his from the moment he first saw her. Occasionally he felt a bit of the winner's sympathy for his fallen adversary. But to have pledged a little sixteen-year-old girl to a mere family friend was unthinkable. Yes, if there was to be a scene, let it come to-day.

These terse thoughts went through his mind like so many pigeons going over, homing always to Amalia. He tied his horse in the dripping woods. This was the end of secretiveness,—on that he was determined.

She was not in the clearing. That would be on account of the dampness. He strode over to the sheep-shed. She might be there hiding mischievously from him. But she was not at that trysting place either. Might she be ill?

With that disquieting thought he started walking over toward the road that led to the house. Suddenly he stopped short. There was no kettle hanging there in the clearing,—only the tipped-over tripod of hickory sticks and the sodden black ashes of the last fire. Something seized him,—a premonition of impending disaster, so that he started on a lope toward the home buildings. A tow-headed young boy, the same who had directed him on his first visit, was coming toward him also with some haste. They met almost at the edge of the timber where the plowed land began.

"You didn't come last Sunday," the boy said in English. "I about give you up to-day, too . . . was just comin' to the clearin' once more. She said to give you this."

And he thrust into Matthias' hands a note directed in the precise and shaded letters of the German script.

As Matthias took the letter and tore hastily into it, the boy stepped away and began pulling bits of bark from the shaggy coat of a soft maple.

Even before he had read a word, Matthias knew it contained nothing but disaster. For a few moments, then,

28

he stood looking at the neat script, frozen to immobility, too fearful of the contents to read.

To speak the language was easy enough,—he had heard it on all sides from boyhood. But the reading was more difficult for he had been to English schools, even to the Princeville Academy for a short time, and the writing of the language had been confined to early copy-book work. So it seemed that he must translate into English as he read.

In his agitation some peculiar instinctive knowledge of what had happened helped him to make the translation. By a labored reading, skipping some of the phrases, he got the gist of it:

> This is news . . . convey to you . . . wagons of church people ready ˙now . . . make long journey . . . new land. Men did not return . . . sent word by letter . . . meet them Nebraska City, Nebraska Territory. There they await us . . . show way to new lands. It is there in Nebraska City I marry.

And something more at the last pertaining to God and forgiveness for which Matthias at that moment was neither interested nor caring.

The words were all swimming together and the earth was falling away from his feet. He felt giddily ill. The boy who had been watching him covertly came up importantly then and Matthias saw him as through a haze. "She said she wanted I should get this one to you, too."

The second note was neither precise nor neat. It was ink-blurred, hurriedly folded, almost it might have been tear stained. In a fever of anxiety to release himself from

the shock of the stunning news of the first letter he tried
to read it quickly.

In his haste the translation seemed to be:

> Matthias, my cruel note under command my father
> was written. This one I send after. The wishes of my
> father . . . can no longer hold out. Many times my-
> self I ask why we met when nothing could be. I better
> could have gone on not knowing you,—indeed, I had
> not been too unhappy.

One sentence stood out with grim sardonic insistence—
"One must not marry outside the church."

Near the last there was a sentence over which he
labored to get just what she meant: *Manchmal sage Ich
mir vielleicht ist es besser unsre liebe zu gedenken als es
war im frühyahr.* And when he got it, he knew it was:
"Sometimes I tell myself perhaps it is better to remember
our love as it was in the springtime."

There was something, too, about the quilt blocks: "Unless I can be with you again, I shall never finish. The
pieces will lie in my box. I think my heart lies there too."

Matthias looked up through the wavering tree trunks.
Dimly he saw the boy walking away. He called to him
and gave him a small coin. "Thanks for coming. What
day . . ." his throat was so dry the words seemed to
crackle ". . . did they go?"

"Two weeks come next Wednesday."

The Wednesday after the Sunday in which he had left
her standing so lovely there, in the clearing. Involun-
tarily he turned his eyes toward the alder thicket not far
distant. For a moment he could see her as plainly as

though she were there in reality. Then the picture grew dim, and nothing remained but the green dripping boughs of the alders.

Mechanically he turned toward Trixie, stumbling blindly into the protruding roots of a tree stump. When he reached the mare he did not mount her but walked along with the bridle over his arm, taking the right trail only because Trixie led him into it. Occasionally she touched his shoulder with her cold soft nose.

The pungent odor of the loosened moist leaves under them came up to him with every step. A meadow-lark sang its liquid notes at the edge of the clearing. Gone. Amalia was gone,—into the great unsettled west,—to be married there. It was a nightmare from which he would soon waken. No, it was true,—the reality after a short sweet dream.

Shaken to the depths, his thoughts tumbled about uncertainly in a whirling world. One emotion after another went flooding through him as the creek waters had flooded the lowlands. A sickening sense of loss and disappointment. Astonishment,—he had never dreamed of any other turn of events than that the seekers for land would first return home as Amalia had said. Self-remorse that he had been so slow. Self-chastisement that he had not forced some means of crossing the river. And then violent anger at man's feeble efficiencies,—at a God who had sent the water to overflow, at the tyranny of the father, at the narrowness of the church, at the weakness of the girl.

His body seemed drained of blood so there was no strength left in him, and he threw himself down on a wet and matted bed of oak leaves where they had turned to brown pulp.

Over and over in his mind he relived the circumstances of their meeting: the love that seemed to spring between them from that very first day, the trysts in the woods, the softness of her lips and the feel of her body in his arms. His *kleine taube*, little dove.

All these weeks. And now he would not hold her in his arms in another week, nor in another month, nor a year, nor a decade, nor *ever*. Never! It rang in his mind like the brassy sound of a jangling bell. There was hollowness in the spring, mockery in the song of the meadow-lark. Life was empty, drained of its reason for being. He threw an arm across his eyes and turning his face down to the sodden earth, shed wild and angry tears.

For a long time he lay there in the midst of the fallen world in which disappointment and disillusion were the only factors. What matter now that the meadow-lark trilled the prairie's love song to the spring? Of what portent that the sun shone? That the sweet odors of the waxy white May flowers near by were heavy on the air? These were not of his man's mind. Over and over he lived the imaginary scenes of the journey upon which Amalia was being taken,—saw the covered wagons pulled through the stickiness of the mud with the father loudly chiding the lovely girl by his side,—visioned the arriving at the territorial town, the Herman of her betrothal meeting her, the marriage against which she was revolting. At that, in his sick imaginings, he felt himself snatching her away bodily from the outstretched arms of this strange man—

Suddenly a thought struck him with lightning-like effect. Immediately he sat up and brushed a hand across his eyes, a dozen things crowding his mind at once. The colonists were to meet the men in that far-off Nebraska City. Amalia couldn't be married until the wagons reached there. How long would it take them to make the trip? Four weeks, perhaps, if there were no delays. They had been gone twelve days.

The town lay hundreds of miles across the Illinois and Iowa plains on the Missouri River, a long, long journey. It had become a sort of gateway to the new country, the hub of the overland trails which stretched from it and on to the west beyond. It was the beginning of the young man's country, the young man's hope of wealth. Hundreds of them were seeking their fortune out there. Why not do so, too? What matter that his uncle expected him to stay and take over the business eventually? The Unknown Land was calling. This accounted for his restlessness, his vague irritation at everything about the little foundry. He, too, must answer the call.

If he could but get to this Nebraska City in some way before the wagons!

He read the note for the dozenth time. Amalia had told him the father's plans for her. Was it a veiled suggestion that he try to follow? To have said "Unless I can be with you again . . ." Did she hope? Did she have it in mind even as she wrote? Well, then, he would not fail her. He did not know just how or by what way, but he, too, would go. Perhaps by taking the river route he could arrive there ahead of the caravan. Then there

33

would be no marriage to a member of the colony. He would snatch her from them, carry her away.

A wild exuberance seized him. His grief passed into a sense of exaltation, as though the thing were already accomplished. He jumped to his feet, shook the soggy leaves and twigs from his clothes, mounted Trixie and was off, crashing through the narrow dark timber road.

CHAPTER V

TO the Lutheran homesteaders the journey out of Illinois and into the plains of Iowa had been a tedious and apparently endless trip. For weeks now they had lurched over trails which took them through prairie grass and sunflowers, down creek-beds and across gulleys, into tangled clumps of wild growth and past an occasional settlement. It had rained much of the time and the crude wagons drawn by stolid oxen and heavy-footed plow-horses jerked through thick black mud or jounced over the uneven dry ground until some of the women were ill from the torture of the constant shaking.

Day after day the prairie-schooners had crept on to the west,—a winding procession like so many tiny, gray-colored bugs following a twisting line on the wide expanse of a school-room map. The cracking of the blacksnakes, the stentorian calls of the drivers, the creaking of the wagons, were all the sounds heard as the caravan made slow and tortuous progress toward the ever-receding rim of the world.

Night after night they had formed in a wide circle around the fires, their cattle and horses corralled by this human perimeter, more safe from any potential marauder than if left outside of it. There was no danger from the redskins in Iowa, they felt,—but of Nebraska they were not certain. It had been only a few years since the alarm had been spread in the town of Omaha concerning the report of Indian outrages, and the militia had gone out to subdue the Pawnees at Battle Creek. No more Indian troubles had been known in the eastern third of the territory for a half-dozen years, but the men said no one could ever tell when it might break out again. On beyond there were tribes of them always ready to steal cattle and to commit various offenses, but it was scarcely to be supposed that they would attack so large a group.

Today, Amalia, riding beside her brother in one of their two wagons, was shaken almost to the point of illness, for never had the trail seemed so rough. Although the household things had been packed together as solidly as possible, sometimes when the horses forded a creek-bed or lumbered down a rough incline the chairs and walnut bureau knocked together, and the new soap-kettle with its perfect rounded bottom took to rocking back and forth perilously.

The menfolks had said they thought they must be getting near the Nishnabotna River region which lay only a few days' journey this side of the Missouri. All indications seemed to point that way. They were rather excited about a possible sight of the Big Muddy in a few days now.

But Amalia took no great interest in this news. She made no inquiry, commented on nothing,—merely clung to the seat of the lurching wagon and lived over again the days of her leaving,—days whose happenings would be forever burned in her memory.

She had been working on her *Baum des Lebens*—Tree of Life—quilt-block in her bedroom, had hidden it quickly as her father came to the door. She could still see him standing there, big and bustling, filling the doorway, dominating the scene, his sandy beard and thick mustaches almost bristling with importance.

"Well, Amalia, I have news."

"News?" she had said, her body going suddenly cold.

"Yah, the men do not wait to return. Instead they have sent word to us. They have found suitable lands many miles to the west of the town of Nebraska City. We are to go as soon as possible and meet them there in that territorial town."

Sitting here beside her brother now, on this endless, lurching journey, she could feel again the faintness stealing over her at his "We go now."

He had shouted it, excited because of the coming important event. "Fritz brings me the letter just now. You I tell first." He laughed at his joke: "You are the favored,—the one of all honored by me to know first."

"We go?" She had repeated it in a whisper.

"Yah! Fritz at once rides to the homes of our people. It is like the *Paulus Rewere* Fritz told us from school. To-day I give the command. Each knows his part. There shall be no delay. It is, as I have said, like an army under orders,—the army of the Lord. You know your part well. At once the extra baking and roasting of the meat. Then, even as these cool, the last of the packing. The sacks of oats and the seed corn at once Fritz loads in the second wagon. Myself I oversee all. Come Wednesday morning we start . . . Thursday at the latest. That day come the Dunbars to take over the house."

Riding silently by Fritz she was living it all over again,

trembling a little now even as she had trembled then. She had tried to tell him.

"Father, I must tell you at once. I do not go."

"Do not go?" The syllables had been lightning bolts.

"No . . . for I cannot now marry Herman Holmsdorfer."

"Have you lost your reason?"

"*Nein.*" At the dear thought of Matthias she had gained a bit of courage. "It is only that the young man at the foundry . . . you recall where we bought the kettle . . . ? Do not be angry, Father . . . he has been here several times since."

"Has he. . . ? He has . . . molested you?"

Amalia flinched again with pain at the memory of the evil thing her father had suggested. How could he have so translated a beautiful thing? How could there ever be evil when two people loved the way she and Matthias did?

"Father! He loves me . . . and I . . ."

"Go on . . . lest in my anger I strike you."

". . . I love him, too, Father . . . so much."

"*Du Narr!*" he had flung at her, calling his Amalia a fool for loving.

Lurching through the sodden wild grass of the Iowa prairie, she closed her eyes now as though she might forever shut out the period that followed, a time as of a great storm which lashed and beat with words, which closed over her in its fury of commands and threats, so that rather than drown in the beating stress of it she had promised obedience.

If only she had acquiesced for once and all at that

38

time, but she must do something which merely made matters much worse. On the evening before they were to
leave she had rolled a few things into a little bundle,
slipped out and started down the timber road toward
Matthias so many miles away. At the sound of a horse's
hoofs thudding behind her she had slipped into the underbrush at the side. But she had not been quick enough,
for the lantern's light had focused itself upon her like an
evil eye, and her father's cold voice had ordered her to
come forth. Well, her spirit was crushed then. There
was nothing more to do.

In two things only had she been deceitful,—in writing
a second letter to Matthias after the dictated one, and in
bringing the shell box with her. She had written her heart
out to her lover in a note dictated by no one, and, when
ordered to leave the dear gift behind for Mrs. Dunbar,
she had pretended to do so. But even now it was in the
wagon wrapped in many layers of unbleached muslin
sheeting.

"What have you there?" her father had asked as she
brought out the yellow-white bundle.

It was then that she had openly lied. "The freshest of
the bread," she had answered. And if God would not
forgive her, she did not even care.

For the first time after all the tragic days, riding now
with Fritz, they spoke of the unhappy situation. The
fifteen-year-old brother had something on his mind which
had worried him for weeks. He could scarcely speak for
the closing of his throat against the words. "I . . . myself I hate, Mollia. This you do not know before. It
was I who told Father I saw you go down the timber road.

I did not then know the reason. I would not . . . would not . . . have harmed you."

"Do not worry. Nothing was your fault."

"Are you then so unhappy?"

"I can never know happiness again, Fritz."

The youth shook his head. "It is bad. You should not be unhappy. You are so pretty. We could have managed . . . Father and I. I am a man now."

It broke something in Amalia, some tight-bound band around her heart and throat which had not been loosed for days. She, who had been like a dead woman for all this time, wept wildly. Her young brother needing her,— her lover wanting her. The church pulling her one way, —Matthias another. Obedience asking one thing,—love another. Why did God bring such agony into the world? They taught you God was good. Was it true?

The wagon lurched on through the miles of sodden grass and sunflowers, thickets of sumac, wild plum and Indian currant.

After a while she calmed. "Fritz, I confide in you. You will never tell on Amalia?"

"*Nein*, sister."

"I am praying that I shall see him again," and did not notice that she was turning to the God about whom she had so recently questioned. "Is it too much to ask?"

"How can that be? So far away?"

"Always in the back of my mind, Fritz, I have it that he might come too, that getting my letter on Sunday after the Wednesday we left he would try to overtake us even though so far away and seek me out."

"It is a big thing to hope for."

"He was like that." She spoke proudly. "And his love was like that."

"I wish for you it could be." He glanced shyly sidewise at his sister.

"Perhaps I wish it so much that I make myself think it could be. Do you think it could come true, brother?"

"It could come true," he answered simply. And if he kept to himself the thought that it was not likely, that no one could ever overtake another in this vast ocean of prairie country, it was out of boyish sympathy for Mollia.

Ahead of them lumbered slowly as always through the sodden grass the other wagon belonging to their father and the two of the Schaffers.

Amalia turned now and glanced back across the wide spaces of the prairie. Behind them on the trail came the three wagons of the Kratzes, the two of the Rhodenbachs, the two of the Gebhardts,—four of them oxen-drawn, three with teams of horses. She knew the outfits, every horse and ox as well as their own. As always there were only these same plodding creatures,—no other.

CHAPTER VI

MATTHIAS MEIER was standing on the dock at St. Louis, surveying the scene before him with both impatience and satisfaction.

A wilderness of steamboats confronted his vision. Some were just leaving dock, the hoarse coughing of their exhaust-pipes making discordant notes. Others were coming in, the screeching of their whistles adding to the already deafening din. Small boats slipped in and out and between the larger freighters like busy waterbugs, twisting and turning with insect abandon. The air was charged with the electric-like energy of movement.

As he surveyed the vessel *Missouri Queen*, in which he was to make the rest of his trip up the Big Muddy, he had the complacent feeling of already having accomplished his objective.

He had arrived in St. Louis without mishap and the overland travelers would be moving much more slowly than he,—of that he was sure. The stolid oxen and heavy-footed horses pulling their clumsy prairie-schooners would do scarcely more than sixteen miles per day. There would be the long halts to make camp. Added to that would be the perverseness of the cattle the settlers were driving, their stubborn stops and futile meanderings off the trail. The rains, too, were delaying the caravan, no doubt. Black Illinois and Iowa mud would be an obstacle with which to reckon. Even at this date he would wager anything they had not gone one-third of the way across Iowa.

Rains would not delay the steamboat, he thought exultingly. She would slip up the Big Muddy and land him in Nebraska City before the colonists had arrived. To see Amalia face to face,—to confront her father,—nothing could then keep her from him. He thought rather shamefacedly of his agony there in the woods when all the time the remedy of it was possible.

He surveyed the vessel now with a boyish sense of proprietorship. Never having been on a Missouri River steamer before he eagerly took in the details of this one that was to house him for his long journey.

She was an attractive-looking craft, one deck above the other, the pilot-house and texas still above those. The whiteness of her newly applied coat of paint made her look very aristocratic riding there majestically on the slow rise and dip of the river, a little like the birthday cakes his aunt had made,—the main deck one layer, the boiler deck another, then the texas, containing the suite of rooms for the vessel's officer, topped by the pilot-house high over the river so that the height of the pilot might stress the clarity of his vision in seeing down into the sandy channels. High above all these towered the two lofty smokestacks carrying their sparks away from the roof and giving a strong draft to the furnace,—the candles on the cake, he thought, and grinned to himself at his whimsy.

Two cannon faced bankward in both directions, probably used now only for the purpose of firing salutes, but carrying withal that gesture of authority for any loitering miscreants.

She was about two hundred feet long and perhaps thirty-five wide, he decided. The bottom looked flat. His curiosity keen, he asked a Negro crew-hand near how much water she drew and was told with much grotesque flapping of large hands that she was "drawin' thirty inches now, boss," but would be down to fifty when the five hundred tons of cargo were all aboard.

That cargo was now being loaded,—great hogsheads of molasses, household goods, horses, wagons, mules, bales of hay and oats for the stock aboard, these latter supplies to be replenished in St. Joseph.

The vessel was propelled by a steam wheel,—two engines on the respective sides connecting directly with the wheel shaft. The last word in river craft, she had steam capstans in the forecastle and two huge spars for that possible occasion when she would have to be pushed over the tricky shifting sands of the river.

"Dis old ribber . . ." the deck-hand contributed, "she done be onreli'ble as a gal."

It set Matthias' mind to working again, momentarily drawn away by the reference to woman and her caprices. Where was Amalia now? Where the ox-train creeping over the plains? What if it were farther along than his judgment had told him? He grew anxious at the thought.

"There must be no delay," he said. "It's necessary that I get to Nebraska City as soon as possible."

At which the dark boy gave a white, flashing smile and threw out those expressive brown flappers. "Yas sah! Ah'll tell old Missie Ribber about dat."

And then they were leaving,—with the hoarse sound

of whistles, bells, chugging of wheels, Negroes' songs, laughter, sobbing, farewells. It gave Matthias a momentary pang in remembering his recent parting from the good uncle and aunt whose disappointment at his going had been so keen, the latter of whom had given him a needle-book, admonitions, a New Testament, mittens, advice and packages of quinine, calomel and catnip.

Leaning on the railing now, Matthias' blood beat warm within him. This was the real part of the journey. On to a new country,—a new start in life! On to Nebraska City in the raw new territory to be there when the Lutheran settlers came in! His enthusiasm over the future knew no bounds. Some of it was an impassioned emotion over the fact that he would still have Amalia, some the natural reactions after his grief and disappointment, some his forward-looking plans for a new business in a new country, and some of it was merely Hope of Youth.

The gang-plank was up now. They were really under way. Crowds thronged the rails. Almost all were calling out their last farewells. It seemed that Matthias was the only one without friends left behind. No, there was one other,—a sun-burned, leathery-looking sort of young fellow apparently about his own age. They were not far apart, and through some interchange of thought, perhaps, just now their eyes met in a quick appraising look. So friendly did each seem to find the other's expression that almost simultaneously they drew together at the rail.

"First trip?" the young chap asked Matthias.

"Yes. Yours?"

"Nope. First one was ten years ago when I was nine.
Mother was a widder woman. Took us up the Muddy
to find a home. Landed at Plattsmouth. Just three or
four houses there then,—Mother knowed one of the
families. Had to sleep on the floor with several other
newcomers. Toward mornin' door opened and three old
Injun bucks come in and stepped around all over us
lookin' down in our faces. Had the hardest time gettin'
Ma to stay and settle. She was all for leggin' it back to
the steamer still tied up to the post and vamoosin' in
favor of returnin' to civilization." And the young fellow
laughed long and hilariously.

They told each other their names and destinations.

"Charlie Briggs."

"Matthias Meier."

"Plattsmouth in the main, but stoppin' in Nebraska
City, claimin' my team I left there and pushin' on to
Plattsmouth 'cross the prairie."

"Nebraska City is where I'm stopping for a time."

There was other information Matthias gleaned from
his new-found friend that first afternoon of their acquaintance. Charlie Briggs had learned surveying. He
had a homestead not far from Plattsmouth but mostly his
younger brothers looked after it while he was off on all
sorts of surveying, freighting and scouting missions.

"Volunteered a year ago last October to help put down
the Sioux Injuns. Saw the Plum Creek massacre in Phelps
County,—got home the very day last April year, the life
o' the best president of these here United States got snuffed
out."

Both were silent for a few moments,—that wordless reverence of all Union men for the fallen leader.

But not for long could Charlie Briggs remain silent.

He knew—and talked of—the great Platte Valley, had been up the Elkhorn, taken one trip to the Republican Valley. The Platte, he said, was flat and by nature treeless. It had shallow, muddy water, swarms of mosquitoes and greenhead flies, prairie-dog towns and rattlesnakes,— the country of the Elkhorn was rich and fine with quite a bit of natural timber along the creeks and rivers. He explained the trails, north and south of the Platte River,— the one on the south with its converging trails like the tines of a fork starting from Independence, Missouri, St. Joseph, Leavenworth, and Nebraska City.

He had all the information of the new country at his tongue's end,—the difference of the soil in the Platte, the Elkhorn, the Republican, and the Loup Valleys. He knew where the native trees thrived—the cottonwood, and the oak, the elm and the ash. He knew the Indian tribes, their locale and their habits,—told Matthias about the old Pawnees that had once lived in the Valley of the Republican, the Kitkehahki tribe, and the chief who at the instigation of the young Lieutenant Pike had ordered down the Spanish flag flying in front of the lodge and raised the Stars and Stripes; related the story of the attack on the Arikara Indians by the soldiers from Fort Atkinson who were joined by the Sioux enemies of the Arikaras, how they overpowered them and feasted on the Indians' roasted corn while the peace treaty was being negotiated.

He had at his tongue's end the history of much of the

territory since the days of Coronado and his Spanish horsemen who had once set out to discover the mythical land of Quivira with its silver and precious stones and its king who slept under a great tree with golden bells on its branches, and found instead a vast plain with wild grass and Indians and queer cows with humped backs.

He enjoyed the telling of these tales and not in all the afternoon did he cease from imparting them. "Follow the prairie-dogs and Mormons and you'll find good land," was one of his sage pieces of wisdom.

It rather fascinated Matthias, the young man's ready knowledge of the territory since an earlier day,—and his own more recent adventures.

"Killed buffaloes? Lord, by the dozens. Pick on your animal, shoot, skin the carcass, let it freeze, chop off a hunk with your ax, throw it in a Dutch oven and a couple hours later get busy."

With no recess for his monologue, he went on:

"Buffalo used to be swimmin' along here where we are most any time. They tell a yarn about a greenhorn seein' 'em once for the first time when he was off in a yawl with a passel o' old timers. This fellow could handle a rope right smart, so they got him to set in the bow with a lasso and the first one they should wound could be roped. Some of the crew fired and wounded one but the greenie threw the rope over the head of one that wasn't hit. The crew shouted and backed oars to get old man Buffalo in deeper waters, but his feet touched bottom and he went up the bank with the boat tied to him and would have took it on a cruise all over the prairie if the stem of it hadn't been wrenched off and carried away by the mad animal. Fellows was left shipwrecked far away from their steamboat."

Matthias grinned his skepticism. "Funny how the fellow couldn't have let go of the rope."

Charlie Briggs spat over the railing: "Never spile a good story . . . and besides rope wa'n't so plentiful they wanted to give any away."

"Any hostility along here now from Indians?" Matthias had carried the question in his mind for some time.

"Naw. Only a few years ago they was barricadin' decks and state-rooms,—keepin' up day and night vigilance. Mostly now any hostilities is above the Niobrara from the Sioux tribes on farther west. Pawnees is friendly."

By dusk the boat tied up for the night,—navigation through the treacherous sand-bars was too precarious. If Matthias chafed at the lost hours, he had only to remember that the overland travelers were making camp too.

He and Charlie Briggs sat out on the deck talking until the mosquitoes drove them in, when they joined the other passengers in the too-crowded parlor-like cabin,—for the most part a motley crowd of fussy old ladies with poodle-dogs, anxious mothers with sleeping children, planters, giddy young girls, whole families moving to the new country, many unattached men. Immigration to the territories of Kansas and Nebraska was heavy.

There was some attempt at music that evening in the stuffy cabin,—a group of young fellows volunteering the tear-jerking "Thou Hast Learned to Love Another" and "Meet Me By Moonlight Alone" and the rendition of "Marching Through Georgia" with an aftermath of sullen remarks and a miniature reproduction of the late war on an after-deck.

Matthias' eyes swept the clusters of young girls coldly in spite of the evident admiration for his stalwart figure some of them plainly showed. Not one was little, dainty, fair-haired and blue-eyed. How could a man care for any other type?

In the days that followed, the boat proceeded very slowly on its up-river journey, gliding along smoothly enough over the turbid water. On the seventh day it put in at Weston for repairs. Matthias chafed over the delay until Charlie Briggs hinted broadly: "Ye'd think the' was some *reason* why ye *got* to git there."

Matthias, however, was non-committal. He would never wear his heart on his sleeve, particularly to one he had known no longer than young Briggs. But unlike as the two young men were, there were qualities which drew them together on the whole trip,—a common love of adventure and progress, sincerity of purpose, and some unnamed characteristic which each felt in the other,—a sort of gallant attitude toward humanity.

It was the morning of the ninth day out before they could proceed. The weather turned cold and disagreeable. There was no more promenading on the wind-swept deck by the giggling girls. There were various rumbles of dissatisfaction from the passengers, too, for eatables were getting low and fare was very poor.

They were in Kansas now. One side of the river bank was sheer steep bluffs, the other vast stretches of prairie, dotted with patches of timber. It all looked very wild.

On the eleventh day they docked at St. Joe. A child

died and was taken ashore by a hysterical family. A doctor was called hurriedly from the passengers to attend a woman in childbirth in one of the stuffy state-rooms. A young bride came aboard on her way to California, happy and blithesome, thinking that all California was a paradise. Life is a loom, weaving gay colors indiscriminately with those of somber hue.

And now the long journey was nearing its end. They would get to Brownville on the twelfth day,—the seat of the United States land office in which Daniel Freeman only a little over three years before had obtained the first homestead in the whole territory just after the midnight hour of the day in which the law went into effect,—the place from which the first territorial telegram had been sent six years before. From there to Nebraska City was but a short journey.

Charlie Briggs in his loquacious way was recounting much of this to Matthias now, recalling some of the anecdotes concerning slaves that had been brought through this section by way of the underground railroad.

The two young men were sitting on deck on the Nebraska side looking shoreward, Charlie Briggs pointing out some distant upstream spot.

"Along nigh about a dozen miles over there is the way John Brown brung slaves many's the time from Missouri by way of Falls City, Little Omaha, Camp Creek and Nebraska City to Tabor, Iowa. Can pint out the barn to ye in Falls City they hid in whenever . . ." His high-pitched voice broke off.

There had been a grinding noise, a quivering of the

boat's frame. With a sickening shiver, as a huge animal might shake in the steely mouth of a bear trap, the *Missouri Queen* stopped.

"Sufferin' snakes!" Charlie Briggs jumped up. "We're on a sand-bar."

CHAPTER VII

WHEN the *Missouri Queen* settled grumblingly into the treacherous sand which had shifted since the steamer's last trip, Matthias was a picture of surprise and irritation. "How long will it be?" he wanted to know at once.

Charlie Briggs who had known the river since his childhood days shrugged lean muscular shoulders. "Can't tell. She may be settin' pretty."

And settin' pretty she was.

Now came the work of the two huge spars which like the legs of some gigantic insect swung into position as though the white bug of a steamer intended to walk over the water and be at once on its way. But the bug stupidly lay thrashing impotent legs and could not move.

With every available means the crew and some of the passengers, including Matthias and Charlie Briggs, attempted to get her off. Men in small boats put out to shore and drove stakes into the bank, around which they would wrap the rope attached to the vessel, and pulling this with mighty tugs attempt to entice the vessel from her sandy bed. And every day she seemed lazily to settle farther into the shifting silt of the treacherous river.

Four full days went by filled with exertion on the part of the workers and with irritation over the delay by all hands.

Matthias was beside himself with anger and worry.

Under normal conditions he would have chafed at the delay. Now he was tormented with the thought that after all these days the ox train might have arrived at Nebraska City. Sometimes he tried to comfort himself with the thought that there would be much more delay for the horses and oxen than this unlooked-for delay of the steamer. He reminded himself of all the minute and trying things which would come up to delay their progress. There would be the shoeing of the oxen, tires to be set on more than one wagon, a broken spoke perhaps, the constant delays for rounding up the driven cattle, early twilight stops in order to make camp, none-too-early starts after a cooked breakfast and repacking of the camp utensils and bedding, and always the black Iowa mud after a rain. But once the steamer was off and on its way again nothing would stop it excepting nightfall.

On the fifth day they pulled off. The next day they were caught again by another sand-bar throwing its treacherous arms across a channel which had been traversed easily on the boat's last trip.

This time Matthias slumped into the depths of despair. This time he was moved to confide in Charlie Briggs concerning his love for Amalia, his friendship for the young chap having progressed to this point. Once he even wildly suggested the possible purchase of a horse from some passenger, swim it to shore, there to take to land. Charlie Briggs dissuaded him from this, pointing out his lack of knowledge of his surroundings, called to his distracted mind that when they pulled off, which might be any time now, their progress would be better than Matthias' blind ride through an unknown country. It took all the weight of his argument to make Matthias realize the folly of the plan. Movement was what Matthias wanted,—to feel his legs moving, the motion of a galloping horse under him,—wings.

Charlie Briggs tried to cheer him. "I know that there Iowa gumbo," he would say: "Haint no mud like it anywheres. As bad any day as a little sand for holdin' you aback. They'll be slowed up fit fer goin' crazy, any the time there comes a rain."

It drew the two young men together,—Matthias' confidences and worry, and Charlie Briggs' sympathy and encouragement because he had nothing more practical to offer. Although they were unaware of it at the time, it was, in truth, the beginning of a long friendship interrupted only by death,—a friendship which was rather unexplainable to the casual observer in the later years of their lives when they appeared to have so little in common.

Charlie Briggs was right. The delay was not so long this time, and the second day they were out of the treacherous sucking sands and into deep water, passing a large Indian encampment on the Nebraska side almost at once.

No more heart-breaking delays! No more anxieties and nervous questioning. The next day—Brownville. A few hours after that—Nebraska City, there to wait for Amalia.

CHAPTER VIII

A ND now near the Iowa bluffs the overland travelers had broken camp for the last time before they were to sight the Missouri River.

Slowly the eleven wagons had crawled up and down the last of the unending Iowa trail. Ploddingly men had walked beside the oxen and cracked the long bull whips which circled over the stolid beasts' backs but never touched them. Patiently the women had sat in the covered wagons for all these weeks waiting this day of entering the new territory in which they were to make homes for their men. Most of them had come on the long trek against the desires of their hearts, for always the woman clings longer to the old hearth.

Young Mrs. Henry Gebhardt had given birth to a child on the way. Anna Rhodenbach had become betrothed to Adolph Kratz. Old Grandpa Schaffer, taken with summer complaint, had died and been buried in eastern Iowa.

But now the endless journey lay behind them,—with the worried forebodings of young Mrs. Henry Gebhardt, with the childhood of Anna Rhodenbach and Adolph Kratz, with the unbroken sleep of old Grandpa Schaffer beside the trail in eastern Iowa.

They were soon to see the Big Muddy. And although several days' journey lay beyond it, still it was the gateway to the new home.

Fritz was continually straining his eyes toward the

west hoping to catch the first sight of the river. But
Amalia turned often to look back along the trail where
the other wagons of the train stretched out like the long
lash of a whip.

"Always, Fritz, I foolishly look for the strange wagon
or the lone rider. Sometimes I think I see it so plainly
that I wonder if I am a little mad."

"There's the river way, too, Mollia. Some one of the
men had a paper printed in the big town of Omaha many
miles to the north. There it said river crafts come up
from the towns to the south and unload their goods."

He unwittingly gave her renewed hope, against which
she strove to turn, fearful that it might buoy her up too
much and make her suffering more keen when it should
come to naught.

And then suddenly from the top of a rise they saw it,—
the River! Almost simultaneously some one ahead had
shouted back the news. And soon others behind were
shouting, too. There it was ahead of them,—the Big
Muddy, its waters tawny with the clay of its high banks,
—rolling on to its union with the Father of Waters. On
the far side,—the Nebraska Territory.

They could see cabins across the wide expanse of water.
Nebraska City that was,—cabins and shacks in a shelter-
ing cluster of trees, and a ferry-boat which must be
summoned from the far side.

Wilhelm Stoltz, as master, was to go across first with
his wagon and the heavy mares whose shaggy legs were
like pillars.

There was the long wait, and then: "Come, Amalia,"
he called loudly. "We go now. You are the first woman

of our people to cross. It is good luck for you. Good luck to meet Herman there, too, huh?" He repeated *"Gutes glück"* many times. He was jovial, excited that the Nebraska Territory was in sight,—had almost forgotten his daughter's foolish idea that she had liked the young foundryman. *Verrückt,* she had been.

The ferry came over, so very slowly. But it did not come too slowly for Amalia. Rather she would have waited here on the Iowa side, prolonged the time before she must meet Herman who might even now be among those people over there on the levee.

They were down on the platform-like boat now, Amalia and her father and the one covered wagon with the shaggy-haired team. So many trips it would take to get all the colony across the river. Fritz must stay on the Iowa side with the other wagon, awaiting his turn.

They were crossing the muddy water now with that feeling of being too close to the dark turbulent waves. Amalia looked down at the turbid waters. They were thick, impenetrable. One could not see one inch beyond the muddy surface. Nor one hour into the future of one's life.

The coming of the ferry-boat had brought a scattering group of people down to the dock. From shore came a confused noise of laughter, braying stock, rumbling wagons, and the pounding of hammers far up on the hill. The wind was blowing hard on the river and Amalia with one hand held to her sunbonnet which rattled starchily in the breeze,—with the other she clutched a hard bundle of unbleached muslin.

The ferry-boat docked with a rattle of chains and the crowd idling about the wharf, pressed forward.

"Prettiest gal I've seen yet. She can have me, Pete," Amalia plainly heard an uncouth tobacco-stained individual say.

"Sst! Careful!" his companion idler whispered. "This here fellow comin' is lookin' for her."

CHAPTER IX

THE *Missouri Queen* had passed Brownville. Charlie Briggs in his self-appointed duty of handing out data to any and all who would listen had been regaling several passengers during the afternoon with all the information he possessed concerning Nebraska City, the destination of many. He was still going strong when the town itself was sighted from the steamer's deck.

"The old Nuckolls House burned six years ago. You should a' seen it." As a matter of fact Charlie Briggs had never set foot in its interior, but that did not deter him from his description.

"The night o' the dedicatin' made river history, I guess. All the toniest of the folks on the river from Brownville, Omaha, St. Joe, even as fur away as St. Louis come. They say champagne flowed upstream agin the current from St. Louis,—that many a sedate and long-faced citizen was cuttin' capers agin mornin' come."

"Did you say it burned?"

"To the ground in the big fire that destroyed most all the early buildin's of the town. Raged for hours, but volunteer fire boys couldn't save 'em."

It was sunset when the *Missouri Queen* docked at Nebraska City, greeted with artillery and a self-elected welcoming committee of countless men and boys on the levee. Most of the passengers who were going on to Plattsmouth, Omaha and Sioux City came on shore to bid good-by to these acquaintances of several weeks. Young girls who had not known each other at the beginning of the journey clung together in tearful farewell. Men promised to send for others if ventures proved successful. Women parted with promises of undying friendship and favorite recipes. Two engagements were announced between fellow passengers. Life acquaintances had been formed.

But Matthias had little time for all this display of emotion. He was anxious to get located, to see the town, most of all to ascertain whether the caravan of Lutheran settlers had come in.

The founders of Nebraska City had displayed a good deal of optimism in its baptismal name he decided. It was not much of a city, he could see, although the town proper looked to be on the bluffs back from the river while crude shacks and cabins clustered around the lower village. Twelve years old now, it had a courthouse, several stores and churches, a school and hotels, so Charlie Briggs had told him. But if Matthias' youthful interest in the little city was keen, it was superseded by the important fact that his rival for Amalia was probably somewhere here in the town at this very moment. He might even be one of these many men down at the wharf.

Just where to go for information concerning the Illinois homesteaders he was not sure, so the immediate call for action was to take his valise and seek out the hotel. He said good-by to Charlie Briggs who was to stay with a cousin in a log-cabin in the lower town which he now pointed out to Matthias.

"If you hear any news of these people I'm looking for, you would let me know?" Matthias questioned.

"I'd do that very thing." Charlie Briggs' little blue eyes twinkled under the tumbled forelock of his red hair.

"As for me, I'll clean up and eat and then start out. Maybe I can hear something." And then Matthias was on his way to the hotel.

At the hotel,—a two-story structure with a porch across the front,—Matthias washed and ate his supper alone under the kerosene lamps' glow. The dining-room was well filled. These were the more comfortably fixed travelers eating here he knew,—most of the incoming settlers would be camping just outside the town.

Apparently that was a bride and groom nearby,—he in broadcloth, white-collared and beaming, she in her bridal suit with pale-blue plumed hat,—and the conversation too low for Matthias to catch excepting the fact that they were hiring some one to take them over the Cut-off trail to Otoe County. Matthias wondered how the brave blue plume would face the prairie winds just now so vigorous.

At the other nearby table a group of men discussed the construction of the new Union Pacific Railroad. The names of Durant and General Grenville Dodge were being used freely, but whether they were two of the men present or were merely being discussed he did not know. The conversation included references to General Dodge having come on to Omaha to take charge of the entire construction of the road, and a protracted discussion as to the respective merits of building it out the north Fork Platte toward Fort Laramie, out the south Fork Platte, or due west where the Platte divides at Lodge Pole creek.

He soon knew that General Dodge was not present in the group but rather under discussion.

"He knows more of the possibilities of the country from the Missouri River to Salt Lake than any other American engineer," he heard, and several references to Dodge's former experiences as an engineer among the Indians who had given him the name "Long Eye" after seeing him use his surveying instruments.

The men seemed elated over the fact that the first sixty miles as far as North Bend had been completed, damned the redskins superbly for giving constant trouble, discussed the possibility of the Union Pacific beating the Pacific Central being pushed eastward in California, referred to "The Moving Town," calling it "Hell on wheels," and laughed long and hilariously at the reply some Jack Casement had given General Dodge when he asked if the gamblers were now quiet and behaving,—"You bet they are, General, they're out in the graveyard."

All this overheard talk of large spaces and big projects filled Matthias with a renewed interest in this raw country to which he had come. What his own part in its upbuilding would be he did not even know yet. He must get into something right away,—something important so that his life work would be started early. He was not without a substantial sum of money,—for that he was thankful. Amalia, first,—to see and take Amalia from her people,—that was of primary importance just now. Then to get into the work of this big opportunity-filled territory and make a place in it worthy of them both.

"You're Mr. Meier?"

Matthias looked up to see a waiter addressing him.

"Yes, sir."

"A gentleman outside to see you, sir."

He pushed back his chair and went immediately to the door which opened on the hotel veranda. It gave him an excited feeling of anticipation as though even now he knew there was to be news of Amalia.

He stepped outside where June bugs thumped about clumsily and the sound of voices and a banjo came harshly from one of the saloons across the street.

Charlie Briggs stood there in the pale light which the hotel's lamp cast across the wooden platform. He came up soberly, turned his lean and freckled face away.

"Reckon' I got bad news for ye, Matt."

Even then Matthias knew he would always remember the expression of unspoken sympathy on the young fellow's homely weather-beaten countenance. Twisted, his face looked, as though he might be in physical pain.

With no word Matthias stood tense and expectant.

"The Lutherans got in day afore yistiddy." Charlie Briggs dropped his usual high-pitched voice to a hissing whisper. "Yistiddy they went on west to their land. The girl was married here . . . just afore they pulled out."

Matthias stood with no word, staring at the burned and leathery face of his informant, just as he had stood in the Illinois woods weeks before and stared unseeing at a younger boy, so that it seemed he was living some portion of his life all over again. But it went through him swiftly that this time there was no way out,—no recourse now from a decision which was beyond his changing. He had a distinct sense of finality, as though life were ending here on the porch where Charlie Briggs' weather-beaten face screwed itself into pain and the June bugs thumped on the wooden porch floor.

There was, then, to be no full fruition of any hope for him,—ever.

With a last grasping effort, as a drowning man clutches for something solid, he asked: "You're sure? There's no . . . no mistake?"

"There's no mistake. My cousin's woman's sister saw the ceremony from her cabin. Two couples was married. 'Twas out by the wagons by the side o' the new Nebraska City Cut-off trail . . . Luther'n preacher . . . 'n all kneelin' near the wheel ruts fer the prayin' afterward. One of the brides' faces was whiter'n limestone, my cousin's woman's sister said, and a Luther'n woman standin' by told her it was account o' a team o' horses sudden rarin' nearby . . . but my cousin's woman's sister said it had looked thataway long 'fore ever the horses acted up."

For a time the two men stood with no more words between them. Through Matthias' mind went a kaleido-scopic turning and twisting of parts of pictures, never forming any whole, merely grotesque and fragmentary shapes,—swollen streams—crumpled letters—rushing waters—dripping timber—covered wagons—driven cattle—Amalia's white face, whiter than limestone,—high cliffs—muddy waves—and always a nightmare of clutching hands pulling his body down into a maelstrom of smothering quicksands.

Sand! Sucking sand! It always held you back from your heart's desire.

Sand! Moving sand! It ran forever through an hour glass.

Queer he had never realized that about sand before. Some sands held you in their slimy grasp and would not let you go. And while they clutched you tightly, horribly, other sands slipped down, down through the hours, pushing time on until everything was too late.

Too late! Too late . . . too late . . .

"Sorry, Matt. If I can ever do anything more fer you . . ." Pain in Charlie Briggs' leathery red face.

"Thanks, Charlie." Mustn't let Charlie see that no one can ever do anything more.

They were shaking hands. The tight grip of Charlie Briggs' two iron hands couldn't help.

Matthias turned and went back into the hotel and up to his room. For a long time he stood in the middle of the floor looking at the wash-bowl and pitcher and the grayish-white towels on the rack and tried to think just what had happened. He had come too late. On account of sand! Sand! Sand that held you back like the tight grip of two iron hands. So that other sand could run through the hour glass and make you too late . . .

Too late . . .

He dropped on his knees, by the side of the bed, burying his face in his arms.

Oh, *kleine taube*, little dove . . .

CHAPTER X

A MALIA rode quietly at the side of her new husband, Herman Holmsdorfer. She had no spoken reproach for her father, uttered no word of rebellion toward the man who had acquired her body.

Herman possessed her now,—he had a woman to keep his house and cook his food and lie by his side at night. He was secretly proud of her prettiness, too, but it would not have done to tell her so. Far more than the prettiness was the fact that she could cook and sew and scrub, tend chickens and help plant when he needed her. Also she would bear him many sons. Seven,—*ach* in the Fatherland one would get something for that. Here they would give bounty only for coyote skins.

Riding along the Cut-off trail he was fully satisfied with life as he knew it. One-hundred-sixty acres of good rich Nebraska Territorial soil for his portion at the end of the journey, a team, a woman of his own,—one of only two children, too, so that when Wilhelm Stoltz died Amalia would get half of her father's homestead. And Amalia being his, the land would be his. Must discourage any sign of remarrying in Wilhelm,—that would not do.

One-hundred-sixty acres, a good team and a woman,— thus did Herman Holmsdorfer gloat on his good luck and although he did not analyze the statement, thus did he grade them in point of value.

Loudly jovial he was on the trip. Amalia had gone to his head like a drink of *roggen branntwein.*

"The best cabin of all for you I build. Not a house of sod as the people far out on the prairies away from a stream, nor yet dugouts from the earth with only boards and branches and strips of sod over them. What think you? Of good logs from the natural timber along the river and creek-bed where is the fine land we have chosen. Say something, woman." He dug a heavy forefinger playfully into Amalia's pink cheek. "Is it not good?"

"It is good," Amalia said quietly.

Very quiet she had been ever since the day by the Cut-off trail near Nebraska City. Tractable, too, she was, and carefully polite to Herman. But something had frozen in Amalia's being that day, as the roots of the lilac bushes back home freeze in the winter. Outwardly pleasant and obedient, her heart had crept into an inner room, hurt and bleeding, to hide forever from the people about her. The *kleine taube,* little dove, had been wounded,—but only wounded, so she could not die.

Thereafter she lived in two worlds,—the practical one in which all these others moved and had their being, working hard when the wagons stopped, taking her turn at the cooking, washing out the necessary clothing in the streams for her father and Fritz, and now Herman,—and another world in which she existed apart from them, entirely aloof in her thoughts and with nothing in common in her emotions. With characteristic docility she submitted to the rough caresses of the heavy-jowled man beside her, but by some cool withdrawal of the spirit found it possible to remain forever away from him.

For several days the ox train headed west on the trail, turned from it at the point designated by Herman and rode miles again across the wild treeless prairie, the long grass dotted with the white of daisies and the blue of prairie gentians.

Twice they sighted small bands of Indians and were frightened, and twice the scare went into nothing.

For a way beyond the Big Muddy the country had been undulating, a succession of rolling hills and prairie land. They rode through hills and valleys, uplands and lowlands, dark sandy loam and black bottom lands, blue joint verdure, and course slough spikes. And the feet of the oxen crushed a thousand wild blossoms in the prairie grass.

Sometimes the way was as level as a floor,—sometimes they went up and down through gullies and creekbeds. Sometimes the skies opened and the wagons stuck fast for hours in the black mire. Sometimes the sun shone and the drying winds blew, and they made fourteen miles a day. Sometimes they passed greenish sloughs, and occasionally near the streams, a virgin timber,—boxelder, elm and willow, burr oak, hackberry and ash, and the tangled vines of undergrowth. A few times they passed cabins, two or three were occupied, some were abandoned claim shanties. Once they halted by a pond of muddy water, warm and brackish, and once by the clear sparkling water of a spring-fed stream. All this where one day there would be villages and towns, churches, schools, countless farms, paved highways, concrete bridges and searchlights sweeping the night skies for the guidance of the mail planes.

Herman rode proudly all this way at the head of the caravan for it was he who knew the way to the new homesteads. On the sixth day he made a sudden halt, got out of the wagon and waved wildly to those few in his vision. One by one the wagons reached those already assembled, the drivers wondering what had caused the mid-afternoon stop.

"It is here that the lands begin," Herman had been saying to Amalia, ". . . here you shall keep my house for me."

"Yes, Herman," Amalia had said,—little Amalia who was to live in the same house with Herman, but always in Another Room.

It was then that three strange young men on horseback rode out to meet them. And now ensued a protracted argument. The young men had arrived during the absence of the Lutheran scouts, broken sod in a sizable area of prairie, built a shack, and what was to be done about it?

It was nightfall before the Lutheran men had come to the conclusion to buy the squatters off. Loath was a hard-working thrifty German to part with good money to English-speaking squatters, but after an assembled meeting of the heads of the Stoltz, Schaffer, Rhodenbach, Kratz, Gebhardt and Holmsdorfer families, they decided to offer the men one hundred dollars to leave. The young men wanted three hundred. The answer to that mathematical problem was as plain as the nose on every German's face,—two hundred.

So the deal went over and the young men settled on land adjoining that of the colonists,—a small enough business deal at the time, but one to be fraught with far-reaching consequences, for it came to be in time that they and their descendants mixed the English language and customs, English schools, and church services, social events and marriages with those of the Germans,—until no longer could one pick out the descendants of those Lutherans from the children of the English.

The business finished, all the new German settlers gathered around the huge central fire which had been built. Wilhelm Stoltz raised his great hand and a hush fell on them. When the least child had grown quiet he thanked God for leading them into the land which would nourish them and their children after them and their children's children,—told Him that He was closer here to his followers than He had seemed in the land from which they came.

Amalia, looking up at the low-hanging stars shining like so many yellow buttercups in a forest clearing, wondered why He seemed so much farther away.

CHAPTER XI

IMMEDIATELY the settlers went to work to lay out the farms. That all might border the river, they figured out a system whereby they narrowed each holding and allowed it to extend farther back so that every homestead might have its full one-hundred-sixty acres. Thus each family could have access to water, and because of the narrower measurements, be slightly closer to each other for protection from the Indians in case there was trouble. They realized that this homesteading out farther than the Omaha area might bring on Indian depredations any time.

For many days Wilhelm Stoltz and Herman Holmsdorfer, Rudolph Kratz and August Schaffer on horseback, with small pocket compasses and the lines from their horses' harness, laid out the acreage into the eleven farms, for there were that many men in the group over twenty-one. Wilhelm Stoltz nearly shed angry tears that Fritz was only fifteen. It seemed such a waste of years to be but fifteen with all this fine land everywhere.

All camped by the wagons near the river while the farms were being surveyed, with every one anxious for the day to come when that particular phase of the work should be finished so that the building might begin. The women cooked and washed at the river's brink, and gathered for the fires the dead branches of trees along its banks and the dried buffalo chips out on the prairie.

This camp was made in more permanent fashion than those of one-night duration on the way. Now several stoves were set up with quilts hung behind them to lessen the onslaught of the wild winds from across the open country.

Many times the two who had come to pick out the land, Herman Holmsdorfer and Rudolph Kratz, were congratulated for their choice. How terrible, the various members of the company said, not to have had this river with its native timber. Several times they had passed settlers on the way who had chosen land far from trees, claiming it was richer or lay more level. It was because they had not scouted about as Rudolph and Herman had done. There was wide, open prairie land here for the good crops which soon would grow, but there was timber, too, even though not large like the Illinois trees.

On a hot day in July with the wind stilled before the sullen approach of a storm, the work of the surveying was finished. It was a momentous occasion, for now came the choosing of the farms. They gathered about in a close circle. Herman Holmsdorfer placed all the numbers of the tracts on pieces of paper. Young Henry Gebhardt wrote all the names of the families on similar pieces. The numbers were placed in one hat,—the names in another.

"Who shall draw?" they asked.

"The two brides," some one said. "Anna Kratz and Amalia Holmsdorfer."

"The two brides," others chorused. "It is good luck for us all."

"*Gutes glück!*" was heard on all sides.

"Hush!" said Wilhelm Stoltz, Amalia's father. "You

talk of good luck. Ask instead the good God for His help and protection."

He raised his great hand high above his head and his loud voice rumbled forth, addressing *Gott im Himmel*. A similar scene had taken place on a far New England shore over two hundred years before. "Thou hast led these Thy chosen people . . ."

Amalia bowed her head. Why were the Lutherans chosen before all others? Was it true? How were they sure?

Love,—a very human love for one not of her church, —made Amalia Holmsdorfer all the years of her life liberal and kind to those who chose to think differently from her own people. Protestant, Catholic, Jew, and Gentile, those of Mormon faith and those of no faith at all found succor at her door until the day of her death.

And now the drawing. Anna Kratz drew a number. "Eleven . . ." she said in a clear, ringing voice.

Amalia drew a name to match with it. "Herman Holmsdorfer," she said quietly.

They all shouted and laughed at the joke. "Amalia is so anxious to get started she draws her own name first."

She looked down at the paper in her hand stupidly. It was true. Holmsdorfer was her own name. She had not remembered for a moment.

In the midst of the laughing and chattering Wilhelm Stoltz raised his hand high again. *"Stille!"* And there was immediate silence, for Wilhelm Stoltz, by some forcefulness of character even more pronounced than the other men also of domineering ways, was their acknowledged leader.

"Of one thing we have not thought. The years will pass. Our children and our children's children will live here on these farmlands. Better they should live side by side those of the same blood. Look you,—if ought happens to any of us,—to be taken in sickness or by death, it should be better that my Fritz and I dwell beside Herman and Amalia that the land may lie together."

"That is good," Herman shouted, and added to himself,—"Three-hundred-twenty acres of land I own instead of one-hundred-sixty should old Wilhelm and Fritz die before me." Almost he was licking his lips at the thought.

It was better so, the men agreed. The women were mere onlookers, consenting readily to whatever satisfied their men.

But one more question came from the lips of young Adolph Kratz. "I am now husband to Anna Rhodenbach. Shall the homestead I own lie then next to my father or her father?"

It was a weighty subject to be settled as the far distant lightning forked in the western sky. Wilhelm decided, this Lutheran Solomon, as he set himself up to be.

"Woman is frailer. It is thought she will die first. It is even so in the English laws. The homesteads of the younger men who have wives of our families shall lie next to the homesteads of the wife's parents. Thus at the deaths of the elderly women the daughter lives next to her father to care for him in his old age."

It was agreeable to all,—this settling so glibly by a

domineering man the entire future of the lives of a dozen families. But this fluent and smooth forecast was by way of being something of a joke,—perhaps the Almighty may have thought so, too,—for it was to be, that years after *Herren* Kratz, Rhodenbach, Gebhardt, and Schaffer had been gathered to their fathers, hardy old *Grossmütter* Kratz, Rhodenbach, Gebhardt and Schaffer met summer afternoons on the porches of their fine farm homes, ate their *kaffee-kuchen,* drank their *kümmel,* and jabbered endlessly in the old tongue, rather to the annoyance of a younger and very American generation.

They now rearranged the drawing, grouping them in clusters as agreed upon, three-hundred and twenty acres to the Rhodenbachs, they to settle between the two families which homestead each should have, three-hundred and twenty to the Stoltz-Holmsdorfers, and finishing the others in the same fashion.

The sky was darker now. The low thunderheads were piling up like a flexible mountain range that constantly changed in depth and height and shadows.

They finished the drawing. Wilhelm and Fritz were to be at one far end of the long line of homesteads, Amalia and Herman next, young Adolph Kratz and his bride, Anna, next, and the others in order.

No roads between these homesteads now: Later, along the side of the vast acreage, a rutty road running as wildly as a vagrant gypsy, dusty or muddy in summer, hard frozen or piled with countless drifts in the winter,—then after a time surveyed and "worked,"—still later straightened and graveled,—then leveled and paved so that cars doing sixty or seventy need not slow down and lose time where the oxen and the shaggy-legged horses of the Kratz, the Schaffer and the Gebhardt, the Stoltz, the Holmsdorfer and the Rhodenbach families once came to a lumbering stop in the midst of the prairie grass at the creek's bend.

CHAPTER XII

IF Matthias Meier drank the bitter dregs of disappointment during those first days in the raw territorial town of Nebraska City on the Big Muddy, there was too much activity going on about him for any continued quaffing at the cup.

It was a time of action, of great physical deeds. Men hewed and dug, sawed and hammered, broke sod and planted. The little town was filled with the sound of pounding, of the crack of the blacksnake, the call to the ferryman, the bawling of tired stock, the creak of wagon wheels.

Scores of wagons, hundreds of horses, mules and oxen still hauled freight from here across the barren plains to Denver. The hot summer winds carried through the town's straggling streets the odors of the river, of alkali dust, of sweating mules and humans, of upturned grass and loam and subsoil. There was the feel in the air of unseen forces,—the push and pull of strange appeals. There was strength and vigor. It was a masculine world, and all men were young.

Matthias, at twenty-one, was stunned and disappointed that his plans for marrying Amalia had gone awry, but found shortly that he was not destroyed. A frustrated life was not necessarily a defeated one. He was too busy to be utterly vanquished by the blow. Whom the gods would destroy they sometimes first make idle rather than mad.

And Matthias Meier was not idle. There was too much to do. It was too good to be a part of the great new country. Out here in all this vast newness one might in time become wealthy, influential, important. Free as the prairie wind itself, he could go anywhere with any of these home-seekers or adventurers. He had only to choose. Or so it seemed to youth.

Strangely enough, then, after those first days of crushing disappointment followed by idealistic dreams of great success, it was something of a deflation of his ego, to find himself again at the humble task of shoeing horses. Even then it was the energetic little Charlie Briggs who suggested it.

Plowshares must be pounded out and edged to turn the virgin prairies. Horseshoes must be forged and shaped. Nails must be made by hand. Much of this was to be done with the thousands of people coming through the Nebraska City gateway to settle westward to the Rocky slope. So blacksmith shops sprang up over night. And Matthias Meier started one.

Charlie Briggs pushed on soon across the prairie to Plattsmouth. Matthias had been sorry to see him leave. Out of the milling throngs he was the one new friend.

"Well, good-by, Matt." He had stood by his wagon loaded with supplies for the homestead which lay between Nebraska City and Plattsmouth.

"Good-by, Charlie."

Neither referred to the intimacy of that hour in which the one had glimpsed the heart of the other and given unspoken sympathy, and yet each knew the other was thinking of it.

"Good luck, Matt."

"Same to you, Charlie."

" 'F ever I can help ye out . . ."

"Thanks, Charlie . . ."

All that year and part of another Matthias Meier worked at his blacksmith shop, shoeing his share of the countless hoofs that came treading through this important gateway to the great plains.

He lived in a man's world, journeying between his boarding-house and the little shop, contacting only the masculine portion of the groups of emigrants stopping there, although many a feminine eye lingered longer than necessary on the young man's stalwart body and fine head set so gallantly on his wide shoulders. But not yet could Matthias see girlish attraction in any one but the shadowy memory of a fair-haired girl standing in front of green alder bushes and waving a farewell that was to last forever.

And now it was 1867 and suddenly Nebraska was no longer a territory. The territorial legislature which had met as usual in Omaha, having drawn up a constitution containing a clause that only white men could vote, found it returned speedily from congress with the rebuke that no one should be kept from voting because of color. Meeting again, it rectified the mistake, and on March 1, 1867, President Andrew Johnson issued his proclamation. Nebraska was a state.

Came now immigration in earnest. Matthias found that he and the settlers of the previous summer had merely come in like the first ripples in the run of the tide.

The great plains of which the newly born state was a part had been dotted by the foot-prints of thousands of people crossing it to the far west. For years settlers had been thinking of it as a great hallway through which they must travel in order to get to those other and more distant rooms where dwelt the Californians or the members of the new Zion in the Great Salt Lake Valley or the Oregon settlements.

Although the soil over which they trod was black and rich and fertile as any beyond, few had lingered. The very vastness of the prairie regions had staggered the mind. So from the days of the earliest fur traders to the year 1867, the great fertile plains beyond the Big Muddy had numbered only a comparative few.

But now they came. Came by the thousands,—especially young soldiers, who having known adventure and having rebelled against the idea of settling down to their old lives in the villages or on the farms of placid New England, turned eyes to the west and let them linger long on thought of the newly formed state with its rolling hills and vast prairies. Many minds decided that the possibilities there were as vast as the green-grown prairie itself.

So the trek began. In they came by boat and by covered wagon,—these strong young men from the northern and eastern states,—American, German, Bohemian, Danish, some of the sturdiest youth of the nation. Some turned to the founding of the villages,—some to the carving of farms out of the raw prairie land, but all to do their part in the building of a great state.

Matthias Meier by instinct clung to the town. Nor

did he intend to shoe horses forever. Already he was thinking that he who would bring in merchandise to sell to these newcomers would make a good profit, or who would loan money out to them for good interest, or set up a lumber business for their homes,—oh, there were many ways to make a good living if one but chose carefully.

Again it was Charlie Briggs who inadvertently helped him decide his course.

The lean-visaged young chap was in Nebraska City en route to Brownville. He sought out Matthias at his shop. It was July and the hot sun beat down on the river town with its dusty streets through which came the never-ceasing procession of ox teams and wagons, with its ferry-boat and its crowded hotels, its steamer in dock from down the river, its bawling cattle in the stockade on the hillside, its unending movement, as though a gigantic gate swung back and forth to let these enthusiastic newcomers through.

Charlie Briggs had news. A committee from the new state's legislature had finally picked the site for the capitol. The news of the decision had just come in. Had Matthias heard?

"No."

"A place on the open prairie out between Salt and Antelope Creeks. Sufferin' snakes, Matt! Open prairie with only three or four log cabins now. Capital of the state! Be a big town some day. 'F I was town-broke . . . But none o' that fer me. I'll take homesteadin' 'n a surveyin' gang 'n a chance to git a gun sighted on a dam' Injun."

Charlie Briggs was right about locating in the newly

chosen capital! Three or four log-cabins on the prairie, was it? How long would that be true,—with a capitol building going up, and the legislature meeting there? Why, in no time at all there would be more houses, a hotel for the legislators, stores, a school, maybe a railroad. No capital city ever stayed a village. Three or four log houses, indeed!

CHAPTER XIII

MATTHIAS MEIER started April first, 1868, for the village of Lincoln, the new Nebraska capitol site, driving his team with a wagon carrying merchandise of the most staple variety,—unbleached muslin, sugar, salt, boots, flour. The wind was strong and cold, and the trail faintly marked over the prairie was deep mud through which the horses struggled with the loaded wagon. By night he had made nine miles.

He had been told he would find a cabin en route and when he sighted it in the late afternoon, a black dot on the bleak prairie, he urged on the team. There he stayed all night with bachelor brothers, graduates of Dartmouth, who had come west to make their fortunes.

The next morning he started out in the rain which soon turned to sleet. All day his team plodded toward the next settler's, never passing a building or traveler. Now and then at the top of a rolling hill he would glimpse another team ahead, always a little fearful that its occupant was making for the same shelter as he was, and from his experience he knew that any house he might reach would be small.

It was after sundown when he drove up to the door of the soddie. A big bearded man stood in the doorway and called out: "Unhitch 'n put the hosses under shelter, friend. Then come in. Always room for one more at Akins'."

Matthias unhitched, led the team to the rude shelter, fed and watered them and then entered the house.

He found it contained two rooms, both of which were filled with people, all the men in the front room around a box-stove in which simmered green cottonwood, the women in the back room urging a small and apparently stubborn cook-stove to put forth its best effort in the way of boiling water for coffee.

He went back to his stock of groceries and brought in a sack of cornmeal to add to the gastronomical part of the evening's festivities. After what seemed endless waiting, and during which time the feeble efforts of the little cook-stove almost died on the altar of all vain attempts, there was supper after a fashion.

Later for the simple reason that it made economy of space, the women and children lay down crosswise of the two beds, while the men disported themselves on the floor after the manner of the spokes of a wheel, with the box-stove and its sputtering green wood contents as the luke-warm hub. In the middle of the night, with the wind increasing to the proportions of a gale and rocking the little house, Matthias, almost frozen, picked himself out of the wheel-like effect rather like a spoke which can no longer hold out, and went out into the icy night to run up and down a somewhat limited space of the open prairie and beat his arms.

With the coming of the sun, as though the two could not work well hand in hand, the wind went down. Soon the sparkling ice had gone and all started on their way, with loud and hearty admonitions from the Akins to be sure and come again. Hospitality on the prairie in an early day may have been only figuratively warm, but never did it fail its fellow man.

At Balls Crossing on Stevens Creek, Matthias made a short stop at noon, and then rode into the prairie wind, which was rising again, facing its rough onslaught, his strong young shoulders meeting its buffeting much as a swimmer breasts the current. But its very robustness gave him a feeling of exuberance, that he could meet the obstacles which would confront him in the new town in the same way that he met the wild strength of the prairie.

In the west, clouds were piling on the far horizon, gray and pink-tinged and gold-bordered by the sun slipping now over the rim of the world, forming castles no airier than his own. For as he rode he had dreams as wild as the wind: that plows would one day go up and down all these hills and valleys, leaving behind them broad new furrows; that endless fields of yellow grain would shimmer in the sunlight; that villages and towns would cut the horizon which circled him now in one unbroken ring.

Fantastic as it was, it persisted,—the mirage of the fields and farms, roadways and villages,—and the picture gave him companionship and comfort in the loneliness of his ride.

If he thought of Amalia, it was neither with the sharp pain with which he had first lost her nor the dull heartache which lingered long afterward. Rather it was with a touch of sadness that he was beginning to forget. His memory of the depths of agony to which he had been cast at the time bade him wonder now how it had been possible to live and enter so whole-heartedly into this new venture.

At that, his mind went forward again in its flight to the new town which was to rise there on the prairie and in whose building he was to have a hand. There were those who said the capitol, even if built, would never remain there,—that the absurdity of locating it on the raw prairie with only a few log-cabins about, was so apparent that a short time would see its removal.

Suddenly he found himself defending its retention, thinking of the newly formed town with a distinct air of proprietorship. It made him laugh aloud,—his air of ownership when he had not even arrived.

He admitted to himself that he had developed a distinct pride in the whole raw uncouth state. This new Nebraska with its few straggling frontier towns, its widely scattered soddies and cabins, its countless acres of prairie grass, its undulating hills and vast open spaces was far more something of his own than ever his native state had been. Into the latter he had been born with no volition of his own. Into this he had come of his own determination and here chosen to stay. It belonged to him.

For a long time he had been sighting black dots on the far horizon and then he knew them for the cabins constituting the town.

The sun had almost slipped away. Nothing remained but a last reflection of its gold on the tip of a cloud and in little yellow pools of light on the prairie.

It was almost dark when he drove to the first cabin. It stood isolated and aloof from any other of the small cabins and the blacksmith shop. The burned walls of what had been a school-house constituted the only other building in the vicinity.

Wide prairie land as far as the eye could see, three or four scattered log houses, a blacksmith shop and the forlorn walls of a little stone seminary! This, then, was the beginning of a midwestern city in which one day there would be countless fine residences and stores, a great University, paved streets and golf courses, parks and libraries, school buildings and churches, and the most beautiful capitol of them all from whose towering top the statue of The Sower overlooks that which Matthias Meier and his kind accomplished for the state,—as though the seed of their early sowing had come to full fruition.

CHAPTER XIV

I N such manner did Matthias Meier and Amalia, the
girl he would have married, begin the years of their
living in the same new state,—the young man in the
village that was to become a city, the girl on a homestead
among her church people,—their lives as far apart as the
vastness of the wild prairie which separated them.

Amalia now put away her love for Matthias, if indeed
one can be said to put away anything which lies always
in the next room into whose silences one may slip at any
time for surcease from trouble.

Always it lay there before her,—the way of escape.
She told no one, could not have pierced the dull stolidity
of Lena Schaffer nor the childish cheerfulness of Anna
Kratz if she had made the attempt to tell them of The
Room which held song and laughter and fragrance. But
many times when the body grew weary of the hard work
which was the portion of all the women, or when the heart
turned sensitively away from the rough ways of the man
who claimed them both, she would slip into this Room
from whose windows one looked into a dim cool clearing
in the woods, and in whose shadowy confines there was
love and understanding.

Happily these little journeys into another realm could
be performed by some magic means simultaneously with
practical work, for otherwise they never could have been

taken. Work was indeed the portion of every man, woman and child.

After the homesteads had been drawn, each family drove to its allotted acreage of one-hundred-sixty acres, living thereafter in the wagons until a house could be built. Eleven units of humanity, dotted up and down the river's bank for several miles, a team and wagon for each, a cow and chickens, a plow and a few household goods,—energy, courage, and hope.

Amalia's house went up in record time, for her father and Fritz turned in at once to help Herman build,—to live in it, too, until one for themselves could be finished on the next homestead. Many times as they worked, they boasted of the fact that they could use logs for the houses, and expressed their contempt for the sod houses of many of the settlers who were away from streams and timberlands, not knowing that the soddies were warmer in winter and cooler in summer than any log house could ever be.

Amalia had something of a fine cabin, rather more elegant than that of Anna Kratz,—for it boasted a partition through it.

In truth, from the moment the initial log was laid for the first of the eleven cabins, there never ceased to be a concealed rivalry in the community over houses and hogs, children and chickens, wagons and windmills. From log houses in 1866 on through frame to the present days of brick and stone and stucco,—from lumber-wagons on through rubber-tired surreys to many-cylindered cars, there lay always under the jovial neighborliness of each family a desire to get ahead of the others. Let a Kratz buy a parlor lamp with a fat round globe and purple pansies on its side, the Gebhardt, Schaffer, and Rhodenbach women could not rest until fat round globes with magenta roses or cerise lilies decked their own parlors. Through all the years, human nature being as it is, two rooms in a log house instead of one, or eight cylinders in a car instead of four was a cause for rivalry.

In Amalia's house, they built the partition of small split logs, not rising to the ceiling but at least above one's head, which would make a good place for hanging washing in bad weather or seed-corn when the big crops should be harvested. When the cabin was finished, Amalia laid her rag rugs over the roughness of the floor, set her walnut bureau against the chinking of the logs and hung her pots and pans on wooden pegs protruding from it. A few household goods, a gun over the door, a willow fishpole beside it, the plow and team, the cow and chickens, —these only with which to conquer the wilderness!

Moving from the wagons into the newness of the little two-roomed house did something for Amalia. It eased the pain which lay always in her heart by giving her a floor to sweep and a hearth to keep clean. An immaculate little *haus frau* to her finger tips, she swept and cleaned and scrubbed her new cabin until even the other women, excellent housekeepers all, began to hold up Amalia Holmsdorfer to their feminine offspring as a shining example of all that a *haus frau* should be, not knowing that her work was an antidote for pain.

For the rest of that summer, hammers and saws were heard all up and down the river until the cabins were finished, one by one. Fritz and his father moved into their own by fall. All broke sod so that a beginning should be made on the land.

If Amalia was known as one of the best of the house-keepers, Herman might have carried the honors of being most adept at breaking the new sod. He seemed to have a knack for it and the others were always calling for him to come and help.

Sometimes when Herman was away at the plowing, Indians came through the prairie grass, in their straggling, single-file way of traveling, and frightened Amalia beyond measure, and often she could see their signal-fires at night on the distant uplands. Sometimes a long loathsome rattlesnake would coil itself in her path when she went to draw water at the spring, and always after sundown she could hear the howl of the coyotes in the timber near the river.

Church services were held at first around the wagons, then in houses. By fall when the last of the cabins had been finished, all turned to the building of a little log church, which would also be the school-house. They chose a site high on a knoll on the Rudolph Kratz place, centrally located, where it would stand like the eye of God overseeing all the valley.

Rock and sand for the foundation were quarried on the land of Henry Gebhardt. The strong capable hands of those who had built the cabins now built solidly and well the house of worship. Ludwig Rhodenbach built the pulpit and benches. But not until fifteen years later was the bell to arrive,—a big one that was to cause the little building to vibrate with its every chime, and whose echoes were to reach far and wide over the fertile fields.

"There will one day be a pastor's house beside the church"—a *pfarr-haus*,—"and when there shall be a grave some day, we shall then build a fence," Wilhelm said solemnly.

And Amalia, hearing him, looked about fearsomely at the assembled group and shuddered. Death,—it could find its way everywhere, even out here on the prairie. Who would it be?

It was young Mrs. Gebhardt's baby. Never strong from the day of its birth on the journey, it sickened and died so suddenly that not even the older women who might have helped with their advice, *flieder tee*, and *pfeffermünz tee* had time to arrive.

Emma Gebhardt was wild with grief. She rocked the little still form and would not let them take it from her. Even when they made a box for it and lined it with a quilt, she clung to the cold little thing and would not let them take it. *Verrückt*, they said she was. And crazy she seemed, until suddenly she broke into sobbing and let them take it away, and they said the crying had saved her.

It was a summer and fall of strange new experiences to Amalia,—of the constant sight of the bend and the dip of the prairie grass, of the loneliness of the cabin, of the fear of marauding Indians and the lurking rattlesnake. And always the hard work and the attempt to please Herman in every way so there would be no loud fault-finding.

Winter came on. The snows came and made of each cabin an isolated island in the vast sea of a snowy prairie. And life became a mere thing of obtaining food. Squirrels, prairie chickens, deer, rabbits, wild pigeons, all fell before the guns of the settlers.

The bearded Herman in his great boots and heavy clothes came and went, caring for his stock, oiling his harness, hunting, tramping in with the snow falling from him and the wild winds rushing in with him. Sometimes he called loudly and impatiently to Amalia to hurry and do some task for him,—sometimes he tweaked her ear jovially or dug his heavy finger into the pinkness of her cheek. And through both moods Amalia was docile and very quiet. Had it not been for the stupidity of his understanding, Herman must have seen that having won her, he had forever lost her.

She put all her mind to the doing of her share of the work. Always she went at it vigorously and with deep responsibility, for it was a fight for their very existence. Nothing was thrown away,—nothing wasted. Every piece of dried *korn brot* had its use, every bone its value to the last moist drop of its marrow. Yes, a good *haus frau* was Amalia.

Sometimes when she was alone she took out the shell box from its wrappings of unbleached muslin. All the time that her father had lived with them while his cabin was being built she had kept the box hidden in the bottom drawer of her walnut bureau lest he know of her deception in bringing it. But even when she was alone in the house and might have done so without detection, she did not open the box, merely dusted carefully between the moon shells and the Roman snails, the angel-wings and the other fragile fan-like shells of a sea she had never seen.

It was as though, if she opened it, she might see her heart lying there, red and bleeding, or a little dead Amalia.

And then suddenly the strangest of all the experiences was neither Indians nor coyotes, nor yet the long dip and wave of the prairie grass, but the fact that she was to have a child. It gave a new thought to living, a queer concern and responsibility for a life that was not her own and yet a vital part of it.

That second summer was hot and trying and a period of such hard work for all that the tasks were never finished. Everything was to be done at once. Herman worked early and late breaking out raw prairie and planting it and harvesting but a meager crop, lending his huge strength to the neighbors in exchange for help from them at other times. Amalia tried to make garden in a spot near the cabin, but the results were painfully disappointing. She cooked and scrubbed, washed and ironed and bent her pretty yellow-crowned head over tiny stitches for the child's simple wardrobe, making the little garments from a voluminous white petticoat of her own.

News of Indian trouble kept percolating into the settlement. A man by the name of Charlie Briggs camped all night with Adolph Kratz and August Schaffer when they went far to the north to buy two cows. He was on some scouting trip in behalf of the Union Pacific Railroad, told the men that Captain North with four companies of fifty friendly Pawnee Indians in each company was protecting the workmen during the building of the road since so many had been killed by the Sioux and new stations burned.

On a late summer afternoon when Herman was away with Fritz and her father cutting wild hay for winter's storage, Amalia, sitting in the cabin doorway to get any breeze that might come through the blinding heat of the prairie and bending to the tiny stitches of the garment in her hand, looked up to see three Indian bucks appearing before her, so noiselessly had they slipped around the cabin from the other side.

She might have fainted,—indeed, she felt the darkness slipping between her and the red of their ugly faces,—but for the thought of the coming child. It gave her an added bravery, the thought of the unborn child to be protected. Fascinated, she could not take her eyes from the paint and the black plaited hair and the muscles of their brown bodies that glistened in the sunshine. A little bird staring hypnotized at a snake was Amalia that summer afternoon.

They spoke among themselves in their low, guttural tongue, seeming amused at her fright. They stepped inside and filled the space so that Amalia could only shrink against the wall petrified with fear, awaiting the end of the torture.

From that time they began a systematic search of the cabin, handling a dish or pan, uncovering articles at will, drinking from the jug of precious molasses which was the only sweetening Amalia possessed.

From the bedroom one emerged with a pillow which they handed back and forth to examine, tearing a long slit in it to see the inside. Apparently they were highly amused at finding feathers which now floated forth into the room in a fine snowstorm of goose-down. As molasses still lingered on their fingers and lips, they could not rid themselves of the feathers which clung tenaciously to both.

For a long time they entertained themselves childishly

with the combination, paying not the slightest attention to Amalia still staring in a frightened mesmerism at the spectacle. Then, evidently tiring of the whole affair, they appropriated the jug of molasses and without a backward glance departed as suddenly as they had come,— riding their ponies in single file across the prairie, until they were merely outlines against the shimmering summer sky.

When Herman came, he looked sober, but tried to make light of it, explaining the difference between these Pawnees and the Cheyennes who were well worth being feared.

But to Amalia an Indian was an Indian, painted, fearsome, dreadful. And although she tried to comprehend the difference, she knew in her heart that had the friendly battalion of Pawnees appeared at her doorstep even under the command of the white Major North she would have dropped in her tracks. The sight of a painted face framed in two tightly bound braids of coarse black hair always gave her an ill feeling, so much so that when she was middle-aged and attending a wild west show she turned her head away and would not look when the Indians under Buffalo Bill's leadership rode in.

The second fall was upon them. The mad winds blew and the tumble-weeds came charging across the prairie like so many brown Indian bucks riding wild ponies.

It was a cold, windy night in November when Amalia knew her time had come. Herman saddled a horse to go for old Augusta Schaffer across the prairie.

When she heard the sound of the horse's hoofs grow fainter on the frozen ground she grew frantic with pain and fear of the strange new thing which was happening.

And then a new fear came upon her, for with the sound of the wind came far-off howls of coyotes on a distant hill. Her blood chilled when she remembered the saying that there were two occasions which brought them near,—times of birth and of death. Each time the little cabin rocked in the onslaught of wind she looked fearfully toward the rattling door to see whether or not it held.

The two of them filled her ears with their howlings,— the coyotes and the wind. When the wind came and threw itself upon the cabin with its wild shrieking, the sounds of the wolves grew fainter. But when the wind ceased for a moment she knew by their blood-curdling calls that the wolves were creeping closer. Once she cried aloud for she thought they were at the window, but it was only tumble-weeds scratching at the glass.

All the time Herman was gone they alternated their eerie calls,—the wind and the wolves,—until Amalia's own voice drowned them both. And when she heard the howl of the coyotes again, the cries of the new-born child mingled with them, and Herman and old Augusta had come.

And then, lying there comfortably after her ordeal, a sturdy man-child by her side, Amalia knew the age-old experience of young mothers,—that nothing in the world mattered but the welfare of that tiny bit of humanity which was flesh of her flesh.

The child, Emil, throve and grew, and sitting in the rocker by the cabin's window with him in her arms, Amalia knew happiness and peace. She told herself that she would never again think of the love for Matthias she had once known, making a sort of childish bargain with God that if He would watch over her baby and protect it she would promise Him this.

But later, when Herman would call her angrily to drop the potatoes faster, or when he would punish little Emil for failing in his baby fashion to mind immediately and unquestioningly in the German way, she would forget her promise and slip away into The Room in which she kept her memories. There she would think of Matthias and all that he might have been to her, and in some queer way which she herself could not fathom, would find a certain surcease from the trials.

CHAPTER XV

ALL the days were filled with hard work for every member of the colony. They were not long enough to accomplish all that the men wanted to do.

To Wilhelm Stoltz, Amalia's father, and to Herman Holmsdorfer, her husband,—to the other heads of all the families, Rudolph Kratz and his son Adolph, to the Gebhardt men, the Schaffers and the Rhodenbachs, the wilderness was a giant with which to wrestle. It must be fought, —more, it must be overcome or it in turn would conquer them.

There were a thousand things to do to make it subservient to their lives, to bring food for the body and safety of living. Daybreak found them at work, darkness only bade them cease from it. New prairie sod was turned, clean-cut with the sharp knife of the plowshare, the planting done slowly and painstakingly by hand. Crops were pitifully meager for all the hard work. Rains held off. In spite of the great snows of the winter, the skies gave only sparingly of moisture. Wood from the river's bank must be cut for fuel. New trees must be planted to replace the inroads being made upon the timberland along the stream. Cottonwood slips were brought to the cabins and planted in long rows to the north for windbreaks. Elm and ash were set near the cabins for potential shade. A shipment of apple and cherry trees was sent out from Illinois and arriving at Omaha was brought on the Union Pacific, completed in 1869. Adolph Kratz and Ludwig Rhodenbach drove an ox team the long miles to a junction to get the saplings for the eleven orchards.

Each man helped the others. Yet this was no communistic colony,—each family fought its own battles, assisted always by the others when occasion arose.

There was eternal vigilance on account of Indians. Sometimes wandering bands came through, begged food and if it were not forthcoming quickly, took it without leave.

There was eternal warfare with the elements,—great snows isolated the cabins so that roads must be broken in order to get through. Cold brought disaster to domestic animals and fowl, so that sheds and barns must be packed tightly with timbers and sod. Heat brought death to priceless horses and spring rains brought floods to the lowlands. It took great physical strength and a knack for careful planning to conquer this Nebraska into which these eleven families of settlers had come. But the German Gebhardts and Kratzes and Schaffers and all the others had them both.

The Annas and the Lenas and the Amalias must do their part,—wash and iron, cook and bake, leach the lye and make the soap, pick the wild fruit,—gooseberry, plum and currant,—patch and sew, work in the gardens, drop the corn, pick up potatoes, and yet bring forth the children who were to carry on the work when these mothers would be gone.

Always the prairie loomed there before them, lonely with silence,—a sullen giant waiting to trap them with blizzard or windstorm, drouth or flood, redskins or red fire.

It was five years now since the wagons, hub-deep in the prairie grass, had stopped at the bend of the river.

Little Emil was nearly four, sturdy and round of face, his hard cheeks apple-red and his hands square and harsh-skinned in the palms as though even now they were fitting themselves for the plow. All Amalia's love was for him.

The world would move from season to season that she and Herman might wrest a living from the soil for this child. The sun would come up each day that little Emil might grow strong in its rays. The night would descend that sleep could restore energy to the tired muscles.

Already Amalia's plans were laid that he was to be a *pastor*. School, confirmation, more schooling, ordination, —she pictured him grown and well known all over this part of the new state. He should be fine and large,— clean and well dressed,—learned and respected.

She pictured him in black suit and snowy white collar going about his pastoral duties,—in fine robe in the high pulpit delivering his sermons robustly after the manner of her church. Long before that time there would be a pastoral house—a *pfarr-haus,*—by the side of the church on the knoll in the Kratzes' pasture. Perhaps Emil would come there for his pastorate. He would marry. But whom? Not Anna Kratz's Elsa nor Lena Schaffer's sturdy little Christine. Some beautiful girl from the cities where he would attend school.

"Lena, I want you should meet Emil's wife." Or: "Little dove" (Emil would call her *"kleine taube"*), "this is my mother's old friend, Mrs. Anna Kratz."

Oh, it was a pleasant picture,—with Emil handsome and finely dressed and so learned, saying: "I am all of this because of my mother."

It was her life now. No longer was it necessary to creep away into a Room for comfort. Her solace was here before her, running about, sturdy and brave, with hard apple cheeks and eyes as blue as her own.

Once she ventured to speak of her dreams to Herman.

He looked at her with but dull understanding. "There are no pastors among the Holmsdorfers. We are all for the land."

Apparently it settled matters in Herman's eyes, but it did not settle them in Amalia's deep blue ones. He spoke of the boy as his, she thought, and felt vaguely that it was not true—that he was hers only.

It was the sixth fall for the settlers,—a mild September afternoon with the air hazy in the distance and a wind from the south.

Herman was over at the Stoltz place helping Wilhelm and Fritz who was twenty now and would soon want to be pushing on to find a suitable homestead of his own.

Amalia was ironing,—hot and ready to drop from fatigue and the heat of the wood-stove into which her irons were set. Always she was sniffing this afternoon, she told herself,—somewhere about her stove there was a faint odor of burning as though a bit of the ash wood was on a griddle. She went all over the top of it with her stove-cloth once more in order to dislodge the piece, but the odor did not stop.

She went to the cabin door, then, with a double purpose,

—to keep an ever watchful eye on little Emil and to see if the faint odor of burning could be located outside.

Once there, she raised her head and drew in a breath from the hot prairie. The smell was outside, somewhere, of that she was sure. The air seemed more hazy, and there was without doubt, now, a far-off telltale odor of smoke.

She had not even time to come to any conclusion concerning it until she could see Herman driving rapidly toward home, the lumber-wagon rattling loudly because of careening about over the rough ground.

Frightened at the combination of the smoke smell and Herman driving home so rapidly, she ran out and called Emil.

There was no answer.

Once he had done so mischievously to frighten her,— made no answer and was hiding behind the oat straw. It had given her such a scare that she had paddled him soundly for his lark. The river, rattlesnakes, Indians,— for these must Emil never leave the immediate ground around the cabin.

But now he was not at the straw stack nor by the log stable nor under the young orchard trees.

Something frightening possessed her,—the smoke odor, the haste of the rattling lumber-wagon, Emil not answering. She was running wildly now, calling here, there, everywhere. On two sides lay the wide open prairie, on one side the dried cornstalks rustling in the hot stiff wind, on the other the timber-land and the river.

Herman was here now, his horses lathering with the heat of their coming.

"Get gunny-sacks," he called. "A prairie-fire."

So there was a prairie-fire coming and little Emil not here.

It took all her strength to say the words and when they came, they seemed not effective: "The baby . . . he is gone."

"Gone?"

"Lost from me."

"Well, then, find him." Herman yelled at her: "Find him before he burns in the prairie-fire."

Fritz was speeding past now across the prairie to the Kratzes'. Years later there would be a bell at the church tower to ring for emergencies, but not yet. To-day must the words be passed by Fritz on horseback.

It did not seem possible that *Gott* would let two catastrophes happen at once,—so did Amalia childishly reason. And so did she call on Him constantly to help her as she ran like a wild woman first toward the corn-field, "Emil . . . baby. Answer mother."

But there was no sound.

Back she sped for another look near the cabin, then down toward the timber and the river: *"Emil . . . liebling! Ach, Gott."*

Up and down the river bank she ran, calling franti-cally, then back to the house, her hair down from its neat braid and flying, her skirt catching on the corner of a wagon-box and tearing its full length.

She could see the low black roll of the smoke now and the air was putrid with the distant burning. Herman was plowing and so was her father. Down in the other direc-tion she could see the Kratz men out too, plowing the strip so that the upturned loam would give the fire nothing upon which to feed and it would die out of hunger for something to consume.

What if the baby were out as far as the plowed strip? Perhaps he had walked even beyond that point and already was between it and the fire. When the blaze rolled in it would bring coyotes running ahead of it and rattlesnakes hissing before it.

And now, calling and running, she had no plan for looking,—was too distracted to hold sane ideas. Fritz was back. The low-running black smoke showed its scarlet flame now like a great black dog, mad and frothing at the mouth, snapping and licking the ground with its slavering scarlet tongue.

She ran toward Fritz and the Kratzes and Herman, calling and shrieking and ready to go out beyond the plowed strip and meet the oncoming red thing if her baby were there too.

Fritz and Herman left the plowing to the Kratzes and came to help hunt. The women were coming up now with wet gunny-sacks ready for beating out any firebrands that might leap the plowed strip when the red menace came near. The thing would not leap the river but it might take all their cabins before reaching the water that was on the north.

Women were hunting now, too,—Lena Schaffer and Anna Kratz, their faces as white as Amalia's chalky one.

"His wagon," Fritz asked, "where is that?"

The wagon was not there. Fritz had made it from timber with round disks cut from a young cottonwood for wheels.

"Where is the wagon, there is the baby." Fritz said and Amalia agreed more sanely.

And it was Fritz who found him. Riding into the cornfield, systematically up and down, so no portion would be missed, he came upon him sleeping by his wagon,—three stubby ears of corn in the little box of it. When Fritz lifted him up, he said sturdily between yawns: "All the corn for winter I husk."

Not even Herman's cross: "See to it you look after him again," could hurt Amalia. She was beyond being hurt when her baby was back in her arms. There was no fear anywhere now but the low sweeping red flame licking closer to the farm land,—as horrible as it was, the finding of Emil had minimized it.

All the rest of the afternoon they worked with plow and wet gunny-sacks. As the firebrands lighted in the dry grass, Amalia beat them like a strong man, for her relief and thankfulness gave her strength.

When the last of the flames died down, the land to the south was a desolate waste, leaving a fear forever branded on the minds of the settlers as marked as the blackness of the scar on the prairie.

Fall came on and the land was mellow with the haze of Indian summer. Amalia cared for little Emil, washed and ironed, baked her *frisches korn brot* and her *kaffee-kuchen,* cleaned and scrubbed, took care of the meat from the hog that Herman butchered, made *met-wurst* and smoked the *schinken* and rendered her lard.

Winter came on and the cabin was isolated in a sea of white so that Herman broke a road to Anna Kratz's and to the church on the knoll against which the drifts packed.

Spring Came On Forever

There were Christmas services with the singing of *"Stille Nacht, Heilige Nacht"* and *"Ein Feste Burg Ist Unser Gott,"* and with little Emil big-eyed at the sight of the green *tannen-baum* and the home-made *kerzen* lighted among its branches.

All winter Amalia hoarded every bit of grease from every rind for the making of her soap. She made her own lye for it, too, leaching the alkali from the wood ashes which she saved all winter long.

When the first spring days came over the prairie bringing the scent of wild things growing and the sound of wild things calling to their mates, she would get out the big iron kettle which Matthias had molded so carefully, and prepare for the soap making.

The odor of the grease and lye was not distasteful to her. It smelled good and clean like the wild free winds that blew over the prairie. And though to herself she seemed like another Amalia than the young girl in Illinois, an Amalia who knew nothing but work and responsibility,—and though it was rather like a song that is half remembered,—yet springtime and soap-time and the lilt of the first meadow-lark brought back to her always the poignant memory of lost love.

CHAPTER XVI

MATTHIAS MEIER was now, in 1872, part and parcel of the new capital town of Lincoln which like a growing youngster gained in size and importance a little every day. There had been a vast change since that April day four years before when he had driven into the settlement of a few log-cabins. In truth, the village was no longer isolated and aloof from the older towns. The Burlington Railroad had arrived in 1870 from Plattsmouth and the Midland Pacific a year later from Nebraska City. Stage coaches were passé. And no longer did Charlie Briggs, through blizzard and scorching heat, freight goods by team from Council Bluffs and Pacific Junction, Iowa. In fact, Charlie had nearly lost his life a few years before, —1869,—with a bunch of frontiersmen and scouts in the Republican Valley. He had been one of fifty-one men standing off the Cheyenne, Arapaho, and Sioux Indians for nine days from a sand-bank in the river. It made Matthias' blood run cold when Charlie came to the store one day and told him some of the bloody details.

There were a dozen or more stores dotted here and there on the straggling streets. Several doctors' shingles swung in the prairie winds and, while lawyers had not descended upon the town in hordes quite equal to the grasshopper scourge, at least a score of them had arrived.

There were a lunatic asylum and a penitentiary and a cemetery, all appropriated by the state legislature,—the cemetery called suitably enough *Wyuka* which is the Indian word for "a place to lie down and sleep." The appropriation of this last showed tremendous optimism on the part of the legislature for it contained no less than one hundred acres, and how can enough people to fill one hundred acres ever lie down and sleep there unless they have first been awake nearby?

The capitol itself had been hastily constructed previous to this with lumber brought in from Iowa and stone hauled from Nebraska City and Plattsmouth, by the tedious team or ox-cart method. It was built on high ground to the east of the village, a cumbersome-looking affair, top-heavy with dome. Paths cut diagonally across the meadow toward it where it stood in solitary grandeur, a miniature Rome with all roads leading to it. The grounds surrounding it were treeless virgin prairie on which the cows of the neighborhood munched the early spring grasses.

But there was no doubt about the growth of the village. Almost could one see the added poundage each month which the growing youngster took on.

Meier's and Collins' Emporium was selling high boots and nearly-as-high shoes, New Orleans molasses and sugar, red flannel and cotton batting, coffee berries, pepper, one or two sizes of rope, two or three kinds of nails, shot and powder, tobacco, goods by the yard running largely to calico, eggs and butter, sometimes slightly the worse for their long jolting trips across the prairie,—but who was there to find fault when there were not any better anywhere?

There were two banks now, the State National and the First National. Ten church organizations had been formed, sometimes with but a mere handful of people in one, but as always, the differences of close and open communion, of dipping and sprinkling, of formal ritual or personal testimony, of conversion in one lightning-like stroke or by the slow process of character building, of foreordination or local option, as it were, drove each citizen of the village to seek his own mode of religious expression, however small the group.

There was a University,—a single building,—classrooms on the first floor and a dormitory above, which like the capitol stood in solitary grandeur on the prairie, and toward which the cows also gravitated as though the grass there might benefit from its proximity to an atmosphere of higher education.

Matthias was energetic, purposeful, one with the neighborly spirit of the little town. He wore a beard,—it gave him added dignity and apparently a few extra years. Twenty-seven he was now,—his partner, James Collins, was twenty-five. Young men were the order of the day.

So busy was Matthias with his store, so ambitious, that he worked early and late, living, in the few hours he was away from it, at a Mrs. Smith's boarding-house with several others of the young business men, where came also some of the legislators in season.

He attended church every Sunday morning in a frame and somewhat flimsy building, and if he had two reasons for going,—one to benefit his soul and the other his business, it has been done before.

His association with young women had been as businesslike as he could keep it, for since his love for Amalia had received its blow, he felt no great desire to form another attachment. Already he was being spoken of by the young women in town as an old bachelor, but an eligible one for all that. Nor was he any martyr to a lost love. He merely put his heart and energies into *Meier's and Collin's Emporium.* Business was his mistress, getting ahead his whole desire. If he no longer thought about Amalia, at least he looked upon no other girl with longings.

He found to his own surprise that he was supposed to be the possessor of a very decent voice. The songs in his head which he had often told himself he could hear so plainly, suddenly proved to be quite capable of arriving in the atmosphere with no little degree of accuracy. At the occasional parties he attended his "Drink To Me Only With Thine Eyes" and "Come Where My Love Lies Sleeping" joined in right nobly with those of the Lunds and the McCurdeys who attended the same church.

It did not take long until Mrs. William McCurdey had inveigled Matthias into the choir of which she was both voluntary soprano and self-appointed leader. The rest of the personnel of the choir included Mr. William McCurdey whose "Rocked in the Cradle of the Deep" reached such utter basso profundo depths after its prolonged descension that half the audience, when hearing it at a home-talent concert, inadvertently put hands to their throats in a sort of mesmerized sympathy of aching muscles.

The tenor was Mr. Anton Lund whose tossing head, rapidly winking eyes and mouth gymnastics supplied entertainment for any deficiencies which his voice might lack, and whose whole facial effect was such that little boys and girls otherwise bored with the services looked forward each Sunday to this particular amusement.

Mrs. Anton Lund was a member of the choir merely because she was Mrs. Anton Lund,—it being apparent to all that she neither added to nor took away from the musical output, her faint little voice never attaining to greater volume than that made by a rabbit nibbling grass. The alto was Miss Dolly Thomas, a good, substantial robust alto, who made up for Mrs. Anton Lund's lack of volume by a full, unshaded, monotonously accurate second part as resonant as a bell.

In this fall of 1872, now, Mrs. McCurdey became filled with zeal to add Matthias, some other as yet undiscovered tenor, and another soprano to the choir. Almost in answer to her prayers, a Miss Ida Carter arrived to open a private school, bringing with her a sweet soprano voice which Mrs. McCurdey immediately requisitioned. After some sleuthing she found one Peter Longshore, a drug clerk, fairly capable of following Mr. McCurdey part way down into the cradle of the deep. These then became the double quartette of the church to which they went long and often for practice, the meetings taking upon themselves more and more of the social side as time went on.

Sometimes the Lunds took Ida Carter, the new teacher, home. Sometimes the McCurdeys took her. Sometimes Peter Longshore and Miss Dolly Thomas. And then one night when the Lunds and the McCurdeys were invited to eat oysters at the Atwood House right after choir practice, and Miss Dolly Thomas and Mr. Peter Longshore frankly disappeared while Matthias was gathering up his music, it devolved upon him to take Miss Carter home himself.

Miss Carter was not pretty. She was merely clean and

neat with rather nice frank gray eyes, and having only a level head and a sense of humor instead of any of the feminine appeal which Matthias knew every man required.

He took her arm down the church steps and through the darkness of the streets, realizing it gave him very little headiness of feeling, a fact which genuinely relieved him. In truth, it gave him such a sense of security that he was rather more courteous and gallant all the way to her boarding-house than he would have been otherwise, slipping protectingly to the inside of the walk when they passed the saloon with its swinging doors and sour yeasty smell.

He saw her into her boarding-house, talked for a moment in the dim kerosene-lighted hallway with her landlady who had rushed out to chaperon the two, bade Miss Carter a formal good-night and departed to his own boarding-house.

Upon arriving at his room, for some reason which he could not analyze, he went to the calfskin brass-bound box in which he kept his papers and took out the leather wallet containing the note from Amalia. He had not thought about her for a long time. She was no longer his,—could never be his. But even so, the sight of the note, the precise and shaded script it contained, gave him more genuine stirring of the emotions than the warm human touch of the young woman he had just left.

He read the letter through twice. It stirred him unaccountably. A sudden wave of longing for her and regret swept over him. He had not felt its like for years, and wondered vaguely why he was experiencing it to-night. Dear, lovely little Amalia! And this was all he had of her,—a fragile note. Not a lock of hair nor a picture, not a flower. Just a note and memories.

Almost as though in answer to the wish, for a moment, then, she stepped out of the letter as plainly as anything short of reality could have done.

Vividly he saw the pansy-blueness of her eyes and the pinkness of her mouth, felt again the warm softness of her lips and supple body.

Where was she now? Did she ever think of him? How had the German husband . . . and the years . . . treated her? For the hundredth time he asked himself why he had been late. Other steamers made the trip in regulation time. Not once in two dozen trips, perhaps, was one delayed so long. But the one he chose had been caught and held grimly by the sands. They had proved to be the sands of time. Why had it happened so? Why? For what reason? What right had Fate to intervene between him and his heart's deepest desire?

He looked again at the note, as though from its six years of lying there in the darkness it might speak. And in speaking, answer the unanswered question.

. . . *it is better to remember our love as it was in the springtime.*

CHAPTER XVII

BUT even though Matthias looked upon Ida Carter
only as a nice, intelligent young woman with whom
he had been thrown in social and vocal contact, at the
end of the next choir practice evening, because she very
frankly made plans to go home with the McCurdeys to
the utter disregard of the previous week's procedure, he
found himself really wanting to take her. There was
something mentally stimulating about her even though
she was so different from Amalia. And she had a sense
of humor such as he had never known in any feminine
acquaintance,—the humor that could laugh gaily at her
own foibles and at his also, but without barbed shafts.

So he took her "home" to the dimly-lighted but
resolutely chaperoned boarding-house that night,—and
many others.

By Christmas time the walk home with her had grown
to be the regular program. By mid-winter he was calling
upon her steadily in the late Sunday afternoon and ac-
companying her to evening church. By February it came
to be a rather settled thing in the intimate little social
affairs of the growing town,—house warmings, oyster sup-
pers, the McCurdeys' tin wedding,—that Matthias Meier
was assigned by the hostess to Miss Ida Carter.

He grew to look forward to their talks. She had such a
grasp of human understanding, could turn a subject over
in her mind so deftly with such reasonable decisions that

she satisfied something in him. He found himself reserving opinions until he had learned her reaction, planning to tell her about problems which came up in his business, even to ask advice outright occasionally. Sometimes he questioned himself closely, tried to analyze just what this type of friendship meant to him,—told himself if this was love, it was a queer kind. There was none of that thunder of blood in his ears he had once felt. He must wait now and see how permanent was the feeling, remembering that when he had loved Amalia there was no question, and no thought of waiting.

So it was that on this Easter Sunday of 1873, a fine one with every one dressed in his best and out on the high wooden sidewalks of the main streets, with many buggies and two-seated carriages tied at the hitching posts in front of the churches, with Mr. Anton Lund's tenor soaring high and Mr. McCurdey's basso profundo rumbling in the opposite direction, that some chemical change took place in Matthias' heart and he warmed toward the young woman sitting in front of him in the choir. He looked at the pretty plum-colored straw hat with its plume hanging over the brim and mingling with her dark hair, at the neat folds of her high collar, and almost before he could question its reason he told himself he was going to marry her.

From that moment on he was lost in a maze of planning. He would build a new house not far from the capitol. He would branch out in other lines of business investments as soon as possible. The town would be twice this size some day. He would never care to live anywhere else. He would always be proud of Ida. His decision sent his mind skyrocketing on an hour of planning far afield from the minister's message.

When the long sermon was over and the congregation poured out on the wooden sidewalks, Matthias slipped his arm through that of Miss Ida Carter, rather to her startled consternation, that gesture being usually reserved for the period following sundown.

With chattering people all about, with buggies pulling up to the edge of the walk near them, and children with Sunday School papers brushing hurriedly past, he said it, as though the saying could not wait, now that he had decided.

"Ida, I want you to be my wife." Now that he had taken the step he found there should never have been any question about it.

No moonlight, no music, no chance for romance. Ida merely saying: "Why, Matt, I am so surprised at . . . How do you do, Mrs. Jamison. Of course I. . . . Good morning, Alice. Yes, isn't it nice? . . . If you think you really want me, Matt . . . Hello, Mose."

In such a way did Matthias make his second proposal to a young woman. And in such a way did she accept.

By night there had descended the Easter blizzard of 1873 which still lives on the pages of midwestern diaries and in the annals of its histories. It caught the people of Lincoln unaware as indeed it caught those of the whole state. It caught Matthias Meier at Mrs. Smith's boarding-house sitting on the horse-hair sofa under the unseeing eye of Mrs. Smith's deceased and framed husband but still within the range of Mrs. Smith's own alert, far-sighted one, also framed, but by the crack of the door.

The blizzard gave Matthias a pleasant background for the thought that soon he and this nice girl with her good sense and humor would have a home of their own shut away from all the blizzards of all time. So pleasing were his thoughts that he was almost unaware of what Ida was saying. But now he heard it.

"Matt, I have something I must ask you. I hate myself for thinking about it, but it seems that if I'll face facts and tell you,—get your honest answer I can conquer the feeling I've been working myself into this afternoon. Has there ever been any other girl, Matt, or am I the first and only girl you have loved?"

He sparred for time. "How can I answer? The way you put your question, Ida, calls for both yes, and no." He laughed a bit as though the whole thing were a joke.

Ida laughed, too,—at herself. "I knew it, of course. There has been. It seems that I can almost sense what you're thinking at times, I have learned to know you so well. Well, I brought it on myself and I've nobody but myself to blame. I wonder why I had to torture myself by knowing? I suppose I'd be far happier if I didn't know all the details to mull over in my mind, but tell me, anyway, Matt. I imagine things like a youngster in the dark. Maybe if you'd light the lamp . . . the bogies would turn out to be shadows."

"There's not much to tell, Ida dear." And because seven years is a long time to a young man, he said: "It was years ago. I was only twenty-one and she was not quite eighteen. It was in Illinois that I knew her. Something . . . parted us. I never saw her again. I don't even know just where she lives, although it's somewhere out here in this state . . . away out farther on the prairie. She's married . . . and come to think about it, I don't even know her married name." He was smiling at the nice girl sitting by him on the boarding-house sofa, slipping his arm about her now. "Pretty dangerous rival, isn't she?"

Ida smiled at that, too. It *had* been silly to punch sleeping dogs. But it was a newly engaged girl's prerogative.

Matthias and Ida did not go to church. No one went to church or anywhere else. The storm raged like an infuriated madman. The room grew cold so that Matthias kept feeding chunks of wood into the sheet-iron stove, not knowing that Mrs. Smith was counting every one.

He stayed all evening as the storm continued its fury. Indeed, so terrible was its raging that he stayed all night, a fact that caused Mrs. Smith so much perturbation that after giving him her own room, she made a bed for herself on a couch in the hall in sight of Miss Carter's door.

CHAPTER XVIII

E ASTER had come to the valley, too.
In spite of the fact that hitherto the winters had
been severe, the seventh one for the settlers, that of 1872
and '73 was unusually fine,—practically an open one with
little or no snow. Not once had Amalia missed church,
nor had she been forced to stay away from Anna Kratz's
for two months at a time as in some of those past seasons.

Almost every other week she had taken Emil to Anna's
and spent the afternoon piecing her quilt,—Anna returning the visit the next week. Sometimes she had to walk
when Herman was busy or angry about something that
had gone wrong with the stock or his tools or the feed.
Then he would storm and rage and Amalia would go
quietly about her work until he had slammed his way out
of the cabin and down to the stable, when she would slip
out and trudge the long way over to Anna's.

It would soon be seven years since she and Anna had
been married the same day by the side of the Cut-off trail
near Nebraska City. Anna had her fourth child this
week,—three boys and a girl now.

Only this Easter morning on the way home from Confirmation services in the log church on the knoll Herman
had thrown it up to her, saying that Adolph would have
help a plenty in a few years and how could one expect to
get ahead and have more land with just one son to work
it with him.

Amalia, feeling bold, had said: "Emil will not be working the land when a pastor he is to be."

It had set Herman off. Even though it was Easter Sunday and he had sung lustily with the others *"O Du Fröliche, O Du Selige,"* already on the way home he was talking of land,—always talking more land and that Emil should hurry and grow up to help work it, and was now in a rage that she was suggesting otherwise.

"The Holmsdorfers have always been for the land."

"My mother was from a pastor's family," Amalia said. "Her father and her grandfather in Germany were well educated and were pastors."

"Let others do the preaching," Herman struck at the horses in his anger so the wagon bounced over the rutty prairie trail. *"My* son works."

At home Amalia changed her dress to her everyday one, built up her fire and prepared her dinner. Wilhelm and Fritz came as always to have the Sunday meal with them. Sometimes several families took dinner together, —once in a while all eleven of them.

The door of the cabin stood open for the day was almost hot with a strong wind from the south. Amalia had worn her straw bonnet—of the fashion of many years ago—to church, so summer-like had it been. For several weeks men had been working in the fields. Only Saturday Herman had plowed all day in his shirt sleeves. Every indication of winter had vanished.

"Everything is getting green," Herman said to the men when he had finished the *tisch gebet*.

Herman made the table prayer no matter what his

mood. Sometimes when scolding loudly, he would stop
suddenly, make the *tisch gebet:*

*"Komm Herr Yesu, sei unser Gast und segne was
Du uns bescheret hast."*

And even though he had said this: "Come, Lord Jesus,
be our Guest and bless what Thou hast prepared for us,"
at the *"Amen"* he would be raising his head and con-
tinuing the loud fault-finding as though nothing had in-
tervened, as though he had never prayed the table prayer.

"Yes. Green and pretty," Amalia added. She was
glad he was so safely over his anger of the morning.

"Of the pretty we do not care," he snapped. "It is the
green for crops we need."

Amalia looked at her plate and said nothing. To Herman there was no need to speak ever of the prettiness of
things. Why did she ever do it when she knew he did
not care? But to little Emil—that was different. Always
she called his attention to the red at the edge of the sunset
clouds and the light on the prairie like lakes of gold. He
was to be a *pastor* and he must see the beautiful along
with the ugly burdens. He must sense the presence of
God in every leaf and wild flower. It would help him in
his work.

The meal went on, a mere consuming of food and talk of
the land and the mares they were buying.

Herman and Wilhelm were leaving right after dinner
for one of the Englishmen's homesteads, that of Mr. Lawrence, about seven miles away. "Together we can manage the mares we are to bring," they decided.

123

"Fritz does not go?"

"*Nein.* If we are late he does the chores for both."

By two o'clock, with the men gone, shifting clouds scudded low across the blue of the spring sky. A little later when surprisingly a slow drizzling sprinkle began, Amalia tied a shawl over her head, put a jacket on Emil and together they went out for eggs.

"So early it is for the eggs," she explained to him, "but later it will rain harder."

Emil was five now, sturdy and strong, his round apple-cheeked face a miniature Herman's. He grasped the basket interwoven with its carpet rags and swung along ahead of Amalia on big stocky legs, calling back German sentences. "I can myself the eggs hunt," and fiercely: "The old hens will I scare."

They gathered the eggs at the straw-stack, Amalia calling out warnings not to go so high, or not go so close to the cow; with Emil, proudly brave, doing the very things of which *Mutter* was fearful.

While they were hunting around the stack down toward the creek-bed where an old hen often stole her nest, the skies grew darker and a chill wind blew in from the northwest. By the time they were in the house rain was falling almost sleet-like in its harshness.

In the midst of the chilling rain, Fritz arrived to do the chores, explaining that he was doing Herman's first and their own later. He wished his father and Herman would get in. "Almost I would say we would have a blizzard if the season was not so late."

When he had finished and gone back home, the clouds grew very black and hung low with a menacing appearance. Amalia watched them from the cabin's small window. The rain turned in truth then to sleet,—then to snow so fine and thick that Amalia could no longer see out of the window. She kept up the fire with the wood from the creek-bed, put Emil to bed very early and sat down close to the stove to wait.

It was a blizzard by now.

She could hear the wild winds of it shrieking about the cabin, feel its blasts shaking the little structure as though the great breath of some insane giant were trying to blow it over. The men folks would not have left the homestead of the Lawrences', of that she was certain. The rain had turned to sleet so early in the afternoon that they would not have started on the long trek across the open prairie.

She crawled into bed beside the sleeping Emil, his rosy face close to hers, and though she said her prayers to the good *Gott* for safety, she shivered with fright whenever the roaring wind shook the cabin. Toward morning she slept,—and because she had been awake so long in the early part of the night, overslept, realizing it when she came to herself with a start.

Sitting up quickly, she had the sensation of a peculiar whiteness about her, as of a strange fantastic light. Everything was white,—the bed blankets were covered with a white powdered snow,—the small window of the cabin was packed solid with it.

Hastily she dressed and leaving Emil sleeping, went out into the coldness of the other room. With freezing fingers she made a fire in the little stove and as its flame tore madly with the wind into the chimney, fearful of setting the cabin on fire, wished she had not done so.

With Herman caught away from home at the Lawrences', she must feed the stock. So she bundled herself in an old coat of his, tied a scarf tightly over her hair and prepared to plunge into the storm.

As she opened the door the fury of the thing was overwhelming. It rushed into the room like a white mad animal. The air itself appeared to be one huge mass of moist and moving snow. The wind howled like so many hungry coyotes.

She stepped out into the welter, scarcely able to pull the door against the fury of the thing, and sank to her hips in a moist and smothering snowbank. Some instinct made her keep one hand tightly clasped to the cabin doorlatch. She held the other mittened one up now to her face and could not see its outline.

For a time she stood there, buffeted, hip deep in the drift, not knowing what to do. But Fritz could not get through this welter from his place she was sure. The stock in the barn needed her,—there were two cows to be milked . . . and the chickens to be fed.

A blast of wind, wilder than the preceding ones, tore the shawl from her head and, unthinking, she let go of the doorlatch to grab for the flying headgear. Immediately she was down in the snowbank gasping for breath like a drowning thing. Frantically she reached back for the door and met only the emptiness of the snow-packed air.

CHAPTER XIX

I AM not four feet from the house," Amalia said to herself, frantic at feeling nothing but the snow-filled air. "It must be here . . . or here . . . or there. . . ."

But it was not there. It was as though the house had vanished, leaving her in a welter of flying, whirling clouds of snow. Arms out, she staggered frantically, her eyes and mouth and nostrils filled with the smothering thing. One thought only possessed her, as it has possessed good mothers always,—her child. She must get to little Emil, alone in the cabin, sleeping there in his bed.

She wallowed, fell, picked herself from the great drifts and staggered about. Frantic, she lunged first in one direction and then another. And then . . . the wall! The good solid wall hitting her suddenly from out a sea of emptiness. *Gott sei dank.* And God be thanked for trees and logs and shelter from the wild elements.

She clung with mittened freezing fingers to the chinks between the logs until she might regain her breath. This way lay the stoop and door. She moved cautiously along, never taking her hands from the wall. When she felt snow piled shoulder-high against the solid thing, she would not remove her hold, but fought the white moist mass with her other hand and shoulders. And it seemed that she would never be able to work herself through the dense mountain. It was so smothering . . . so . . .

She was through. But strangely, here was a corner of the house. How could there be a corner? She must have hit the cabin on the narrow side that first time she had found it in a sea of snow,—shuddered to think she might have missed it entirely.

And now there was this other side to be traversed. It seemed hours that she fought her way through, clinging always to the logs lest for one instant she lose their feel.

And then she stumbled, and the thing that had caused her to stumble was the stoop. With numb hands she clung, worked them slowly up through the hard-packed mass, not seeing, doing all by sense of touch. The latch! With one last exertion of her body she flung herself onto the latch,—into the room,—pushed the door back against the mad white giant, drunk with the power of his strength, trying to follow her into the house.

She must have fainted, for when she knew what was next happening, Emil in his flannel nightgown was bending over her, pulling at her eyelids, calling *"Mutter,"*— and she was down on the floor in a slushy bed of snow that had dropped from her garments.

All day and all night the storm raged. Wild white fingers plucked at the little cabin standing lonely on the prairie, a continent away from the other cabins on the adjoining homesteads, as far away from Fritz in his log house on the next acreage as though a sea separated them. Indeed, it was an ocean that parted them, with snow-drifts for water and Death riding the waves.

All day and all night with the snow blowing under the door and seeping in through every crack, Amalia tried to make her supply of wood last. In the afternoon of the second day she went to bed with Emil clasped in her arms, both fully dressed, and with the quilts wrapped about them. If only they could have foreseen how bad it was to be, Fritz would have stayed here with them for safety and for company. Many times she thought of her father and Herman, thankful that the blizzard must have come on before they started home.

On the third day the storm abated, and the sun came out upon a world devoid of color. White everywhere,— nothing but a sparkling white world and a blue sky, as though an inverted blue china bowl met the rim of a white plate.

Fritz, after nearly a half-day's work through the drifts, managed to get to Amalia. He told her tales she could scarcely believe,—his horses had stamped so much snow under their hoofs that their backs were near the shed roof. Frozen prairie chickens were everywhere and a deer lay dead between the house and the barn. The trees along the river banks were not visible,—only a great solid white wall traced the way of the stream.

Out at the stable he found a horse nearly embedded in snow, frozen chickens, a calf almost lifeless so that he brought it into the house, much to Emil's excited delight.

He agreed verbally with Amalia that the storm would have struck before the menfolks started home, but each knew the other in his heart was not entirely confident.

All day and part of the next Amalia waited to hear from the two men.

And then Ludwick Rhodenbach and August Schaffer

found Wilhelm Stoltz lying against the wagon-box which he had turned on its side to protect himself from the onslaught of the storm. He was unconscious, his feet frozen stiff.

They took him home. When he gained consciousness and could talk, he said he did not know where Herman was,—that he had set out across the prairie for Rudolph Kratz's house. Later a doctor came on horseback across the prairie from the far-away new town of Westville, and amputated Wilhelm's feet,—the feet that had walked with unceasing energy beside the ox-cart all the way from Illinois.

The snows began to melt under the April sun and the river rose. Every hollow and ravine that ran in an easterly or westerly direction was filled with snow from rim to rim. Shacks had been unroofed and people in them frozen. Travelers caught out in the wild onslaught were found when the drifts melted weeks afterward.

The Kratzes out hunting for their horses came across the dead body of Herman. It was at the head of a small canyon pocket, his gun by his side. Evidently he had died on his knees having crawled into the narrow place to get such slight protection from the cold as its walls would afford.

They brought him home to Amalia.

Mrs. Rudolph Kratz and Anna came ahead to tell her. They wanted to break it gently. As though Death is ever gentle.

But when Anna saw Amalia standing at the stove cooking *suppe* for her sick father and thought how the two

couples were married the same day so romantically outdoors by the side of the trail, and how she would feel if
it were Adolph, she threw her apron over her head, burst
into wild weeping, and could not tell.

So the older Mrs. Rudolph Kratz said it bluntly:
"Amalia, you have lost your Herman. They find him
dead."

Amalia stood as one paralyzed and yet wondering
sanely how one can lose something one has never had.

In the days that followed she could not sense what was
happening. It was too strange. She moved in and out of
the cabin and went over to her father's bedside while
Mrs. Rudolph Kratz and old Augusta Schaffer bathed
that which had been Herman and dressed it in its black
suit.

She shed no tears, and for that they whispered among
themselves that she would go crazy if she did not cry.

The neighbors brought *met-wurst* and *kuchen* and all
their children, set the table and ate a great deal and
talked of Herman,—how good he was at turning the new
sod and breaking colts and how mad he would have been
to know the two mares he had already paid good money
for, froze to death on the way home.

Amalia let Mrs. Kratz and Augusta Schaffer swathe a
great black veil around her head that made her feel
suffocated and from which she asked frantically to be
let out at once, for behind its thickness it seemed that
she was in blinding black snow and could not breathe nor
find little Emil.

Herman was buried while Wilhelm still lay hurling
his huge bulk against the wall in the throes of death.

With the prairie soggy from the melting snows and the teams of the settlers hitched all around the log church on the hill, Amalia sat through the long services for Herman, and saw him lowered under the sod that he had known so deftly how to break. And now some one else had broken a little patch of prairie sod for Herman. Who was Herman? A man whose house she had kept and whose bread she had baked and by whose side . . .

And then she thought of little Emil, whose hand she held so tightly, and suddenly burst into wild sobbing.

At that all the women in their black funeral clothes pursed their lips and nodded solemnly to each other across the soggy pile of dirt. She was now all right, having passed the tearless stage. Now she would not go crazy. She had cared so much for her man she had been on the way to going insane. *Verrückt.*

But Amalia was not crying for having thought so much of her man. For herself she was like a stone,—she had no feeling. She was crying because every little boy ought to have a father, and now her little boy had none.

Three days after Herman was buried, Amalia's father died, too.

It was a hard death that old Wilhelm Stoltz had to meet, far harder than Herman's painless sleeping in the snow,—gangrene from the frozen feet, amputation, and after that a lingering and terrible passing.

Never sick a day in his life, always his own master and dictator of those about him, when he realized that he was not to get well,—that, like Herman, he too could never again crack the blacksnake, never break the new sod or plant or reap, never face the wild winds of the prairie or buffet the storms,—he grew hard and bitter and turned on the God whom he had addressed so fervently and for whose worship he had come into the new land. But at the last, with the fever consuming him, when he was worn and spent with his ravings and knew that he must obey the absolute Dictator, he grew meek and muttered humble supplications.

But even then he could not leave his authoritative position without a last strangle-hold upon the lives of his children. He called Fritz to the bedside, bade him bring the big Bible.

"Put . . . your hand on it. A promise make me."

Fritz obeyed. He had always obeyed.

"You will never marry. To look after Amalia and little Emil you will stay single."

Fritz swallowed hard. His bronze face paled. Twenty-two he was, warm-blooded and ready for a wife. Already in the church services he had cast longing eyes toward Minnie Rhodenbach, a young widow with a small child. He could not speak out his mind that it was cruel to expect such a promise. He could scarcely have done so if his father were well. How could he, then, when Death hovered over him?

"Before God . . . you promise?"

Fritz's tall lanky body shook as though he, too, felt the coldness of the grave, and saw its darkness. This looking on at a passing, it was a fearsome thing, at this Death that laid low the two huge frames of his father and brother-in-law. He wet his dry lips. "But if Amalia marries and has protection?" he ventured.

"It releases you. But you will not tell her of your oath. Promise."

Fritz turned frightened eyes toward the log church in the distance as though he might there see the soft round face of Minnie Rhodenbach with dimples at the mouth's corners.

"Promise." Wilhelm heaved himself fearfully on his elbow, his deep-set eyes, glassy in death, piercing those of his son. *"Gleich!"*

"I promise."

They buried old Wilhelm, too,—not old,—but seeming so because of the weatherbeaten countenance and the huge gnarled frame and his long years of hard work beginning in the German mines when he was twelve.

There were four graves now on the high knoll of the church acreage. Sometimes the fierce sun blazed down on them and the hot southwest winds blew. Sometimes the tumble-weeds rolled over them and the crows circled low. And sometimes the great prairie snows piled high between the mounds.

But wind or sun or snows, it was very quiet out there where Herman and old Wilhelm lay.

CHAPTER XX

IN the strange days that followed Herman's death and that of her father, also, in the Easter blizzard, Amalia could not seem to adjust herself to the new way of living. She appreciated the kindness of all the families, knowing how little they had to give from their meager supplies and seeing how generous they were in their giving. For all of them came now bearing gifts to show their sorrow to one who was never anything but kind to them and gentle.

The women brought home-made *käse* and wild *pflau-men-butter*. The men drove in to see about the stock and corn-planting.

She thanked them all, but told them Fritz was going to move over here with her, and bring their father's stock and equipment. She and Fritz would get along fine. She even laughed at a little joke she made that Fritz had always been her favorite brother, when they knew she had only Fritz. Anna Kratz was ashamed for Amalia that she had joked that way before the men, and Herman so recently taken.

"But maybe Fritz wants a wife now and farm his father's place for himself," Elsa Rhodenbach suggested, having been sent as a sort of official spy by her sister Minnie.

But Amalia only laughed aloud at her,—twice to-day she had laughed. "Fritz isn't looking around any yet."

She had a queer feeling of deception; that she was

135

pretending to be something she was not,—that she was two women, the real Amalia and one who must act a part.

She had shed tears over the passing of Herman and her father, and neither death had touched that which was away down inside her being.

She had been shaken by the shock of both tragedies and the awfulness of the presence of death in the house; but a few days later something inside her had soared as at a release. She would have been ashamed to have any of the women know it. From Anna Kratz who mourned over her constantly because of the double marriage and the closeness of their friendship, she must always keep the knowledge. But it was true. She felt free without Herman's loud orders and his clutching hands upon her, without her father's constant commands and the fear of his opinions. Only for little Emil was she sad. But she and Fritz would teach him to mind them without fear. She and Fritz would be all that Herman had been and more.

In the late summer she unwrapped the shell box which Matthias had given her and left it openly for a few weeks on her walnut bureau, so that all the feminine contingent of the Kratz and Schaffer, the Gebhardt and Rhodenbach women might see and admire and envy, but never know from whence it came.

Fritz, seeing it there with its shining Roman snails and angel-wings, moon shells and fragile fan-shaped ones, said suddenly:

"Amalia . . . you are a young widow. You are . . ." he was embarrassed, ". . . are free."

She had thought of it too. She had known how wicked

it was, but how could she help it,—who had loved Matthias so?

"You would write . . . a letter, Amalia?" If poor Fritz was thinking of Minnie Rhodenbach more than of Amalia,—no one knew it, so who was there to chide?

Amalia shook her head. "Don't speak of it, Fritz. It is not right . . . and seven years is too long. I would only hurt myself to hear of his marriage."

So it came about that Fritz, his mind working a little slowly perhaps, but with stubborn persistence, one day wrote the letter himself, painstakingly, in the German, telling no one, and mailed it to the iron foundry in Illinois.

CHAPTER XXI

BACK in the growing town of Lincoln Ida Carter gave up her private school in June. She and Matthias were to be married on September 20th, the wedding to be at the McCurdeys', for the trip back to her home in Massachusetts would have been long and expensive. The two had now definitely come to another decision, rather a queer one and with Matthias a long time in coming to see it as Ida did,—she was going in the store with him. At first he had thought it all wrong, later came to agree with her that a woman's taste and intuitions might be a good thing in the business.

"When we make our first fifty thousand dollars, I'll stop," she had said laughingly, so that Matthias laughed too at the huge sum.

They were going to live at the boarding-house. "When we get to making money and I stop the store work, we'll have a fine home," she told him.

All summer she was having her new dresses made, the making of a dress taking far longer than the recent making of the new state constitution, the latter not having pleats, panniers, and panels.

The town to a man was interested in the coming event. Plans were secretly under way for a charivari. Matthias had a new horse and high buggy, and the sight of the two fine-looking young people,—Ida with her gray dress and cape and small straw bonnet, Matthias in his dark suit and high hat and with his black beard trimmed in its neat square-cut style,—driving around the dusty streets or through the splashing mud was a sign for much attention from the sidewalk portion of the population.

Mrs. McCurdey was rather beside herself with importance, many cakes to be baked, an elderberry drink to be made and saying often: "Oh, if only there could be such a thing as plenty of ice in the summer."

The invitations were to be mailed out the sixth of September.

On the fifth Matthias received a letter from Fritz Stoltz sent on to him by his uncle in Illinois.

He cut into it at the desk in the back part of the store, not knowing whose stilted German-looking script was before him. When he saw it was from Amalia's brother, he was as surprised as amazed.

It was formally written, the penmanship painstakingly done as by a small boy, although Matthias knew Fritz must be a young man by now.

He read it slowly, carefully, his pulse beating rapidly at this first word in all the seven years concerning the girl he had so loved.

Amalia was a widow, the letter said,—the man she had married because of her father's wishes had been frozen to death in the Easter blizzard of last spring, and their father, too. Matthias shuddered as he read it, remembering the fury of the storm the night he had stayed at Ida's. He had read of many deaths out on the prairie at that time. One of them, then, was Amalia's husband and one her father, and he had not dreamed there was any one frozen to death of whom he had ever heard.

Amalia was free now, Fritz said, but did not know he was writing, would never know that he had done so. He could say that he knew Amalia still loved Matthias although she had never said it in so many words. When he had spoken to her about him, she had said he was no doubt married by this time. If this was true, or if Matthias had forgotten Amalia, he need never take the trouble to answer. But it seemed only right and truthful to let him know that Amalia was free.

Concluding the missive Matthias felt a combination of emotions,—sadness for the cruelty of the girl's mismanaged life, an irritation that the letter had come in just as the invitations for his marriage were to go out, an annoyance that the brother had written at all, but in spite of all this, a revival of love for the little Amalia which would not down. The affair had been as a book that was closed, or a song that was sung,—and now the pages were fluttering open, a strain of the old music was in the air.

All day he went about his business with the letter on his mind and a mixed group of emotions within him. He listened to the merry quips of friends who made bold to speak of the coming event and was provoked that they had taken upon themselves the freedom to do so. He was angry at Fritz for writing and angry that he had not done so sooner.

It weighed so upon him that when he went to Ida's in the evening, he was preoccupied, not himself. Ida, with her quick intuition, caught the mood, asked him about it.

"If there's anything troubling you, Matt,—don't you think it's a better way to begin our married life by talking it over? If I'm wrong for asking, forgive me. It's only . . . that I care . . . and want to help."

How good she was and capable and understanding. Suddenly he wanted to tell her, to go to her as a boy would to his mother, and let her know this upsetting thing which had happened.

He showed her, then, the letter, translating it from the German, for she could not read it. It eased his mind. Already he felt the weight of the burden lifting that she was knowing about the matter.

"I'm glad you have done this, Matt." Ida was cool and poised, keeping from him how it had shaken her to the depths. "I appreciate it. It makes me know how frank you are, and how honest you would have been with me."

" '*Would have been,*' Ida! You can't . . . This doesn't mean anything to me . . . not *anything* now, excepting a bit of sorrow for . . . for her. You must know it. I shouldn't have shown you the letter . . . I was . . ."

"Listen, Matt." She was firm of voice, still poised, but he did not see how her hands were holding each other tightly, each trying to keep the other from its trembling.

"There is something I must know . . . to-night . . . just now . . . before the invitations go out to-morrow. You owe it to me . . . to yourself . . . to her. Answer me this, Matt. Everything depends upon what you say. I can't go on until I know. If we two—this other young woman and I—were side by side in this room. . . . If she . . . just as you knew her . . . and I . . . just as I am . . . were here together. . . . If you walked in here and we were waiting, which one would you choose?"

She was looking bravely at him, her gray eyes steady and unflinching, watching to ascertain how the question affected him, and yet not wanting to see.

Matthias did not hesitate. He looked back steadily into the honest depths of her eyes. "All right," he could even smile now. "You are here . . . and she is here. I am to choose between you. But you have omitted something. What you have forgotten to say is that two Matthias Meiers would walk in here, a twenty-one-year-old one and I. You and I don't care much which one the young cub would choose, now do we? What concerns us is that I . . . the man standing here beside you, would choose *you*."

"Unqualifiedly, Matt?" She searched his face.

"Unqualifiedly. Does it satisfy you?"

"It satisfies me. You're good to put it that way. I think you believe it. I'll never mention her again."

He kissed her,—more tenderly than he had ever done. She cried hard for a few moments so that he comforted her but could not understand the tears. They were the last she shed for any hurt from Matthias, for she was not the crying kind.

In his boarding-house, he went over the queer quality of the question . . . Ida's intensity, the unusualness of her suppressed emotion, his satisfied feeling that the answer he made had been the right one.

But he could not get to sleep. For a long time he lay listening to the early morning sounds of the small town,— a milk wagon going through the street, its cans rattling together, a night watchman's tramp of feet on the high wooden sidewalk.

Just as he was dropping off, dimly between him and the window he saw Amalia, pink and white, infinitely sweet and alluring, heard vaguely for a moment the sound of a meadow-lark and the honk of wild geese flying.

He called to her, his arms seeking her, but she was gone. He woke and lay very still, breathing hard, shaken by the queer thing he had dreamed.

The next day the duties of the store, the meeting with people who spoke of the coming wedding and congratulated him on the young woman he was choosing, Ida's natural talk about her preparation for the wedding, drove into the realm of the unreal the momentary pangs he had felt concerning the girl he once loved so deeply.

In the evening he wrote an answer to Fritz,—several of them. "I am going to be married" was the theme of one,—"I am married," of another. "Remember me kindly to Amalia" and "Give my love to your sister."

Then he wrote one to Amalia herself, trying several ways to express that which he wished to say, realizing his written German was atrocious, and disliking them all; for how could he put into it the delicate touch that would convey to her all that she had once been to him, tell her that he, too, was living in Nebraska now because of her,—that he had tried to get to her but had been caught by sucking sands,—and yet hold her aloof?

He destroyed them all,—and wrote no other.

CHAPTER XXII

LIFE among the German neighbors in the valley went on in much the same way that it had gone on before the deaths of Wilhelm Stoltz and Herman Holmsdorfer in the Easter blizzard.

Wilhelm and Herman both would have said in their arrogant way that the settlers could not get along without their help and advice,—that Fritz and Amalia would not know what to do with no daily commands to guide them in their work, that they would lose the stock and bungle the crops and nothing would be *recht.*

But life closes over the vacancies and goes on. The settlers managed very well without the two, through some of the most trying years of the state. Fritz and Amalia did as well as the others, which is not saying a great deal, for the first few years following the Easter blizzard were lean years.

There were prairie fires and blizzards, grasshoppers and drouths, Indian raids too close for comfort. Prices for farm products were so low that it did not pay to haul the scanty crop to market. So Fritz and Amalia along with the neighbors began burning corn for fuel. In the little shiningly polished four-holed stove of Amalia's neat cabin it would snap and crackle and hold its heat as well as any coal would have done. They burned hard twisted prairie hay, too, at times.

Amalia made the garden, in the good German way, but

she would not go into the field with Fritz as Lena Schaffer and young Mrs. Henry Gebhardt and some of the others did for their menfolks.

In spite of the hardships that confronted them always, the entire colony stayed just a little out of the reach of starvation and failure. The unceasing labors and good management of the homesteads by the men,—the thriftiness of the women,—these brought the settlers safely through a half-dozen years which drove those of less thrift and stamina from the scene.

To Amalia it was pleasant to have Fritz around. Even-tempered, a little jolly at times now that he was his own master, Fritz was a comfortable companion. He took a great deal of pride in Emil too, teaching him masculine chores,—taking him down to the creek for muskrat trapping, allowing him to drive the big team when by his side on the high wagon-seat, letting him husk corn so that his hard little palms grew more calloused. It caused Amalia to say one day to Fritz: "A good father you will be some day, Fritz,—kind and understanding."

But Fritz did not answer, and walked off to the stable hurriedly as though cross at her saying so.

The day that Minnie Rhodenbach was married to Karl Schaffer, Fritz went away to Westville with corn for the grinding, so that Amalia was ashamed he had gone and made excuses why he was not at the wedding festivities which lasted all day, and neither would he later go to the christening of Minnie's baby, little Christina, so stubborn about it he was.

The fall Emil was seven, Amalia got him ready for the Parochial school held now in the log church. She made him a suit out of an old one of her father's, every stitch in it tiny and neat, each one a thought or a wish or a prayer for the sturdy little son.

"You will now learn all there is to know in books," she said to him. "Then you will be a fine pastor."

"Yes . . . a pastor I will like to be . . . I can shout and the pulpit I can pound harder than any."

Amalia laughed at that. "Oh, but there is more to do than shout and pound. You must know books and all that is in the Bible. You much preach wise sermons. You must be kind, and know when to give advice. You must live right and have every act a good one. You must not sing loudly and pray loudly and then after that say and do unkind things. That is not Christianity."

Amalia would not have said: "You must not do this way as your father and your grandfather did." But in her heart she knew she was drawing pictures of them both.

The morning Emil was to start, Fritz brought the team and wagon up to the cabin to take him part of the way. Amalia had his lunch put up in the smallest egg-basket. One would have thought from the contents she expected her small son to stay a week rather than a day. From a larder more meager than usual since the grasshopper siege, she had managed to furnish *speck* and *korn brot* and *äpfelschnitz,* which the English neighbors would have called side meat, corn-bread and dried apples.

Emil was excited, loud and noisy. He ran in and out of the cabin with the slate that had belonged to Fritz under his arm.

Amalia thought she could not stand it, could not bear to see Emil go away from her to the school. But she must be brave, must not let this trouble her, for after his fourteenth year and Confirmation, he must then go on farther away for his learning. Then would it be time to be troubled at his leaving.

But now that the day had come for schooling and he was sturdily climbing high over the big wheel of the wagon, she called to Fritz to wait, ran and got her shawl and her bonnet, set her *korn mehl maus* back on the stove, and went with them.

At the last half-mile, Emil did not want them to go with him farther, told them to stop here, so he could get out and walk the rest of the distance, that the other children might not know he had been brought in a wagon.

"He is a real boy," Fritz said, watching him trudge through the rank prairie grass, brandishing a stick toward a host of imaginary enemies.

But Amalia, sitting in the wagon and gazing after him, could not see what Emil was doing; so blurred a little figure did he look that he seemed swimming in the liquid prairie grass.

Always, these years, Fritz worked constantly. Even when others, far from lazy, were through their work and would congregate in groups to talk over the drouth and the 'hopper damage, the war with the Sioux, the rush into the Black Hills for gold, Fritz must be on the go. The first one in the morning at work and the last one at night must Fritz always be. Often Amalia, looking at him, wondered what was driving him so. Every one worked hard, but he hardest of all.

Sometimes she would say to him: "Fritz, are you never going to get yourself a wife?"

He would laugh at that. "For the girls I do not care," he usually answered, but once when she said it playfully, he turned on her fiercely: *"You* should ask that." And went out to the field, although he had just come in, so that for a long time Amalia tried to think why he said that peculiar thing.

By 1878, times began to be better. When the colonists came together now, there was not so much head shaking, not so much talk of drouth and poor crops and hardships, —more talk of railroads being built,—of the Republican Valley being settled, of the Pawnees all removed to Oklahoma, of the north part of the state being opened to settlers. Crops were better. Fritz was raising enough to eat and even selling a little corn.

There were noticeable changes in the twelve years. A few fences were here and there around door-yards and gardens. Old wagon trails over the prairie had the appearance of real roads. The trees had made unbelievable growth, especially the cottonwoods with their merry leaves, never gloomy, never silent, always dancing in any kind of weather. There was a whole flock of children who had not come in with the wagons,—native-born little Schaffers and Kratzes, Rhodenbachs and Gebhardts. And there were six graves there where the tumble-weeds rolled in the autumn and the sun blazed down in summer and the snows piled in winter.

And Amalia was changed too. Although she still braided her once-golden hair neatly and wound it around her head, it was now rather like sun-burned straw. And the rose-petal of her skin was gone, too, and in its place a redness seared into the delicate flesh by the prairie winds.

So now with times looking up, and Fritz and Amalia such good managers, they built a new house to take the place of the cabin, twelve years old and grown too small and shabby.

Fritz told Amalia to pick out the exact spot of ground she wanted for it, and while she was making her selection she had a swift thought that Herman would not have been so considerate,—that like her father he would have dictated both place and the plans as he wanted them. Amalia was rather happy these days with her brother Fritz and husky Emil, now eleven years old.

Fritz built sturdily and well, even though it took him all through the year, for he must do his regular work first. Amalia drove the team to Westville several times, a day's trip, bringing lumber home.

There was a little cellar this time into which they could put the potatoes and pumpkins, turnips and onions for winter's use and into which they could go if a storm threatened. Amalia was more proud of her cellar than any other part of the house. Fritz built a slanting outside cellar door upon which she could sun her milk crocks, and Amalia set out wild gooseberry and currant bushes close by. Almost was it going to seem like the farm-house in Illinois where she was born. There were four rooms,— a sitting room, a kitchen and two bedrooms. Oh, it was rather grand. Amalia could scarce keep the pride from showing when Anna Kratz and Lena Schaffer and the Gebhardts and the Rhodenbachs all came to see the skeleton of it going up there on the prairie.

On a day in November, an Indian summer day with the

sun shining hazily on the wide brown prairie and the trees over by the river's brink yellow and bronze, and the sumac flaming red, Amalia moved into the shining new four-roomed house.

The wooden floors were scrubbed until one almost saw one's face in them and the new rag rug which she had woven was placed exactly in the center of the sitting-room until such time as they might have carpeting. The walnut table held the Bible and a conch shell, and on the wall were hung the two pictures from the old home,— the *Gute Nacht* and *Guten Morgen,* two chunky semi-nude little girls with daisies in their hair. There was a motto too, which Amalia's mother had worked in the old country in dainty stitches, *Gott Segne Unser Heim,* as though God seeing it there constantly would not fail to bless their home. Two rocking-chairs and a book-shelf that Fritz had made from ends of the lumber for the few German books completed the furnishings.

The kitchen held the table and the cook-stove with the iron hearth, the pots and pans and four straight chairs. Fritz put wooden pegs on the walls for the coats and hats, made a fresh new wood-box, and for Amalia's birthday bought a gay blue mirror with tin comb-box underneath. In Amalia's bedroom was the heavy walnut bureau from her mother, and sometimes she was greatly torn between leaving it there or having it back in the sitting-room where strangers stopping on their trips across the prairie could see it.

It started a perfect disease of unrest among the neighbor women; followed by an orgy of building. "If Amalia Holmsdorfer can have a new home of boughten lumber, so can I," became almost a slogan up and down the river.

Anna Kratz had a new house with five rooms, where-upon Lena Schaffer could not rest until she had six. Oh, but the German colony took upon itself the appearance of more comfortable circumstances.

All of these years Amalia had been very close to her boy. Always she was talking to him of lovely things, of the beauty in nature, of the way God manifested Him-self,—showing him the gentler side of life and the more tender. She walked with him in the timber along the river and talked of the trees as though they were humans,—the ash and the willow, the cottonwood and the wild sumac. She taught him many things for which Fritz had no time or inclination. Together they picked the violets and the ground-plums, the black-eyed Susans and the trillium, bellwort and bloodroot and wild colum-bine, although Amalia's names for them were not always as these. Together they found the meadow-lark's nest in the prairie grass and the place where the owls hooted the night away. She stood with him on the church knoll which looked over the valley and had him repeat with her the Psalm of walking through the valley of the shadow of death and yet fearing no evil.

She had him climb and put back a woodpecker's young one that had fallen from a nest, called him each night to stop work for a moment and see the sunset's after-glow, and bade him note that all things happening now were still like miracles of old.

Sometimes Fritz grew cross at these teachings. *"Du wirst ihm ganz verzärteln,"* he would say disparagingly.

But Amalia knew she would not make him a softie, that
it did not make a softie of any one to love beauty in nature. And a *pastor,*—how could a *pastor* better understand humans than to see God in everything?

So time went on and spring came and turned into hot
summer with the meadow-larks' songs stilled in the heat.
Summer turned into fall with the corn ripe in the shock
and the dried tumble-weeds rolling across the prairie like
so many brown waves of the sea. And almost before
Fritz and Amalia could realize it, Emil was nearly fourteen,—nearly to his Confirmation. After that would come
going away to more schooling in preparation for his work.

On this spring day Amalia was thinking how it would
seem next fall without him. But to sustain her in the
loneliness it would mean she had only to vision him in the
pulpit in his black robe, and she knew she must make no
outcry about his going. When the other boys of his age
were at their farm work, he would be studying away at
the Lutheran college, and the thought filled her with an
ecstasy of pleasure. She would work her fingers to the
bone for Emil's schooling, and Fritz would help her.

Even as Amalia was cherishing these pleasant thoughts,
Emil was sitting near the opened window in the little
school-house looking out at spring coming over the prairie
country, as though it were a person and he could see its
tangible form. It was in the call of the crows, in the
warmth of the sun, in the odors of the loam.

He fumbled the dog-eared reader, looked at a para-
graph which contained no meaning: *"In-zwischen hatte
Johann Hus die Schriften von Wycliffe gellesen."*

152

As though he cared that in the meantime Johann Hus had the writings of Wycliffe read.

Back to the window he turned his lack-luster eyes. Over by Willow Creek there was a faint tinge of green against the gray of the branches. The rolling prairie stretched as far as the eye could see. On the top of a knoll far off, a man and team and plow were silhoueted against the horizon. Maybe it was Uncle Fritz. For a moment they were all poised there as though drawn with pencil,—then they passed out of sight.

Something broke in Emil. Some queer condition arose in his whole being over which he seemed to have no control. He took the two other thumbed old books out of his desk and a cracked slate with red flannel binding, tied them to the reader with a frayed piece of rope, and stood up.

The master rapped sharply on the desk: "What are you doing, Emil?"

"I go home."

"What do you mean? Sit down."

Emil, already on his way to the door, turned and shook his head stolidly.

The teacher advanced toward him, ruler in hand, but he broke into a clumping run, passed the bucket of water and was at once out on the moist prairie grass, from which vantage point he turned and gave a delicate thumb-to-nose gesture of farewell.

He could not have told just what happened,—did not fully sense that he was happily freed from the intricacies of arithmetic and the geography of unknown and undesirable countries, of memorizing hymns and Catechism and verses. All he knew was that the school-house had caged him, that spring called,—and the Land.

As he walked over the spongy ground just released from its frost, he felt rather than thought about the world around him. There was the first warm sunshine, and the odors of the prairie ground from which the new grass would soon shoot. As he looked a long V-shaped line of wild geese went over. He watched them until they dropped into the north swampland, then turned on his heel and broke into a run toward home.

It was nearly noon when he arrived with his lunch still untouched.

Amalia, seeing him coming across the open field, ran out to meet him. "What is it?" she called. Nothing but illness or trouble with the teacher would bring him home.

Now that he was here he did not know quite so well how to handle it.

Fritz came up from the stable. Emil had not thought of this contingency. Twice Uncle Fritz had licked him when his mother told him to. He could feel the last thrashing yet. Uncle Fritz didn't dare now. If Uncle Fritz touched him he would light in and thrash too.

"I come home," he said stolidly.

"I see," said Fritz. "But why?"

"I'm through school," he swallowed hard.

Amalia was pale to the lips,—it took schooling and much of it for the *pastor's* work.

"But why?" Fritz shouted.

Emil turned his head from them. "Never going again," he muttered. "Going into the field. Going to be a farmer."

Fritz's face relaxed. The shadow of a grin rested on it.

"There goes your pastor, Mollia," he said gruffly, and to Emil: "The ground is ready to-day . . . get the plow."

But Amalia went into the house and shed bitter tears.

CHAPTER XXIII

SO EMIL decided for himself he was to be a farmer like Uncle Fritz, and Amalia with many a secret sighing over the disappointment put away her dreams of his schooling and a *pastor's* robe and a beautiful girl from some city whom he would one day marry.

But Emil did no sighing,—he was happy and content, and threw his young strength energetically into the work.

To a certain point he was Herman all over again, energetic, loud of speech, noisy with laughter. But at that place where Herman would have been ruthless toward another's feelings, commanding arrogantly, or scolding loudly,—Emil's manner would break into something less formidable as the ice breaks in the springtime, turn gentle with Amalia and end the scene in mere joking. So to Herman's gifts of physical strength and ceaseless energy had been added something of Amalia's own,—a bit of her thoughtfulness and tenderness, a little appreciation of the red tinge on the prairie clouds.

By 1885 the land was largely fenced. Crops were good. Some of the out-buildings were new,—corncribs and a hay barn. Trees were much larger,—the cotton-woods and the elms. Orchards were bearing,—Amalia could make *äpfel-butter* and *pflaumen-butter* every year. There were elderberries, choke-cherries and wild grapes in the woods, and gooseberries and currants in the yard. All the land was taken. Homesteads were now farms. The whole community took on an appearance of prosperity. In addition to Amalia's and Fritz's farm,—up and down the river valley stretched the neat places of all the Gebhardts and the Schaffers, the Rhodenbachs and the Kratzes. If there had been keen rivalry over houses and barns, children and crops, it had made for progress.

There was a road to Westville, clogged with snow in the winter and muddy or dusty in summer, but at that, something better than the unbroken trail of prairie grass over which they had first come.

Trains passed daily through Westville, the western portion of the state was being settled. Every day people going west stopped in their wagons at some one of the farm-houses on the river for water or directions or to stay all night. Some were bound for the Republican Valley, some to the Black Hills of the Dakotas, some to the grassy plateau in the sand-hills.

The German families had grown more friendly with the English ones,—the Kirbys and the Blacks and the Lawrences. The women came sometimes to see Amalia, and every so often she and Anna Kratz would hitch up the spring-wagon, drive to their homes and return the calls.

Amalia had a hard time understanding them, and with some embarrassment and laughter tried to make them know what she was saying. But after all, a sick child or a new design for a quilt or a jar of *gurken* or *kraut* is a common denominator in all feminine language, and they got along very well.

"I bring you apple-jelly," Mrs. Kirby would say.

And Amalia, like a devoted parrot would repeat: "I brin' you äpfel-chelly."

All the weeks she would try to remember this, and when she would arrive at the Kirbys' next time, she would be gay with laughter, jelly, and the surprise of her English for Mrs. Kirby. "I brin' you plom-chelly."

But she could not muster a "w" nor a "th,"—ever, all her life,—nor some of the English words.

"They are water-melon," Mrs. Kirby would say patiently.

"Dey are vater-mel*o*nen." And so far as Amalia was concerned vater-mel*o*nen they stayed.

For several years the old log church on the hillside had been gone and in its place a substantial frame, white-painted, with a spire pointing its long finger to the way all the settlers must look for guidance.

Ludwig Rhodenbach had made the pews and a high pulpit, and all the men had turned in and helped build the *pharr-haus* for the *pastor*.

There was a great bell, too, in the tower of the church, that shook the building and reverberated up and down the valley.

At a passing, it tolled the number of years the dead one had spent on earth, so that when old Rudolph Kratz died it echoed up and down the valley for a long time with its eighty-two strokes, but when Lena Schaffer's little boy died, it gave only a single tap that was heard by scarcely any one but the caretaker who rang it and the prairie-larks and Lena Schaffer many miles away.

Emil worked side by side with Fritz all through his

'teens, strong as a young ox, for he had never known anything but hard work. Amalia was glad the two got along so well. If there was an occasional disagreement, it soon passed. Fritz was always quiet. But Emil, noisy and loud, might rant for a time, start to say ugly unnecessary things as his father before him, and then, looking at the gentle face of his mother—suddenly something would break and his ranting go into nothing. Amalia did not know how this could be. It just was so.

In 1887 Emil was twenty. The two men had cut a great deal of wild hay and stored it and there was to be plenty of corn in the cribs. The combined three hundred and twenty acres were yielding well. No one gave a thought to the ownership,—that there might have been some legal question whose land it was after the death of the two original owners. Fritz and Amalia and Emil thought of it only as "the place," all working long and hard to feed and clothe themselves and "put something by."

And now this year, the biggest change, since Herman's and Wilhelm's deaths, was upon the family. In the late fall or early winter when he would have passed his twenty-first birthday, Emil was going to be married. To Anna Marie Rhodenbach! That was Minnie Rhodenbach's daughter, the child of the Minnie Rhodenbach upon whom Fritz had cast such longing eyes when she was a young widow with this little girl. And curiously enough Anna Marie at eighteen was almost the exact replica of Minnie at the time Fritz had given his solemn oath never to marry.

Fritz and Emil were building the new house in the

very yard with Amalia's house, although over on the next rise of ground beyond the slow-growing lilac bushes.

When they started to plan it, Emil had brought Anna Marie over to talk with Fritz and Amalia about it.

Anna Marie was chubby, her soft round face had dimples at the corners of her mouth, and when she laughed, which she did very often, she looked exactly as her mother had looked at eighteen.

Looking at her sitting there so pretty and soft and demure, Uncle Fritz said suddenly: "Emil, why don't we build this one very grand? The place will all be yours some day. This house, it should be of stone . . . finer than any one's in the valley. You will have a family . . . they will grow up in it. Who knows maybe *their* children too, would live in it. It should be solid and big. I would like to build one so that all the settlers come to see it. I would like the best one in the whole county for you. It would take the year but we could do it fine. What say you, Emil?"

Amalia warmed so to Fritz's kindness. What a good boy he was. And why would he want to put so much labor on something for Emil?

He was thirty-seven now, thin and hard and gnarled, and never had he looked at a girl.

"You should for yourself be making one." Amalia chided him.

But Fritz laughed at that. "What girl would look at a gnarled old bachelor, nearing forty?"

"Oh, there's a plenty," Amalia told him. "I could name as many as fingers on my hand. Shall I name them?"

But Fritz would not stop planning to listen to the naming of them. "The good ones are all married already," he said laconically, so that Amalia pondered it quite awhile.

Fritz and Emil hauled stone from a quarry down the river. It took a day to come and go. Before he was even fifteen, Fritz had learned something of the stone mason's craft from his father so now he built carefully and well.

All the summer and fall of 1887 the two worked on the house every moment between the necessary crop work. The big thing rose slowly on its sturdy foundation, every stone solidly placed, every studding nailed securely.

"It's so sturdy Anna Marie and I will have our golden wedding in it," Emil told them.

"I shall then be ninety years old," Amalia laughed.

"Yah," Fritz said. "You will live, Millia, to see children and grandchildren and (*vielleicht*) great-grandchildren living in it."

But Amalia could not believe that—it seemed so very far in the future. Yet it happened to be true,—Amalia was to live to see Emil and his son and his son's son living in the honestly built stone house.

It was large for the time and for the young state no older than Emil himself. There were a parlor and a sitting-room, a dining-room, a bedroom and a kitchen downstairs, and three more bedrooms upstairs. If not overly artistic it was strong and sturdy and as honest as Fritz Stoltz. People came from miles around to see it. Not in all the days of the settling up of the river valley had there been put up so big and so good a dwelling. It sent Anna Kratz home with a sick headache that her

Frederich was to live for awhile in her own discarded cabin.

Amalia could scarcely get used to the idea that Emil was to be gone from home. But the two houses were only a short distance apart, something like a town block over at Westville. She thought with a warm little feeling of pleasure how nice it would be to have another woman so close. She and Anna Marie could exchange *kaffee kuchen* and *spatzen*. Her twenty-two years here had been only with menfolks about.

She had a dozen quilts ready for the young couple and now every day she sewed carpet rags, great balls of them ready for the loom. If all the carpet rags she sewed that summer had been laid end to end . . . but luckily they never were, but were made instead into much hit-and-miss striped carpeting for the rooms of the big stone house.

Anna Marie made quilts, too, and bleached quantities of tan-colored muslin, sewed petticoats with a great deal of tucking in them and yards of rick-rack and made many pillow-cases with crocheted ends.

Emil bought new things,—the most stylish of all, a walnut bedroom set with marble top to the bureau and a looking-glass built solidly on the back of it. This was called a *dresser* in English, and for all the world as though the dresser had a child, there was a small one just like it called a *commode*. There was a wash-bowl too, and a pitcher, with three fat red roses on the side of each one. It seemed that company washed right there in the very room in which they slept instead of in the kitchen or wash-house. Amalia preened a good deal when she showed these to Anna Kratz. And she bragged sometimes about her brother Fritz. "Nothing is good enough for Emil in Fritz's eyes. The shirt off his back he would take for Emil. Wanting Emil always to have the nicest things in the house." Or so it seemed to Amalia.

Christmas time passed with the church services and the *tannen-baum* set up so prettily at the pulpit and the tallow *kerzen* lighted and twinkling among its branches, with the *"Stille Nacht, Heilige Nacht"* heard everywhere, —at church, in the houses, at the stables, on the prairie road from sleighs.

The wedding was set for January twelfth.

The house was finished. Fritz Stoltz surveyed his handiwork. Emil had worked day and night with him, but he had been the builder. He felt an indescribable pride in the great solid structure. It would stand until long after he was up there on the hill with his father and Herman. He had, after all, something to leave behind him. It wasn't a son, but it was a sort of monument,— for Emil . . . and Minnie's little girl.

The wedding was a big event. It took place in the church on the hill in the morning at ten,—Anna Marie in white India linen and hand-crocheted lace with a veil. When the ceremony was over, all went by buggy and lumber-wagon, spring-wagon and carriage to the new stone house for the wedding feast.

Anna Kratz and Lena Schaffer, young Mrs. Henry Gebhardt, young no longer but going by that name for twenty-five years; and Amalia took charge of the great wedding dinner set out on the boards placed on saw-horses down the length of the combined two new parlors.

There were *schinken* and *gebratene hühner*, which the

163

English neighbors called ham and fried chicken, and *hühner* pressed into loaves. There was *met-wurst* and *käse*. And there were *bohnen* and *pastete*, which Mrs. Kirby told Amalia were called in the English, beans and pie. There was *kümmel* in which the toasts were openly drunk by all, and there was the strong *roggen branntwein* slipping about surreptitiously among the men who kept their eyes peeled for any approaching and potentially protesting wife.

It was the finest kind of a day. On all sides one heard remarks about it,—January the twelfth and like spring. Yes, it was as soft and mild as Anna Marie's dimpled face.

"It is a sign of your married life," Lena Schaffer said, ". . . the way the day is. Ours was stormy, having thunder and lightning." And she cackled loudly and poked a fat forefinger into August Schaffer's lean ribs.

Through the feasting the doors were all open. The sun shone almost warmly, so that men removed their coats and went out into it that they might boast of it in years to come,—"I remember like yesterday at Emil Holmsdorfer's wedding,—January twelfth and I was out o'doors in my shirt sleeves."

There was moisture on the sides of the elms and the cottonwoods. Hens scratched in the damp steaming ground of manure piles and on the south side of the straw stacks.

The crowd from the gorging of much food grew less noisy, settled for a time into an after-dinner lethargy. The women washed countless dishes. Babies bawled and were put to sleep upstairs on the new beds high with feather ticks and Amalia's intricately-pieced quilts. The men drank more *kümmel* openly for old friendship's sake and a little of the *roggen branntwein* surreptitiously for any fragile reason that presented itself. Then Elsa Rhodenbach came in and started the dancing. "Come! Don't be old. This is a wedding, folks; not a funeral."

It revived the faltering food-stuffed company. August Schaffer and Adolph Kratz got out their *violinen* which the Kirbys called fiddles, tuned them up and activities began.

In the midst of the dancing some of the men came in to say it looked stormy in the north,—maybe they must go and do chores if they were to come back for the evening. Several of the women went out to look, too.

The north sky was the color of burned-out camp-fire ashes. There was a hushed quiet over the whole country-side,—that portentous quiet which is more ominous than noise. Several of the older men began hitching up, but the young folks danced on. Fritz slipped away to his barns for early chores. Amalia called something after him about her chickens. Even as she did so, a single icy blast snarled down from the low-swinging clouds, the wind whipped her new silk dress as though it were a rattling garment of paper.

The storm that followed the initial blast went down into history as the blizzard of '88.

The snow in great packed masses threw itself at the countryside, drove its fury all over a snow-bound land. It lashed at the wedding party, held captive, like a wild thing mad with the knowledge that it could not hurt the great stone house which Fritz and Emil had built so well.

Those who had started home, remembering the fate of

two of their original company of settlers so many years before, sought shelter at the nearest farms, some greatly in danger of losing their lives before they could fight their way to houses and barns.

It threw a pall over the gaiety,—the worry about those who had gone home for the chores. Even Fritz did not come back, could not make it through the storm from so short a distance.

In the big stone house, the dancing took the minds from the mad fury of the elements, the food luckily prepared in such quantities, held out, the *kümmel* sustained the thirsty. Only the drinking of the *roggen branntwein* came to a sudden termination for the simple reason that with Adolph Kratz, it, too, had gone home to do the chores.

So now Amalia was thirty-nine, her son a married man, and never any more did she think of romance for herself or crave it.

Twice during the years had she been asked in marriage. Several times young Fred Gebhardt had come to spend Sunday evening when Emil was small, but Amalia, pretending that she did not know the reason, kept Fritz from leaving and allowed Emil to sit up long beyond his bedtime so they could all make merry together with popping *korn* and making molasses candy, until Fred asked her and she refused him under the noise of the popping *korn*.

And once from beyond the valley Otto Weis had driven in rapidly, explained his matrimonial intentions, given her gratuitously an inventory of his cows, pigs and chickens, and explained a little breathlessly that if she were so minded to take them all on as well as himself, he would appreciate it if she could come before threshing.

Amalia had laughed in his face and told him to go to the fourth homestead down the valley and hire Lizzie Gebhardt for two dollars a week.

No, Amalia craved no more romance for herself. But sometimes when the sun was gone and there was a moment to spare after the supper dishes were done, she sat on the porch of the small frame farm-house and looked across the darkening fields and pastures. From there she would watch the first stars come out, a night hawk dip low and the new moon get caught in the branches of the plum thickets,—would listen to the breeze stirring the leaves of the cottonwoods and to the cicadas and the good-night call of the robins that had come of late years,—would catch the scent of the hay fields and the petunias that bordered the path to her gate. Then she would open the rusty-hinged door and go into The Room.

She could not have explained it to any one,—certainly not to Emil or Fritz, and not even to her daughter-in-law, Anna Marie, or to Anna Kratz or Lena Schaffer. But it was always there,—a little chapel more beautiful than any church, built in a clearing in the woods.

CHAPTER XXIV

FOR SEVEN years after Ida Carter's marriage to Matthias she worked side by side with him in the store, never missing a day nor a chance to help her husband earn a penny. On hot summer mornings she rose with the sun and was ready to go with him through the dusty streets when he left for work. On winter mornings she was up long before daylight, breaking the ice in the pitcher for washing, dressing in her flannels and woolen dress, and was off with him in the dark and the cold.

There were hard times for town people as well as the country folks in those years after the Meier marriage. Every grasshopper cast its tiny reflection into Matthias' store, until the whole became a dark shadow over the counters. Drouth took its toll of the customers and so of Matthias himself. The little town had seen its citizens go out to fight a prairie fire which came rolling in with no apparent regard for the capital's importance. It had seen an uprising among the convicts in the penitentiary several miles away so that Matthias shouldered a gun with other citizens and went out to help quell the riot. It had seen the burning of the Atwood House with its big twenty-thousand-dollar loss.

All these seven years Ida Carter lived in her small suite of rooms in the boarding-house looking forward to the day when she would have a nice home. But the boarding-house was good enough, she insisted, until she could stop work and devote herself to a home.

And then in 1880 her child was coming, so that she must stop her work at the store. They named the boy Carter and he throve and grew even as did the little town into which he had arrived with such welcome.

Even before the baby's coming, the new state had begun to pull out of the hard times, and with these general conditions bettered Matthias' business took on noticeable gains.

Life was very pleasant to Matthias these days. Ida was comrade and friend as well as wife and mother. Any word of hers concerning the business was worth heeding. And then came word of the death of Matthias' uncle, and wholly unlooked for, a fair-sized legacy. Rather suddenly then he sold his share of the store to his partner, bought stock in one of the banks and became an officer of that growing institution.

The town had thirteen thousand inhabitants now,—the University had graduated several small classes. Eight daring young men on the flying trapeze of their enthusiasm had organized the Sigma Chi fraternity and were nearly expelled for their pains. The huge west wing for a new capitol building had gone up.

There were more convicts in the pen, more inmates in the asylum,—and many people had been taken out to the acreage in which to lie down and sleep.

So now Matthias and Ida were to have their new home. It was of red brick and sat far back from the wooden sidewalk of a popular residential street, where it seemed to draw its red skirts away from the splashing of mud all spring and the clouds of fine dust rolling in through the hot midwestern corn-curing weather. It was rather awe-inspiring in its massiveness, dwarfing as it did the modest homes on both sides of it. There were ornate trimmings over the long, narrow windows, and a tower high above the second floor could have served as an excellent Indian lookout if there were need, for from its lofty interior one might gaze over the undulating prairie as far as man's vision could function.

It was one of the town's most showy residences, but scarcely had its final oak balustrade been placed, its last piece of ornate grill-work set in the archway between parlor and library until plans were laid by the William McCurdeys for a new house with more oak grill-work and two towers.

They followed each other like mushrooms after rain,— the huge frame house of a merchant, the red brick one of a banker, the gray stone of an attorney, all dignified and elegant at the time. It was only in the light of after years that they looked fussy, like old ladies bewigged and rouged and loaded with jewelry.

Other town-shaking events were happening. Whereas one had hallooed lustily heretofore from his porch to the neighbor for whom a message was intended, or sent the swiftest-legged member of the family, one might now talk to him through the huge box fastened on the wall. A half-hundred business houses went up, many times that number of homes.

When the Meier house was finished Matthias and Ida gave a housewarming. While scarcely true that half the town came, the impression was there. Young swains and their ladies danced the Virginia reel and the mazurka on the intricately inlaid pattern of the newly polished floors,—a few tackled the schottische. Young Carter, a big healthy boy, was allowed to stay up until nine. Ida had succeeded in making him look almost as effeminate as she desired in his velvet suit with lace collar and cuffs, his hair in curls to his shoulders. Ida herself had a new striped heavy silk dress trimmed with bead passementerie over a huge bustle.

Oyster stew was served in the basement, moist yet from its fresh mortar, the ladies squealing a little and holding up their trailing skirts when descending the long, narrow stairway. Some of the guests had driven to the party in their fringed canopy-topped carriages, those close by had walked, tip-toeing across the puddles on the wooden sidewalks, carrying their party shoes in bags, but a few souls out for adventure and feeling particularly devilish had taken the new street-car to the nearest corner.

Charlie Briggs came, looking a bit incongruous among the other guests with his baggy clothes, his oiled red hair, and his voice rolling out in the same tones he had employed when he snapped the bull-whip at the side of the oxen. But Matthias would have him, and Ida was good-natured about it, laughing heartily with Charlie when they showed him around the new house and he said he'd swum in all sorts o' rivers 'n lakes 'n buffalo wallers, but never swum yet in a big soup-bowl like that there one in the bathroom.

Aside from a *faux pas* or two on the part of Charlie, the whole affair was a huge success.

The newspaper said it was one of the most pleasant

occasions ever known to Lincoln society, that youth and beauty were rampant, that the Meier residence was a model of elegance, its proud owners unexcelled in hospitality and the collation the most appetizing of which ye scribe had ever partaken.

Matthias and Ida were exceedingly pleased over the write-up, felt a curiosity tinged with impatience to see the one which would follow the McCurdeys' housewarming in a few months. When it came out, it said that the party was one of the most pleasant occasions ever known to Lincoln society, that youth and beauty were rampant, that the McCurdey residence was a model of elegance, its proud owners unexcelled in hospitality and the collation the most appetizing of which ye scribe had ever partaken.

Life now to the Meiers took on no small degree of prosperity which in turn gave them their place in the social sun of the little city.

They went to hear Oscar Wilde lecture and Bill Nye,— to the Funk Opera House to see Edwin Booth and Modjeska, Lily Langtry and Fannie Davenport trod the boards. They joined a whist club and kept up their choir work even if somewhat under fire by visiting evangelists for combining the two.

Ida joined with a group of her women friends in receiving calls on New Year's Day to which the gallants of the town in Prince Alberts made yearly pilgrimages by way of a livery hack.

At the turn of the decade came one of the outstanding social events,—the opening of the Lansing Theatre. Matthias was forty-six now, a little pompous looking with

his shovel-cut beard and a gray patch above each ear,—
quite the picture of a bank vice-president. Ida was forty-
three, heavy too, deep bosomed and molded into her
stays, wholly the picture of a bank vice-president's wife.
Her heavy brown hair was piled high on her head in
doughnut formation. In the privacy of her room she
pinched her cheeks to bring color to them.

Carter at eleven was to be allowed to go to the great
opening. "He can't begin too young to hear and see the
best things," Matthias had said, to which Ida assented
with reservations that he mustn't expect to go often.

The great building towering all of four stories high
was a blaze of light. The boxes were filled with notables.
The Governor was there in the dress circle, and the new
young congressman, William Jennings Bryan, and his
wife. The proscenium was a dazzle of splendor and the
audience beautiful and manly if one may take whole-
heartedly the newspaper accounts of the day. A painted
scenic representation of Thalia, the muse of comedy and
bucolic poetry, in an undieted condition, largely covered
the sounding board with a languid pose of nonchalant
snootiness surrounded by corpulent cupids.

Lillian Lewis and her company played. The orchestra
rendered exquisite strains between acts. One would have
said it was like a Chicago event. Culture had come to
the prairie.

On the way home Matthias and Ida in their carriage,
with the man driving who doubled in yard work for them,
asked each other what more one could wish for.

Ida said it didn't seem possible all this could have come

to pass in the raw village to which she had come nineteen years before.

Matthias responded with a rather uninspired: "No, it doesn't," . . . thinking, and yet not being able to tell even Ida, of his long journey alone over the cold, wind-swept prairie twenty-three years before, and of his dreaming that one day a city would stand there on the horizon where stood four or five log houses. He felt a little awe-struck to-night,—it seemed too much like sorcery,—as though the magic of his thinking had turned the dreaming into fact.

CHAPTER XXV

THERE were changes again in the German neighborhood in which Amalia Holmsdorfer lived with her brother Fritz. Changes in the farms, certainly, but more among the people. Deaths, births, marriages,—they roll in on a community like the tides of the sea. Most of the marriages had been among the various families which had come into the state together.

But another element was entering in. Lena Schaffer's boy married a Kirby girl who was what they called a *Congregationalist*. Tsk! Tsk! Probably not a Catechism in the house and calling a *pastor* a minister. Young Henry Gebhardt's girl got into trouble with one of the English Brown boys,—the trouble not being so bad as the mixed blood.

And the biggest change of all to Amalia,—she was now fifty years old and a grandmother. Emil and Anna Marie had a little son, Joe, aged ten now. Three times since Joe's birth, Anna Marie had expected a child, but after a few months could not carry it. Anna Marie had now lost her chubbiness to something more substantial. Fat, in no uncertain terms was what she had come to be,—a mound of quivering fat which seemed in no way to detract from her lightness of foot. Looking at her sometimes Amalia wondered how a fat woman could walk so springily. She had all the qualities of a rubber-ball, and even though she had to walk sideways down the porch steps of the big stone house, she seemed to bounce down from step to step.

Emil was a good husband to Anna Marie. Often Amalia talked about it to Fritz, wondering in her mind if he remembered their father's and Herman's harsh ways, but saying nothing about it. When Joe was born and those other times of her illnesses, Emil brought home neighbors' girls to work. He bought a two-seated carriage for her, too, and though Fritz and Amalia rode yet in the spring wagon, Anna Marie never went anywhere excepting in the carriage where she sat alone in her grandeur in the back seat because of her bulk.

Sometimes Amalia would hear Emil telling his wife not to put so much labor on the house, to let up a little in the work, that since the new eighty was all paid for, they would be getting ahead. Four hundred acres in the family now,—that was good. Amalia knew Herman and her father would have been elated at that news.

Only this spring Amalia had seen an example of Emil's thoughtfulness of his wife.

Anna Marie had just pulled the old soap-kettle from the back porch out to the yard, walking sideways up and down the steps in that balloon-like way of hers, when Emil came up from the barn.

"What are you going to do?" he had asked in the German, for although they both could speak some in English they chose the easier way.

"Make soap," Anna Marie had said, "and I'd rather take a licking than stand and stir."

"Why do you then?"

Anna Marie laughed good naturedly, her dimples making large holes in her cheeks. "I think because my mother did before me and her mother before her, and for no other reason, for it is one of the things I do not like to do."

"Don't do it then."

"But, Emil,—I have all the grease saved and the lye is leached."

"Throw it away. You do not have to do it any more. A bushel of corn or two will pay for the soap you would make to-day . . . maybe make yourself sick too!"

So to Amalia's amazement, she saw her daughter-in-law take the pans and waddle lightly down to the edge of the orchard, bury the grease in the ground, throw the cracklings to the chickens, and sit down on the big porch to rock comfortably all the rest of the afternoon. Tsk! Tsk! Such a waste.

At night Emil took the iron kettle down to the hog-lot and cooked mash in it for the little pigs.

So, even though large families were the order of the day, because of Anna Marie's inability to bear more children, Joe was to be Emil's only son and Amalia's only grandchild.

It may be for this very reason Amalia centered all her love in him. So devoted was she to little Joe that he seemed her own, that she had borne him herself in some distant year with the pain and the worry now all forgot.

He was less noisy than Emil had been, quiet and uncommunicative. One had to guess what was on his mind, withdrawing it by questioning.

"What is the matter, Joey? What have you on your mind that troubles you?"

"Nothing."

"Is it that you cannot go to town with father?"

"No."

"Is it that the little calf died?"

A long silence,—and Amalia knew it was that the little calf died.

Although he was boyish, full of energy for the farm activities, never a day passed that he did not come down the path between the petunias, to the frame house where Amalia and Fritz lived. She kept cookies in a big stone crock always for Joey. She kept a bed made for him so that when Emil and Anna Marie would want to go somewhere without him, he could stay. She kept a flannel nightgown there for him and a pencil and paper and slate should he want to do his school work.

And that was another change in the community. Joey went to English school and did the German work up on the hill with the *pastor* only for a time in the summer vacation. There was a country school-house on a corner of the Lawrence land called the Evergreen School. It was under a county superintendent, and all the children, both German and English, must attend.

Joey could talk the English just like the Kirbys and the Lawrences, but he could talk the German, too, and usually did with Amalia. But sometimes, in proud boyish way, he wanted to give her an English lesson and although it was tedious and tiring to Amalia, she was patient for the little boy's sake.

"It is a nice day."

"It iss a *schön* day."

"No, Grandma. *Nice.*"

"It iss a nitze day."

"This is soup."

"Dis iss *suppe.*"

"No, Grandma. Soup."

"Sss . . . oop."

And the lesson would go only into laughter and the eating of more cookies.

But in one way, Amalia's association with Joe was identical with that of her own little boy, Emil,—the talking to him of all the lovely things about the farm, of the beauty in nature and the way God manifested Himself. She walked with him in the timber along the river,—a little less buoyantly now because of her fifty years,—and talked of the trees as though they were humans,—the ash, the willow and the cottonwood, and the wild sumac. Together they picked violets and black-eyed Susans and trillium, bellwort and bloodroot and wild columbine, and although Amalia's names for them were not always as these, Joey knew these very words in the English and taught them to her.

Together they found the meadow-lark's nest in the grass and the place where the owls had hooted away the nights in the woods for thirty years. She stood with him on the church knoll which looked over the valley and had him repeat with her in German the Psalm of walking through the valley of the shadow of death and yet fearing no evil.

Fritz did not reprove her as he had done when Emil was small, did not tell her she would make of him a softie. Fritz was nearly fifty now, himself, and someway in the years, he had learned that it is not always softness to be tender.

Sometimes she asked Joey if he would not like to go away to school and study to be a *pastor*. But Joey's answer was always the same, that he would farm all the land and buy more and be the biggest land owner in the county.

So the farm work went on,—a thing of plowing, harrowing, planting, cultivating, laying by the corn, picking it to toss into the wagons, husking it in the big barns,—of wheat planting and harvesting,—of butchering, smoking *speck,* making *met-wurst* and smoked *schinken,* of discouragement over low prices, chuckling pleasure over high ones, of occasional seasons of drouth and short crops, and others of too much moisture followed by rust, of the eternal vigilance over the management of the place which is known only to natural-born farmers. And always one eye on the weather. Rain, dew, sleet, hail, drouth, snow, frost, ice, sunshine, cloudiness, wind,—every morning Emil and Fritz and Joe stepped out of the house with the question on their lips,—which, from the long list of his cohorts had the weather man marshaled for the day? By the small margin of difference in the various combinations would there be success or disaster.

Most amazingly Joe soon went to High School over at Westville. When he had read all the readers and studied all that the country school-teacher had for him, Emil sent him over to the town school.

"Parochial school was good enough for me," Emil said, "but I want Joe to have better."

So with his books tied on the saddle and his lunch in a

tin box, he rode his pony every day to school over the road no longer grass-grown but worn hard and black now from the travel of the thirty-five years. Sometimes he even stayed after school awhile to play baseball and, though Emil needed him badly, he did not swear at him and scold as many of the fathers did, but said: "Get around home a little quicker to-morrow and help with the corn."

It was a great night for the Holmsdorfers when Joe graduated. It was called "the Class of 1907" and four of the graduates were from the families of the old friends in the valley,—Joe, Rose Schaffer, Henry Gebhardt, the third, and Nora Kratz, Anna Kratz's grand-daughter.

Amalia was so proud of Joe one would have thought she was the mother instead of the grandmother. She was fifty-nine now, with not a semblance of the lovely girl she had once been, but an old woman, wrinkled and worn from much hard labor. Fritz was fifty-six and he, too, looked older than his years, gnarled and thin and weather-beaten from his long seasons of battling with the elements.

Joe had something of a time getting ready, what with carrying a wash-tub up to his room for a bath and when almost dressed having to run over to Amalia's for the tie stick-pin he had left there.

But they were all ready in time, although they went in three different rigs. Fritz and Amalia had owned a buggy for several years and they went in that. Joe, excited and not knowing just when he would leave "the bunch" after the exercises, took his own rubber-tired buggy.

Emil and Anna Marie went in the two-seated carriage. From the window Amalia saw them leave a little before she did,—Emil driving up close to the porch and Anna Marie coming sideways down the steps, but lightly like a balloon, and then sitting alone in the grandeur of the back seat as they drove away.

The exercises were very fine, Amalia thought, and although neither she nor Fritz could read a word of the programs, they studied them diligently between speeches.

Rose Schaffer looked as pretty as her namesake, the prairie roses. They called her by a frightfully long name and although Amalia whispered to Fritz to ask if he knew what the word printed there meant . . . that one,— V-a-l-e-d-i-c-t-o-r-i-a-n, Fritz shook his head.

But although there were seventeen in the class, Amalia had eyes only for Joey with his fine shoulders thrown back so proudly, and his nice suit Emil had let him pick from the catalogue. They spoke and sang and received their papers rolled up and tied with ribbons, and last of all they gathered in a group and yelled something which sounded louder and worse than the time the Indians yelled around the molasses jug and the feather pillow.

When Amalia and Fritz went out of the "opera house" to leave for home a fog had fallen over everything. It enveloped the night like a ghostly presence so that Fritz had to let the horses walk and feel their own way. Never had the road seemed so long. They knew when the horses turned the corner on the valley road, and later hearing the grate of the iron tires, knew they were crossing the railroad track, at the curve. Other than that, they scarcely knew their bearings until the faithful team turned in at the farmyard.

Several times Amalia peered out to see whether there was a light in the big house but never seeing one for the fog, she went on to bed.

It was an hour later when the voices sounded outside the door, lanterns flashed, and some one was calling Fritz.

Something terrible seized Amalia, a premonition of impending disaster. As she pulled a dress over her muslin nightgown and lighted a lamp, her hands shook, so that the matches went out twice. She was trembling so she could scarcely get to the door, asking "What's wrong?" in the German.

Fritz was ahead of her, and together they stood, lamp high, in the doorway peering out at Karl Schaffer and young Adolph Kratz and his wife and Anna Kratz, Henry Gebhardt, and back of these old friends two Westville men standing apart, and at Joey coming from beyond them, running, pushing through the fog, pushing through the men and the women, elbowing them aside, white, wild, crying and calling:

"Grandma,—Father and Mother are dead."

"Was ist, Joey?" Amalia was confused and the English words only added to it.

"Vater und Mutter sind todt."

And then Amalia understood.

Emil and Anna Marie, alive and well and proud of their fine boy two hours ago, were not now alive and well, and were quite incapable of further pride in their fine boy.

At the railroad crossing by the curve in the dark of the fog it had happened when the night passenger came through. The men thought Emil must have mistaken a

183

headlight for a light in the Lawrence farm-house. Or
so it might have been.

There were details which they were keeping from Joe
and Amalia, one gathered. But Amalia was strong. No
one knew where or how she could obtain all that reserve
strength, nearly sixty as she was, little, too, and almost
frail. She went from the small house to the big one and
back in the days that followed. She saw the *pastor* and
gave directions for the services. She picked out the
things for them to put on her boy and his wife, and comforted Minnie Rhodenbach Schaffer, Anna Marie's mother,
who came with her other sons and daughters.

She sent Fritz, broken up as he was, out to the horses,
knowing that he always found comfort in their sleek hides
and their gentle nosing of him. But most of all she
helped Joe pull himself together.

"It is happy for them, Joey," she said steadily, although
it took effort to say the words. "Always from the time
your father was seventeen, there was no one but your
mother for him. He loved her, and she loved him and no
other. That is a very happy thing. So few people are of
that way. They loved each other. They were fine people.
They gave you life. It is your gift from them. And now
they go where there is nothing but more happiness . . .
for them . . . and they go together. That is the nicest
way of all . . . no long sickness, no worries about leaving
their boy . . . just suddenly . . . and together."

And Joe threw up his head and went bravely through
the long ordeal because of what his grandmother had said.

He could do all this because she had put her own

strength into him, and because he did not know that in her own bedroom after she had watched him fall asleep these nights, she dropped on her knees and cried aloud in her anguish, finding it hard to walk through the valley of the shadow of death and yet fear no evil.

CHAPTER XXVI

ONLY Amalia, Fritz and Joe were left now of the family. It was crushing. One could not sense the thing that had happened so suddenly in the midst of their ordinary everyday life.

"Im mitte des leben sind wir in tode," the *pastor* had said that June day when all the countryside came, so that the road winding up to the old white church was packed with carriages. *In the midst of life we are in death.*

There had been wild roses that day, tangled everywhere in the prairie grass on the hill and a pair of thrashers had flown scolding over the heads of the people for disturbing their young. The bell had tolled forty long slow strokes for Emil whom every one respected,—thirty-eight for Anna Marie whom every one loved,—and then because this was so strange a service, the caretaker had added nineteen full, resonant strokes for the years of their married life together. All over the valley were the solemn notes heard, so all should remember that in the midst of life they were also in death.

The fields that had called to Emil were calling yet. But now it was Joe who answered, who plowed and planted and harvested.

Fritz and Amalia moved to the big stone house and left the small one standing vacant and a little forlorn. "Some day when Joey brings a wife home to the stone house, we shall come back," Amalia said to Fritz as she moved her things, carrying in her hands her shell box carefully wrapped in its unbleached muslin.

So in the next few years Amalia and Fritz were mother and father to Joe just as they had been to Emil, his father, before him. But things were quite different now. Emil had stayed so closely on the place, going only to services and to see Anna Marie and sometimes on the wolf hunt or taking part in some other mannish activity. But Joe had his rubber-tired buggy and a pair of slim, fast-stepping horses. He seemed restless. No one worked harder, but always after the work he was cleaning up and leaving. Sometimes he told where he was going,—more often not. Amalia worried about it a little. Such a close-mouthed boy and so hard to understand.

There was new machinery on the place. The old cradle and reaper were falling to pieces in the weeds behind the barn. There was a binder. One might ride now at the plowing. Tsk! Tsk! Like going to town.

Joe was all English now in his talk, would seldom offer to put anything into the German for Amalia and because he did not do so of his own accord, Amalia felt a certain pride in not asking him and would try so very hard both to understand and to express herself. In truth, the whole colony was changing in that respect. A Kratz had married a Lawrence. A Gebhardt had married a Black. Two of the Schaffers were at this moment keeping company with two Kirby sisters. All was changing.

The old white church on the hill was gone this last year and in its place a solid red brick and the *pfarr-haus* for the *pastor* matched it. Only the old bell was not worn out although it had called to worship and tolled and caroled for thirty years. More than these material changes, the services were part English,—there had been almost a rumpus over it, and again over whether to have a short sermon in German and another in English immediately following, or the German every other Sunday. They said they must do it to hold the young folks. Hold them, thought Amalia. How queer! No one could have made her miss church when she was young. What would her father . . . what would Wilhelm Stoltz have said to that, —getting the colony to come out here so they could keep together and retain their customs?

And then rather suddenly Amalia found out where Joe was going this summer of 1910. It was to see Rose Schaffer who had graduated in his class three years before.

It relieved her immensely and pleased her too. Rose Schaffer was everything that Amalia would have wanted for Joey. Pretty, neat and clean, so pleasant to every one. Oh, but that would be *schön,*—no, nice. She could hardly wait to tell Fritz when he came in from the field. They were cutting the new alfalfa which Joe had insisted on sowing. Fritz was all for the old things he understood,—Joe for the new. Fritz was sixty-one, not so young any more, but hardy as a hickory tree. He had given up readily enough about the alfalfa. He was easygoing and, anyway, it would all be Joey's place,—four hundred of the best acres in Nebraska.

"If he wants to plant pepper-nuts," Fritz had said, "nothing will I say."

Amalia had laughed heartily at that, for *pfeffernüsse* were Christmas cookies.

So Amalia was full of excitement over the news that she had just heard from Anna Kratz whose daughter had told her that *her* daughter had told *her* that Joe was keeping steady company with Rose Schaffer.

"Maybe we shall soon move back to the little house, Fritz. See to it that you keep it well painted and repaired and that it always stands ready."

Fritz laughed at that, teasing her whether he should start to pack.

And then others told it about and every one seemed to know it.

Amalia surreptitiously began making a quilt for Joey,— the Jacob's Ladder design. Joe, himself, said nothing. Such a boy,—one never knew what he was thinking. Always doing his work so silently and well. Perhaps she couldn't expect him to confide in his grandmother. But sometimes she wanted so badly to know how things were with him that she hinted, not quite subtly: "What's come of all your old class, Joey,—what's come of Rose Schaffer? Do you never see her any more?"

She would be asking in the German, he replying now in the English.

"Sure I do, Grandma. I saw her last night. We went over to Westville to the band concert."

"And how was she?" as unconcerned as though it were mere conversation, and not the vital thing it was.

"Oh, she's always up and coming."

Amalia was satisfied,—entirely pleased with his choice. If Joe had sent her out on a shopping trip for a wife she believed she would have returned with Rose Schaffer.

Life took on a new interest now. It would be like living over Emil's young days to have Joe bring Rose to the big stone house. She planned every day for it, expected any time now that Joey would tell her the news. She could even anticipate the conversation, so well did she know her Joey.

He would approach it like this:

"Grandma, what would you think if I should bring some one else here to live with us?"

"Oh, Joey,—do you mean it?" She must be surprised.

"Yes . . . I've been thinking of it."

"You mean a wife, Joey?"

"Yes. What would you say to my bringing Rose Schaffer?"

Oh, she would like it,—like it very much indeed. Kind, substantial Rose with a pleasant word for every one,—a girl who would be like a daughter. And it would be nice to live in the little house again and have only the work there to do. Let's see, how old was she now? Almost sixty-two. Time to take it easier. Yes, she would welcome the change,—with Rose nearby for company.

And then the corn was in and the butchering done. The fall winds blew cold across the country bringing a flake of snow or two as though messengers had been sent ahead to remind the countryside of what would soon follow.

Amalia, standing at the kitchen window of the big stone house on a Saturday morning, rubbed away the steam to see out. Across the dark fields and the bare brown stubble she could see the big comfortable white farm-houses and the red barns of two of the neighbors,—the Adolph Kratz place and the Gus Rhodenbachs'. Everywhere the fields were precisely laid out and fenced, square-shaped or long like Joey's dominoes,—not much like the old days of patches of crops here and there with no fences. On the main highway some county commissioner had tried a new-fangled idea of having little stones and gravel hauled for people to drive over. Joe was all for it, Fritz against it. Joey always for the new, Fritz for the old.

What had been wide sweeping prairie was as cut up now as roads and fences could make it,—so much for wheat, so much for corn, this square for pasture and that one for the new alfalfa hay. People scarcely used the word *prairie* itself any more, so subdued and tamed was the wild thing of an earlier day.

As Amalia looked she saw two men with guns crossing the Kratzes' cornfield. That was a part of the wolf hunt to which Joey had gone.

Joe, out on the wolf hunt, swung along over the frozen cornlands, his gun pointing as his father had taught him. He had sighted a coyote once and heard the wild call of others not long before. Far across the field he could see a couple of the hunters, probably young Jim Rhodenbach and his dad taking their cut across the field. Outside the fences down the road, teams were tied and the Kirbys' new automobile was nosed up to the pasture. Noisy things—these automobiles—scare all the horses to death.

The cold bit like a steel trap. Had almost forgotten

what it felt like after the hot summer harvesting and the mild fall corn-picking.

The finish of the hunt would be somewhere near the Schaffers'. He was glad of that,—could drop in and get a cup of hot coffee and see Rose a few minutes. Pretty fine girl,—Rose. Queer how he had never thought very much about her in High School,—merely given her a lift to town occasionally or talked over some lesson a few minutes. But it was different now.

He grinned cheerfully to himself,—she was his girl now all right. Ever since the High School Alumni banquet in June. Something had happened,—he didn't know just what, but things had been different since. He had gone alone, stagging it as usual. She had come with a couple of the other girls from the old class of 1907. Out three years now. Gosh, you couldn't realize it. Seemed as though the class had drifted apart,—Chick Adams and Ray Hostrop and Fat Leaman all going away to college that way. Fraternity fellows now,—with college yarns to spring. Two or three of the girls, too, were back from college or girls' schools. Couldn't blame them for hobnobbing together with a lot of things in common. He'd like to have gone too, but father and mother . . . just then. . . . Not much use in it either, would have just come back to farm anyway and you didn't have to go away to school to learn that. You knew all about that from the time you were a kid.

They had sat side by side at the banquet,—he and Rose. That was when it had happened and for the life of him he didn't yet know *what*. All he knew was that before he went he hadn't thought any more of her than of any other neighbor girl. When it was over and he had taken her home in his new yellow-wheeled rubber-tired buggy he knew she was his girl. And Rose knew it too. He hadn't asked her to marry him yet. Seemed silly to have to put it into words when each one understood, but he supposed he'd have to. Christmas Eve,—that would be the time. Christmas exercises at the church,—ask Rose after those—have the diamond ring in his pocket,— a pretty nice one too,—could use some corn money— seventy-five, or eighty dollars, maybe.

They were closing in now. Men were shouting. The guns opened up. By an almost miraculous watchfulness on the part of a kind providence no human's life was sacrificed, although practically all were in jeopardy, for in the last stages of a coyote round-up shots were as wild as the wolves themselves.

There were seven gray gaunt forms thrown on the pile. There were some drinks and much smoking and whacking of cold hands together to take away their numbness,— then Joe was off through a creek-bed and up a ravine, across a pasture to the Schaffers' house.

He tapped on the kitchen door with a simultaneous opening of it and stepped in. Odors of newly baked cinnamon-rolls and fresh coffee assailed his nostrils as the spices of Araby might have assailed a traveler. Rose was flushed from the baking, but pretty enough to kiss. His heart warmed to her and he was crossing the room, sud- denly inspired to carry out the suggestion when he stopped short, for a young girl came from the Schaffer dining- room and stood in the doorway,—a dainty little thing in a blue kimono held tightly around her cute form. Her eyes swept Joe with a soft pleading expression.

"This is Miss Bates, Joe, the new teacher to take Miss Ray's place. She's going to stay here. Miss Bates, my friend, Joe Holmsdorfer."

The new teacher's name was Myrtie,—Myrtie Bates. She had a delicate flower-shaped face, coming to a sensitive little pointed chin. Her big blue eyes were as soft and innocent as a baby's. She smiled on Joe so gently, with something so vaguely sad in the smile that he felt suddenly sorry for her, but just why he could not have told.

CHAPTER XXVII

NOVEMBER slipped into December. The Christmas exercises this year were partly in English. It disappointed Amalia. The older she got the more she clung to the old ways. Perhaps she should not do so, but it was hard to change. When the young folks sang: "Silent Night . . . Holy Night," Amalia hummed it too under her breath, *"Stille Nacht . . . Heilige Nacht."* It sounded sweeter the old way, and more tender.

Joe was there with Rose and another girl who, Fritz told her, was the new teacher of the Evergreen School. She lived at Schaffers'. Joe had been over to Schaffers' so much lately,—Anna Kratz told her she always watched from behind the curtains to see when he went by in his buggy. Anna said sometimes she could see he had two girls with him. That Anna! *Alte klotsch!* Old gossip, Joe called it in English.

The exercises over, she and Fritz drove home. There was no snow, but the moonlight was so bright it gave the appearance of white everywhere.

When Fritz put the team away and came in, something depressing seized Amalia. It was Christmas Eve and no time for feelings of this sort, but getting home this way from the exercises with Fritz brought it all back, that other night three and a half years ago when they had come home through the fog. And even though she put her packages for Fritz and Joey under the tree and tried to make it seem a happy occasion, she could not do so. Something made her wish constantly that Joe would come, made her listen for the thud of the horses' hoofs on the hard frozen ground.

She could not sleep. Joe had been late before,—dances and candy pulls,—but never like this. She got up. Three o'clock. The weirdness of the moonlight worried her as much as darkness ever had done. She went back to bed. She thought how queer it was that Joey was her grandchild and yet he was her son. It was as though she had borne two sons,—Emil and Joey. You never outgrew that maternal feeling for a child for whom you had cared. That was why people could adopt children and feel the same toward them as toward their own flesh and blood.

Four o'clock and he had not come.

By five the roosters were crowing. She got up and dressed. Something had happened and she could not stand the strain. The agony of all the things that had ever troubled her seemed to return in a great nightmare of foreboding. Always she was losing the people for whom she cared: Fritz and Joe were all that were left, and if anything happened to Joey, there would be no least reason for living.

Six o'clock. The stock was bawling. Fritz was up. Amalia walked the floor, peered from the windows into the gray of the dawn which was coming. Then she heard the team come in. She slipped back into her bedroom and closed the door, sat on the edge of the bed trying to think what could have happened. Some of the thoughts she put from her as unworthy. Whatever it was, she must be kind,—be motherly and patient.

She got breakfast, made a cheerful remark or two and busied herself at another task while Joey ate. They opened their presents, but there was no Christmas feeling among them. Joe went silently about his work during the forenoon. There was Christmas dinner, but though she lighted *kerzen* and put them on the table, the meal was not Christmaslike. After supper Joe hitched the team, came in and dressed up, said shortly as he left: "Don't leave a lamp for me."

Amalia lay in her bed and looked at the black walls of her room. Of all the crosses that she had borne,—of all the hardships that life had brought her,—there was something about this that was the most frightening. She could not have told why she was so shaken. It was as though a strange person had taken the place of her boy,—as though the air about her that was recently so clear was now smoky with gases,—poisonous and stifling.

In the morning she heard the team come in and looked out to see Joey helping a girl out of the buggy. Amalia could have laughed and cried with relief. She saw it all now. He was bringing Rose home just as she had known he would do. That would be Joey's quick way—no fuss, no plans, no talk,—just bring her home when the time came.

Amalia started out to meet them. But when they came up on the porch, she saw it was not Rose. It was a strange girl,—a pretty little girl with a flower-like face and big eyes like a baby's.

"Grandma, this is my wife," Joe said. "Her name is Myrtie."

"How do you do?" the girl said coolly.

Amalia thought she would faint. "Vy . . . vy. . . ." Always she talked more brokenly when under stress. She wiped her hands on her apron and held one out to the girl "Welcome to *unser heim* . . . our home."

But Rose! Rose! What about Rose? Her mind was asking it so loudly that she was afraid it could be heard.

All morning Amalia was confused,—so upset that she had to stop in the kitchen every little while when doing her work and think it all over. Joey had married a girl and brought her home. A strange girl, *not Rose*, not even German. Every time Fritz came into the kitchen with milk pails or to warm the chicken feed, she would look at him with questioning eyes and whisper in German: "Why is it so?"

But poor old Fritz did not know why it was so,—could have no way of knowing that a girl with wide baby blue eyes and cuddling ways and no deep sense of loyalty would deliberately take a man away from her friend,— even though it was a good-looking young man with four hundred acres of the best land in Nebraska. How could Fritz know this,—who had the kind of ethics that would always keep a promise?

Amalia got dinner. She had roast chicken and mashed potatoes and gravy, cole slaw and a pie from her Greening apples in the cellar. And she got out the good pink-flowered dishes and set the table in the dining-room, turning the plates over carefully and putting her stiff new

napkins upright in the drinking glasses. She could think
only of the queer thing that had happened, but so often
had she roasted *hühner* and baked *pastete* that she did it
all mechanically.

Myrtie sat in the big sitting-room and looked at the
album and the few English books in the corner bookcase
while Amalia prepared the dinner. She ate heartily for
such a little delicate-looking thing. Joe could scarcely
take his eyes from her at the table. He helped her to the
white of the chicken and wanted to know if she would
rather have peach-sauce than her pie.

After dinner when Joe went to the barn to look after
his team and Amalia washed the good pink-flowered
dishes, Myrtie went into the cold parlor, wrapped herself
in the crocheted afghan and took a nice long nap on the
red plush couch.

For a week Amalia did all the work in the big stone
house, and always a little worried, kept wondering what
was best to do. Then she broached the subject. "Joe,
vielleicht maybe Fritz and I *besser* over in de old house
geh . . . go. We can fits it up." Amalia must always
talk the English now as best she can for Myrtie does not
know the German at all,—not a word. Fritz, too, should
speak it always. Amalia must remind him of it. She
felt a little cross with Fritz now, sitting and looking at
his plate so timidly, as though this new girl could make
Fritz feel not at home in the house he himself had built
over twenty years before.

Myrtie spoke up immediately and answered for Joe
that it would be a good plan to move.

"I vould before go," Amalia said, "but I t'nk maybe I

should de vork do." She spoke slowly and carefully, thinking it out.

"Oh, no, no." Myrtie said pleasantly. "You can go. We won't need you. I'm going to keep a maid,—can't I, Joe?"

"Vass ist . . . a mait, Joey?" Amalia questioned.

"Myrtie means a hired girl, Grandma. Yes, I guess we can manage that . . . all right."

Myrtie turned soft baby blue eyes on Joe and said: "Another thing, we're going to have this house all made over, aren't we, Joe?"

"Sure," Joe said, "any way you want it, Myrtie."

So Amalia moved back to the old house. Myrtie acted gracious and bubbling with good nature the day they left, told Amalia to take anything she wanted; for she and Joe were going to have all new things.

It worried Amalia. Of course everything they had was Joey's and always would be, but farmers were not rich people. And all those things new when Anna Marie and Emil were married,—the red plush parlor set and the dresser, and its child, the commode, and the wash-pitcher and bowl! Tsk! Tsk!

But Myrtie gave them all as graciously to Amalia as though she had owned them the twenty years instead of a week, told her to take all the rag carpet and the sale carpet too, for she was going to have Wilton and Axminster rugs. So Amalia took the walnut corner cupboard and the high-backed bedstead, the dresser and commode, the album and the pictures of the fat semi-nude little girls with daisies in their hair. Fritz backed the wagon up to the side porch and he and Joe put the furniture into it and

200

some of the small things, but Amalia walked down the path, grass choked these last four years, and carried her shell box wrapped in unbleached muslin.

It seemed quite like old times to be settled with Fritz in the little home. Anna Kratz came over and spent whole days, so exciting was it to see all that was going on at the big house.

For, all winter and all spring, repairs and rebuilding went on. There were workmen there for weeks. Myrtie had them put wire all over the fine old gray stones and cover them with little pink sand that glistened in the sunlight. Delivery wagons from Westville came into the driveway nearly every day with furniture which Amalia, pretending that she had always known so, told Anna Kratz was called Mission furniture.

Myrtie had the walls of the two big rooms decorated in large-figured paper that gave the appearance of gilt bamboo-poles slanting across the Aurora Borealis. She had the floors varnished a shining dark red over which Amalia must walk charily on the few occasions of her going over to the big house. She used some of Amalia's beautifully pieced quilts for pads under the mattresses and her hand-woven rugs for wiping feet.

She had Joe paint their own bedroom blue, and because Joe was no artist, either by natural instinct or acquired knowledge, he got too much ultramarine in the mixture so that results gave one a rather nightmarish impression of a storm at sea. But because Myrtie liked it, Joe liked it too. Amalia scarcely knew what she thought about it, excepting to experience a stifled feeling of wanting to get

outdoors away from it under the soft blue of the sky and
the new green of the elms and maples.

All this change about the house took so much of Joe's
time he could scarcely get into the field.

As Myrtie had done none of the work herself, only the
planning, she was not especially tired these evenings so
she coaxed Joe to clean up to go to dances or band concerts
in town every few nights.

When the home was all finished Myrtie would not let
Joe come into the main rooms, or for that matter, any
farther than the kitchen, explaining to him in her cunning
babyish way that it must be kept nice for their friends
out from town to see.

Rose Schaffer was holding her head very high these
days, going into town with her father and brothers as
though nothing had happened. Sometimes she even drove
the sleek carriage team herself, their black manes tossing,
and the lines pulled taut over their shining dark bodies.
People began hearing that Rose had gone to help at a
neighbor's where there was sickness,—that she had stayed
by old man Rhodenbach all three days that the death
noise in his throat sounded louder than a child's rattle,—
had nursed a Kirby child through lung fever, saved it too,
the doctor said, with the steam from a teakettle and pine
resin dropped into the water,—queerest of all, had helped
a strange girl through childbirth in the school-house on
a stormy Saturday night.

Anna Kratz came waddling up the path between
Amalia's petunias one day, out of breath from her efforts,
to tell the news. Rose Schaffer had gone to Omaha to

learn to be a nurse, although Anna was dubious over what one can learn about it.

"You are a nurse or you are not," she said in German to Amalia. "Augusta Schaffer, Rose's grandmother, was a natural nurse. What can a young upstart like Rose learn that God does not give you?"

"Augusta lost babies sometimes when she helped," Amalia said, also in German.

But Anna Kratz settled that question easily: "It was God's will."

By this time Amalia could see that Myrtie's fragility and her ethereal beauty were misleading, for she began guiding all the destinies of the farm. Whenever the occasion demanded, she could wind Joe around her little finger by any one of the simple processes of wheedling baby-talk or big childish tears or an imitation of hysteria.

One afternoon in the summer when she and Joe had returned from town, she came over to the little house. Amalia saw her picking her way daintily through the bluegrass path under the apple trees past the big lilac bushes, then the petunia-bordered path.

"I've got a big piece of news for you, Grandma." She was excited, sparkling, clapping her hands like a child. Already Amalia had learned that Myrtie was always gracious for a little while after things had gone her way.

Amalia stood in the center of the little sitting-room, a broom-straw and pot holder poised in her hand from testing her *kuchen*, awaiting the news.

"What do you think? Your name isn't Holmsdorfer any more. You'll never have to be saddled with that old German name again. It's just Holms. You're Mrs.

Amalia Holms. We had it changed . . . in the courts. Joe and I. We're Mr. and Mrs. Joseph Rhoden . . . not Rhodenbach but Rhoden. . . . Mr. and Mrs. Joseph Rhoden Holms.

Amalia looked dazed. She called to Fritz to come in and help her interpret this astounding thing. Fritz stood timidly in the background, looking at the floor, as he always did before Myrtie. Amalia asked about it again, as though she could not understand the calamitous thing that had happened. You couldn't change your name like your dress.

When Myrtie explained some more that she had always been ashamed of the big long name and had Joe change it, and that Amalia was Mrs. Holms too, Amalia only stood and shook her head, so that Myrtie lost her graciousness and stamped her foot because of Grandma's stubbornness, and said: "You wouldn't be so dumb as that I hope."

But Amalia was firm. "You . . . *vielleicht* . . . maybe . . . Myrtie, you and Joe. But not me."

CHAPTER XXVIII

THE gay nineties had their good points in the growing city of Lincoln where Matthias Meier lived with Ida and his son Carter. For one thing, the bank in which he was vice-president had blossomed forth in electric lighting. The old horses on the street-cars were turned out to pasture and some of Mr. Edison's discovery took their place. There was a very grand new hotel built called The Lincoln. Matthias helped organize a Board of Trade and Ida a Woman's Club. University registration almost reached the unbelievable figure of two thousand. The first automobile honked its noisy way down "O" Street, a large portion of its inwards immodestly exposed to view.

Matthias, Ida and Carter went to the World's Fair in Chicago, returning with souvenir spoons, much Mexican drawn work, and pictures of Mrs. Potter Palmer and the Ferris wheel.

Upon her return Ida found the salt water pool in the new hospital opened to the public, and having been brought up on the Atlantic shore she took a great deal of pleasure in joining society around the huge affair. She had an entirely new outfit for the occasion,—a navy blue flannel suit gathered becomingly just below the knees with wide ruffles, the waist even cut a bit away from the neck, and the prettiest sort of gathered cap over her large head of hair, also finished in a wide rubber ruffle. With this, naturally, she wore her thigh-high lisle stockings into the water. One in her position had an example to set for the young ladies of the social set who were sometimes in these modern times threatening to leave off their hose when they swam.

At the beginning of the nineties there was drouth, and because nearly all crops were failures, the effect threw its shadow over all business. Settlers out on the prairie lived on what they had saved the year before, and Matthias Meier's bank drew on its reserve,—both rather like camels living on their humps.

There was a panic in 1893 and Matthias and his fellow officers figuratively bailed water night and day to keep the bank afloat. As though that were not enough to bear, the next year a hot seething wind blew across the mid-west and again ruined crops.

By 1896 the state was represented for the first time in a race for the presidency. The platforms created a general upheaval in the country. Gold democrats were bolting and rallying around William McKinley,—silver republicans were bolting and rallying around Matthias' friend, William Jennings Bryan. It gave Nebraska its first but not last political attention. Matthias himself had dipped into politics as far as the state legislature where he was responsible for one or two of the most important bills of the times. Sometimes he cast a speculative eye toward Washington, but "I better stay here and saw wood," he said to Ida,—and then laughed with her that he might not have had any other choice.

Between the years of 1898 and 1902 Carter was in the University,—one of the rather popular young bloods;

when he graduated, he stepped immediately into the bank of which his father was a vice-president and told every one that fellows who said it was hard to find jobs had bats in their belfry.

At twenty-seven he was married to Miss Lucile Bondurant, daughter of one of the other vice-presidents, at an elaborate church wedding. They went to Atlantic City on their honeymoon, and upon their return moved at once to their new home in Cedar City, a nice growing town in another county.

All this was by way of being something of a cataclysm to Matthias and Ida. But Carter, having evinced a great desire to run a bank himself and "run it right," had argued long and volubly before his marriage that he could never have matters his own way in this present job with a group of middle-aged men ahead of him to say nothing of several of their sons.

It had its points, Matthias agreed with him,—helped him purchase the controlling stock in the State Bank of Cedar City, sent him on his way with trepidation successfully concealed, remembering the days of his own ventures in a country that was raw and unsettled.

CHAPTER XXIX

EVERYTHING seemed different to Amalia at the farm since the coming of Myrtie. Sometimes she had a feeling that she and Fritz were visiting here or perhaps living on charity,—a queer enough feeling, too, when you stopped to think that the first two homesteads had belonged to Wilhelm, her father, and to Herman, her husband, and that only the newest eighty had been purchased by Joe's father from the Kratzes.

Life at the big house was so different now that she and Fritz did not go over very often. Myrtie was expecting a child and was so changeable in her moods. Sometimes she grew restless and had Joe take her to town every day. Sometimes she said she was nervous and would shut herself in her bedroom, not answering when Joe tapped on the door to ask what he could do for her. She did no work at all, having May Gebhardt there to keep house.

Amalia tried to smooth it over with Joe. He dropped in at the little house every day now and Amalia would laugh at his worries. Myrtie was all right. That was the way they always acted. But Amalia knew she was fibbing in order to bring oil to troubled waters,—knew that was not the way she had acted long ago, being so busy making garden and cooking and baking, washing and ironing and cleaning. It was not the way Anna Marie had acted, cheerful and laughing good-naturedly at her own shapelessness, pleased that she was bringing life into the world, heart-broken those times she could not carry her babies.

But she would soothe Joe, and feed him cookies from the old stone jar, so that he would leave whistling.

She could see that he was patience itself. Looking at him so eager to please and so willing to do everything Myrtie asked, Amalia wondered sometimes if he would ever tire of that babyish petulance, ever break over the traces and throw patience to the winds. When the time drew near, he paid the trained nurse to come much sooner than necessary so Myrtie would not worry. When she constantly wanted the doctor, too, and the nurse said there was no need, she cried hysterically and would not eat. Joe was quite beside himself with alarm. And Amalia comforted him, but even while she did so, she was remembering the wind and the shaking cabin, the loneliness at the birth of her child, and the sound of the coyotes howling.

The baby was born in September,—a boy, normal and husky, his sturdy little limbs a joy to see. They named him Neal, and Joe was as proud of him as a turkey-cock. Amalia could not comprehend that she was a great-grandmother. Because she and her son and her grandson had all been married at early ages, she was a great-grandmother at sixty-three.

And now, soon, life took on something of its old interest, for by the time Neal was three, Amalia was having much of the care of him. Joe took the little fellow with him on short journeys to the timber or barn or cornfield, and Fritz did likewise, so that it relieved Myrtie of a great deal of responsibility. She had many interests outside her home by that time, belonging as she did to so many organizations in town for the betterment of her mind, and one or two for her soul. It necessitated having a woman for housework and a second girl occasionally, even though Amalia took so much care of Neal. But it was a little hard to run the house as it had always been done, for there were guests out from town so often that the girls seemed never able to accomplish anything excepting to prepare for entertaining. As a consequence, the birds took the cherries, plums rotted on the ground, and apples turned to sour mash. But Myrtie said it didn't matter, now that one could conveniently get canned fruit and jellies in the stores.

She had a discontented droop to her pretty mouth much of the time now. Joe bought an automobile for her,—a fine red four-cylinder affair with top and lamps and windshield included, which materially increased her trips to town, but inasmuch as she never learned to drive it, Joe had to come in from the field almost every day to take her and once more to get her. As she insisted on his clothes being changed each time, this had its disadvantage from the standpoint of the farm work, so that he was obliged to take on another hired man.

When Neal was six, Myrtie was made secretary of a lodge in Westville so she bought a man-sized desk for her clerical work and turned Joe's and her bedroom into a semi-office. The desk just fitted into the corner where Joe's share of the twin beds stood so she retained only her own and put Joe and Neal upstairs. As Myrtie said, it was a very satisfactory arrangement for sometimes she liked to work late at her desk and then sleep late in the morning.

To Amalia, seventy now, fell even more of the care of Neal. But Amalia loved it. Even though she was old and tired, she loved it. What would life have been to her without this lively little boy? It was now as though she had her third son. Emil . . . Joey . . . Neal. Sometimes when he trudged by her side chattering so gaily, she caught herself thinking that which was not right and which she straightway corrected in her mind,—that of all three she loved him most.

Never had she seen so happy a child. Remembering Myrtie's pouting and her nervousness, old Amalia wondered how this had come to pass. One would have expected him to be cross, selfish, discontented. He was none of these. Everything tickled him, the dog running after a jack-rabbit, the martins frightening the sparrows, old Fritz dropping his upper teeth when he was in the corncrib. Neal's smile was always sunny. His laughter rang out at the slightest provocation. How could this be?

Myrtie's love for him took on a queer expression for a mother. Apparently it consisted for the most part in wanting him to be talented and courteous and to show off before her friends. Amalia could not put her finger on the queer quality of it, excepting that whatever he was doing openly and however he was appearing seemed to be of more importance to her than that which lay behind these external qualities.

Sensing this, Amalia bent all the time of her contacts with him to these very things which Myrtie passed over so

casually. She made him go all the way back to old Anna
Kratz's to return a small and unimportant wheel he had
brought from there without asking about it. She labored
a half day with him to get him to tell that he had taken
fruit *kuchen* from her pantry, caring not in the least for
the *kuchen* but only that he should be honest.

Together they walked in the timberland even as she
had walked with the little boy's father and his grandfather,—not buoyantly now, but slowly for her seventy
years. She talked to him of the trees, old now like Amalia
herself,—the hoary old cottonwoods and willow and ash
and the great thickly knotted clumps of wild sumac. Because it was too hard for her to stoop, Neal picked and
brought to her the violets and black-eyed Susans and trillium, the bellwort and bloodroot and wild columbine.
But it was only the English names of these that Neal
knew, for not one word of German could he say but *"Ich
liebe dich"* which Amalia had taught him was "I love
you."

Together they found the meadow-lark's nest in the
grass and the place where the owls had hooted away the
nights in the woods these fifty years. She stood with him
on the church knoll with its fine brick buildings and well-
kept cemetery behind iron gates looking over the valley,
and had him repeat with her,—she in German and he in
the English,—the psalm of walking through the valley of
the shadow of death and yet fearing no evil.

And this time Fritz was not here to make any comment,
either to tell her that she would make a softie of the
little boy as he had when she instructed Emil so, or
to admit that it is not softness to be tender as he had

with Joey. For old Fritz, himself, was lying back there now behind the wrought-iron gates. Old Fritz, himself, the year before, had walked through the valley of the shadow of death, fearing evil for a time, until Amalia by his bedside, holding his gnarled old hand and thanking him for having been such a good brother to her, made him fear no more.

It was lonely these days without Fritz, but much of the time it seemed to Amalia he had not gone away at all. When she was baking she often forgot and let a pan of *kuchen* get browner because he liked it so, and very often, unthinking, she set the table for two.

But Neal, dashing in then, full of life and laughter and staying to use the other place, would drive the loneliness away and fill her heart with happiness.

CHAPTER XXX

IT was this year of 1917 that strange things came to pass.

The country was at war. Amalia remembered the news of the Civil War when she was twelve, the drafting of several of the men in the neighborhood, the great pride the Illinois people had taken that old Abe was in the presidential chair, the company coming home when she was sixteen.

It had seemed unbelievable that war could touch her again. Even the Spanish-American War of which she had heard had been unreal, for no one from the immediate neighborhood had gone. There were three brave Nebraska regiments, they had told her,—one had gone to the Philippine Islands, wherever they were,—one to Tennessee, and one had crossed to Havana.

But this war was so different. It was coming into the neighborhood. It was asking for the young men. It was making trouble,—was causing bad feelings right here between old neighbors.

There could be no more German in the church on the hill. It must all be English,—not a song, not a sermon, not a psalm could be in the old tongue. Tsk! Tsk! How could one sit through and understand it all? How could it harm the country to say the Psalms in the German?

The *pastor* had been told to leave, had been given a

few days to get out of the neighborhood for making wrong statements. Anna Kratz came over every day now to talk. Almost in a whisper Anna talked to her in the German, looking about furtively as though the walls might have ears. Adolph had been in town, he and Karl Schaffer and Henry Gebhardt had been talking on the corner about the war; some men had come up to them and said to cut it out, meaning, so Adolph said, to speak no more in the German tongue.

Worst of all Myrtie made more trouble. She talked constantly to Joe about the relatives, put strange notions into Neal's little head so that he said: "Grandma, you shall say no more German words to me ever. I am ashamed of them."

"Not even *'Ich liebe dich'?*"

"No, it is not nice."

When the Christmas exercises were held in the church and they sang "Silent Night, Holy Night," Amalia hummed the song below her breath but with no words at all, for the English were too difficult and with the German she did not dare.

Oh, it was a trying time. Sometimes Amalia was wishing with all her might that Fritz were here to talk the queer situation over with her. Then, remembering Fritz's hard time with the English and the things some of the neighbors were saying, she was glad he was not here to be hurt.

Joe was irritable. Not even the high price he was getting for wheat—so much money—could pay him for the mean way he felt, torn by his loyalty to the oldest of the Kratz and Gebhardt and Rhodenbach people and by the harsh things Myrtie and her friends were saying.

And then he was drafted and Amalia and Myrtie were drawn together for a time by their common fright. But the scare went into nothing when the lawyer filled out the answers to the questions that Joe was sole manager of four hundred acres of farm land and must stay home to attend to raising the wheat.

Rose Schaffer was one of the first to go over-seas.

One of Karl Schaffer's boys died of pneumonia in camp. A Gebhardt boy was killed in France. Elsa Rhodenbach, who was a widow living in town now, had two sons leave the same morning together. Elsa got breakfast for them, said good-by, walked out of the house when they did, and never went back. All summer children used to stand on their tiptoes and peek through the woodbine covering the windows, seeing the dishes there on the table, the unmade beds with the boys' shoes under them and their ties and night-clothes thrown across the backs of chairs.

It was over at last,—the war. The whistles blew in town that it was over, and the train coming through, shrieked its way all across the countryside, through the villages and past the fields which had raised so much of the wheat for the armies. The bell in the tower of the big brick church on the knoll, rang, too, for in what language does a bell worship or toll or carol?

It was over for the neighborhood,—all but the scars left by the things that had been said, and for the fact that the Gebhardt boy and Karl Schaffer's boy did not come back, and neither did Elsa Rhodenbach's sanity.

Over, excepting for all of these things and a wild aftermath of economic and moral breakdown that swept into every village and farm.

Joe was making a good deal of money these days. His car was big and new, six cylinders now. The land brought in such good returns that he was anxious to get more. Myrtie was having a great many very nice things; clothes and company and a trip to Chicago with friends. She was back home now but so busy with several social affairs that Neal was still at Amalia's.

To-night while his parents were away, he was making a crude little boat in Amalia's kitchen . . . pound . . . pound . . . with Amalia sitting near looking over *reis* for to-morrow and watching him. Seventy-one she was. Did a woman never outgrow her motherliness? Neal was her little boy just as Emil and Joey had been. Emil . . . Joey . . . Neal! Son . . . grandson . . . great-grandson. The years had all run together so that they seemed three brothers with no great difference in their ages. Three little brothers, and she the mother of them all. How could it be like that?

Neal dropped his hammer now and leaned back against the wall for a time, eyes drooping and hands listless. Even as she was peering questioningly at him, he came languidly over to her. "I don't feel so good, Grandma."

She had him in her lap, was feeling his hot face, his rapid pulse.

"I'll say, *'Ich liebe dich'* Grandma, if you want me to. It is not bad. It is just as good as 'I love you.' "

"Oh, Neal-*liebling*." She pulled him to her, frightened at the premonition of a sickness for him. And he did not even rebel at the endearing word she had said to a big boy of eight.

Old Amalia kept clean night-clothes here in her house for Neal because she had him here so much,—a queer word they called them, pajamas. She never could remember to say it,—"night panties" she called them instead. She got out his night panties now and got him into them, her fingers stiff and slow but tender as always. Already he was dozing, shivering a little, too, and rousing to whimper. She covered him, got drinks for him, sat by the bed, comforting him.

It was late when she heard the automobile come into the yard. Joe would be down in a few minutes. He never failed to come down to see if everything was all right, whether to leave the little boy or carry him up home. Joe was a good father. Sometimes she thought he was father and mother both. In bearing Neal, Myrtie had apparently paid off most of her obligations to motherhood.

When she told him about Neal, he was at the bed in a second bending over his little son. Then out again for the doctor the moment he had seen his flushed face and how he was thrashing about.

Spanish influenza they called it, and it went through the country like the prairie-fires of the old days. People dropped over at their work,—young Mrs. Henry Kratz was frying chicken, fainted, was buried the third day with no one allowed to attend the funeral. A sixteen-year-old boy died, a sixty-year-old woman, a baby,—the whole countryside was panicky.

Myrtie's hired girl took it, then Myrtie.

Joe was beside himself with worry and sleeplessness.

He phoned to Westville for a trained nurse, to Lincoln, to Omaha. None was available. They said they would put him on the list but gave no hope for immediate relief. He plodded between the two houses, staggered almost with loss of sleep.

Old Amalia did everything for Neal the doctor said to do, but with her intuition she sensed he was not confident about his own orders. She carried out his orders fully, adding a few old-fashioned cures of her own, *flieder tee* and *pfeffermünz tee*. She had waged a fight like this many times for Emil and Joey,—now it was for Neal, her third little boy.

It was toward evening of the fourth day when Joe, haggard, unkempt looking, just back to the cottage from caring for Myrtie, was standing by Neal's bed, that the door of Amalia's sitting-room opened. Startled, they both turned to it. Rose Schaffer stood there in a white dress and over-seas cape, a little black satchel in her hand.

"Rose!" Something jumped so plainly from Joe that Amalia, relieved as she was at Rose's coming, turned away from him in embarrassment. As long as she lived Amalia knew she would carry with her the memory of Joe's face when he turned and saw Rose in the doorway. And now Amalia had this secret she must never divulge, must never even remember. And who but old Amalia knew what it meant to have married the wrong person?

"I came to help, Joe." Rose took off her hat. Her clear gray eyes, her serene mouth, her strong capable hands,—how good she looked!

"You're . . . so good, Rose." It was all he said.

Rose went at her work with no other explanation. Joe went out to do his chores.

For two more days and nights Neal was not out of danger and Rose scarcely took her eyes off the child. Then the fever broke and the great sweating sapped his strength.

Joe coming in found Rose crying by the bedside and was almost too frightened to speak: "He's . . . he's worse, Rose?"

"No . . . he's better. He'll get well if you're careful."

"Then why . . . are you crying?"

Amalia saw him start to put his arm around her and then drop it quickly.

"Just . . . a sort of reaction. Silly . . . isn't it?"

But old Amalia, who had lived seventy-one years, knew why Rose Schaffer was crying over Joe's little boy.

CHAPTER XXXI

CARTER MEIER and his wife Lucile had adjusted themselves ably to conditions in the smaller town of Cedar City.

"The smaller the town the more often they tack on the word 'City,'" Lucile had said.

But Carter had called her attention to the fact that when a town gets its baptismal name its sponsors in fancy see it stretched out over half the county.

"Like babies, I suppose," Lucile said with sarcasm, "with the mother always thinking her youngster is to be president or the first lady."

In 1913 Lucile herself had no sarcasm for the situation, but very frankly admitted that her baby was an eligible candidate for the first lady's place. The child had dark red ringlets, creamy petaled skin and hazel eyes. They named her Hazel, but Matthias sometimes facetiously called his only grandchild "Reddie."

He and Ida took their honors solemnly. Because Carter had not been born until they were thirty-five and thirty-two,—and because the child Hazel did not arrive until Carter and Lucile had been married for six years, —it followed that Matthias and Ida were well along in years,—sixty-eight and sixty-five,—before they experienced this ownership of a grandchild. It was almost overwhelming.

They drove out to Cedar City at the least possible excuse, taking advantage of every national holiday, every birthday, and even, so Ida said, April Fool and Columbus Day.

Matthias was out of active business now. He looked after his property, advised Carter on any and all matters that came up in the Cedar City bank of which he owned some stock. Once he and Ida had been abroad, several times to Florida and California.

Ida, at sixty-five, looked the part of an amiable duchess,—snow-white hair in a becoming coiffure, solid pink cheeks, her heavy figure straight and trim in its hard stays. Her word had weight in the Woman's Club,—church organizations asked her to make decisions, every charity included her name.

Matthias, too, was straight as an Indian, his shovel-shaped black beard of the old days white-washed by the years and trimmed down to Scotch-like closeness.

They belonged to the Country Club, ten years old now. Matthias swung a mean club in the newly introduced game of golf, and Ida could hold her own at the card table. Sometimes they laughed at the old days. "Imagine how I used to play croquet in a long trailing skirt!" or "How I ever had the nerve to sing in a choir . . . !" And then quite often the statements would be followed by "Just the same they were the good old days," spoken together like the chorus of a song which they both knew.

The child Hazel could not, if she were able, have chosen more satisfactory grandparents.

Carter's business was good. The State Bank of Cedar City was paying ample dividends spring and fall. Matthias admitted his son had used his head when he went into the smaller bank on his own. His success made Carter Meier rather unsympathetic with failure of any sort. One did with life as one wished. Or so he thought.

Lucile had everything to make life comfortable for her, —sufficient clothes for the exigencies of the small town and for the times when she would go to Lincoln to be entertained by her own people or Father and Mother Meier, —a nice home, plenty of help, her own car, a healthy and attractive little daughter.

Carter worked day and night during the World War, —his own business in the daytime, war work at night,— questionnaires and applications for release from the draft for the farm boys. He was a part and parcel of the smaller town as his father had been of the small Lincoln, grown by this time to fifty thousand people.

To the west twenty million acres of sandy soil held fast to the earth's breast by coarse, tough grasses since the glacial period were being loosened by plows to feed a fighting Europe.

It was easy planting. No forests to fell, few stones to remove. Peel open the top soil with a plow, seed it, scratch it with a harrow, and Mother Nature did the rest. As the crops went in, the soil grew finer, became more powder-like.

A few shook their heads at the unthinking procedure. Once when old Charlie Briggs dropped into Cedar City to see Carter, his old friend's son, and a bit of fine dust was coming through the air on the wings of the west wind, old Charlie lifted his head like a fire-horse and sniffed.

"Dirt from the Panhandle," he said. "Powder, that's what the ground is being pulverized into. It might turn into gunpowder one of these days. A body can't tell. Wheat may get to be scarce. Bread might be a luxury right here in the heart of our own country. Ain't I heard somepin' about a French Revolution startin' over a bread riot?"

Carter Meier laughed a lot about old Charlie Briggs and his ideas.

In 1919 with Spanish influenza sweeping the country, Ida Meier died suddenly in her Lincoln home. Only four days of sickness, and with Matthias employing every means at his command,—doctors, specialists, nurses, oxygen,—she slipped away.

He was too stunned to comprehend. Why, Ida was a part of him. She was one of his hands, one of his feet, one side of his mind, half of his heart. If Ida was dead, that meant half of him was dead.

But he pulled himself together, lived on, imposed his feelings of loss on no one. He sold the old home to the Pi Beta Chis,—when some of the "actives" came in to look it over, closed his ears to their merry quips about the ornate grill-work through which they could hang their neckties, and how they would play checkers on the inlaid woods of the entrance hall. Still, Ida would have laughed merrily if she could hear their humorous sallies. All right, he would laugh too, then.

He moved over to Cedar City to be near Carter and Lucile. They built a larger house so he could have his own suite of rooms. He went down to Carter's bank every day. Carter depended a great deal on his judgment.

Hazel was Matthias' comfort. He watched her grow, —eight—ten—twelve—fourteen. How the years rolled on. She was not quite so pretty now,—her hair was lovely, but she was at the gangling age,—a brace on her teeth, freckles on her nose. The former would come off in time,—it was questionable about the other.

She was athletic,—always on roller skates, ice skates, a bicycle. A tennis racket was her insignia,—"I can beat you" her life's motto. She went hither and yon with the wind. Sometimes he tried to take a hand and tame her down,—tell her that she would soon be a young lady, that ladies should be more demure, that the young men cared more for that kind, and how could she expect to have any young man ever care for her?

"But I don't *want* any young man to care for me," she would respond. "It would just drive me *nuts*. I'm going to be the champion swimmer—or a circus woman—or maybe fly in a plane."

Whatever could you do with a young girl like that? Such times as these were. No modesty, no womanly graces.

Fairly often old Charlie Briggs came to see Matthias. Lucile and Carter laughed a little at the old codger.

"Whatever Father can see in him, with his long-drawn tales of the 'airly days,'" Lucile would say.

"Search me," Carter would respond indifferently. "With all Father's travel and culture, I believe he hangs more on every word that old fellow says than any one I know."

But Hazel always stood up stoutly for him. "I like him. He's a nice old man. He shot an Injun once right in the belly when the Injun was trying to slip up on him."

"Hazel . . . how terrible! Why do you listen to all

225

that gore? Anyway, it's Indian, not Injun. And do, for pity's sake, say he hit him in the stomach if you *have* to say it at all."

"Charlie Briggs says it's Injun. And your stomach *isn't* your belly. Your belly . . ."

"Hazel. That will do."

". . . is below your stomach."

"Hazel. Do you hear me?"

"Anyway he knows more about our own history than anybody. He knows all about the Vigilantes hanging the horse thieves in summer 'til the crows pecked their eyes out . . . and about sticking them down through ice holes in the winter."

"Oh, Hazel, you have such a delicate sense of the æsthetic."

"And I'm going some day to see where old Charlie Briggs and Grandpa got off the boat at Nebraska City . . . and John Brown's cave where he hid the runaway slaves. And Charlie Briggs can show me yet, he says, where the overland trails all began. He bets he can find ruts some places yet where the wheels of the prairie schooners cut. I can go, can't I, Dad?"

"Sure. Anybody as history-conscious as that ought to be allowed to poke around a bit."

CHAPTER XXXII

TIMES had changed again slowly. The highway was hard packed with gravel. The Evergreen School was closed and a bus came by daily to take Neal and the other pupils into town. When Amalia got out Joe's tin bucket that she had saved carefully and offered to put up Neal's lunch for him every day, thinking how much pleasure it would give her, he rolled on the floor in his mirth.

"Grandma, you are so behind the times. Don't you know I buy a hot lunch in the cafeteria?"

"In de calf . . ."

"Cafeteria . . . where you can buy the food you choose to eat,—soup and hot meat and potatoes and salads,—a balanced meal to keep you healthy."

Tsk! Tsk! And the cold *met-wurst* and the *schinken* and the *korn brot* and *äpfel-butter* she had put up so many times! And who had been more healthy than Emil and Joe?

There were other things about which Neal laughed hilariously.

Once she asked him hesitatingly,—for perhaps, already she knew his answer,—"Neal, vould you . . . vouldn't you like to be a *pastor?*"

Giving it, as she did, the emphasis on the second syllable in the German way, Neal was not sure of her word.

"Pas*tor?* You mean a preacher?"

"So. A preacher."

Neal rolled then on the floor in mirth and shouted. "A preacher! All I would like about that is being invited to all the big dinners in the country."

No, there was no use. No one of her three boys a *pastor* would be.

Myrtie's latest argument with Joe these days was that he should get out of the hog business altogether and depend only on selling his crops.

Joe groaned when she began, for never since their marriage had Myrtie dropped a subject upon which she had once set her mind.

The grain from four hundred acres would bring ample income, she said, and pigs were such dirty things,—you could hear their grunting and squealing away up at the house, too, company or no company.

At first Joe only made joking answers, that he'd have some one in to instruct them at their eating, that the day Mrs. Meredith, the banker's wife, and the lodge ladies came out from town, he would speak to the old porkers himself.

But Myrtie would not joke. She ran instead the full gamut of her little tricks,—teasing, baby-talk, wheedling, tears, hysteria. It was not often that she had to go so far, but Joe set a good deal of store by his Berkshires, and it required her entire bag of tricks before he capitulated.

After the hogs went, she began on Joe about the chickens. She said eggs were so cheap it was foolish to look after those chickens and cackling hens every day, and when they wanted one to eat, Grandma would let them have one of hers.

So they, too, went,—and the farm was exactly like a town home with its nice sloping lawn, no pigs or chickens on the place, and Joe, dressed up, driving the car up to the side porch whenever Myrtie called.

As there were no pigs or chickens to be fed, there was no mash to be cooked. So Myrtie told one of the hired men to scrub up the old soap-kettle, paint it copper-colored, fill it with dirt and bring it onto the front lawn. There she had him cross three stout hickory sticks in camp-fire style and hang the kettle on them by a gilded chain. Then she had the hired girl plant white snow-on-the-mountain in it, and red geraniums under it. And people coming out from town said it looked cute, just as though there were fire under it and steam coming out of it.

Only old Amalia, standing in the doorway of her small house, shading her watery eyes from the sunlight to see the finished article, failed to think it looked cute. She thought the old kettle looked out of place and a little silly.

By the time Neal was through the grammar grades and ready for High School in the fall of 1926, Myrtie's desires took on more radical form. Specifically,—she wanted Joe to retire.

"Retire?" Joe laughed heartily at that one. That one should be in the funny column, he said,—maybe in the department called "Slips That Pass in the Night."

When Myrtie would not laugh, but persisted day after day in referring to a potential retirement, Joe grew irritated. It was too foolish to waste one's breath on it.

"Retire? Say, what do you take me for?"

"Yes . . . retire." Myrtie's little rosebud mouth set in a straight and stubborn line.

229

"Can you beat it for a cracked idea?   Retire when you're thirty-eight."

"Age hasn't anything to do with it,—if you're able financially to retire at thirty-eight."

"But I'm not."

"Oh, you just think you're not.   Just that old Holms-*dorfer* idea that you have to hoard."   The accent on the *dorfer* which had been dropped and the slur which it implied angered Joe more than Myrtie had ever seen him angry.

"See here, a Holms*dorfer* was good enough for you to want to marry.   And you leave the old folks out of this. If you and I are ever half as good as . . ."   He caught himself, said more evenly: "I don't call it hoarding to earn your living by hard work so you can have something to depend on in your old age."

"You'll have plenty, never fear."

"Not if I quit while I'm still a young man, I won't. And don't forget that last eighty from the Gebhardts,— costing twenty thousand dollars because the improvements were extra good,—five thousand only paid, only two really which was cash, the bank holding a seven thousand note of mine, Henry Gebhardt an eleven thousand mortgage.   That sounds like retirement in a pig's left eye.   Oh, excuse me for mentioning pigs."

And when Myrtie's little mouth trembled and she looked misty-eyed, he asked querulously: "Retire . . . *where?*"

"Over to Westville of course, or even to Lincoln."

"In *town?*"   Joe was really disturbed.

"Of course."

"But I wouldn't *like* it, Myrtie. I'm a farmer. My father . . . and my father's father and *his* father . . . maybe back to Adam for all I know were *land* people. It's my *work* . . . my *life*."

"There's a lot more to life than a farm."

"I know it. I want to get things running here smoothly so we can take a good trip every year. Canada . . . I'd like to see those real wheat farms, . . . California, maybe, . . . the old Spanish ranchos I've heard about. . . ."

"Farms . . . ranchos." Myrtie said it in the same tone one would speak of tarantulas and scorpions.

"Then there's Neal," he went on. "He's to be thought of."

"How do you mean . . . 'thought of'?"

"Why, that everything shall be in tip-top shape for him."

"Where?"

" 'Where?' Why, *here*."

"Neal will have something to say about that."

"Of course, and he'll say the right thing, too. Natural-born farmer . . . look at his 4-H Club work . . . his calf prizes."

At that Myrtie would walk into her own room and close the door.

But a mere walking off by no means closed the argument.

It went on many times after that. Sometimes Myrtie was quietly insistent about it, sometimes she was tearful, and always she kept it over Joe's head. Sometimes she said Joe ought to be generous enough to do it for her after all she'd been through, at which Joe could scarcely restrain himself against asking just what that had been. Sometimes she remarked that he was blind not to see it was for his own good. Often she said it was too bad that he couldn't do that much for his only son.

At that Joe would explode: "My only son's a spoiled kid with everything in the world from his first little velocipede on through town school,—a boy's camp,—asking for his own car at fifteen now,—the promise of one on his sixteenth birthday. At his age I was up at five with my dad, doing my share of chores. . . ."

That would be about the point where Myrtie would cry and take a headache tablet.

Joe, dropping down sometimes on the steps of the old home and looking across the long sloping lawn to the paved highway and his fields beyond, lush with purple alfalfa, to the corn lands and the pastures, and his sleek cattle, tried to think how any one would want to live anywhere else.

He worked hard, of course, but who didn't? Lots of discouraging things,—bad crops, hail, prices slumping, one battle after another with chinch bugs or blight or cutworms. If it wasn't one thing it was another. But wherever you were or whatever you did there was always something. He bet even the banker had his troubles. He'd rather battle his enemies out here in the open.

Sometimes he thought of Rose Schaffer. At first he had put her from his thoughts as disloyal to Myrtie about whom he had once gone off his head. Then, he didn't care whether it was disloyal or not. He liked to think about her. How contented Rose would have been on a fine farm and how efficiently she would have managed. Oh well, she was probably doing just what she was cut out for,—head nurse or some such title in one of the Omaha hospitals.

And now Amalia was seventy-nine, tiny and weather-beaten, her hair in a hard little knob like a walnut, her skin a network of wrinkles, deep rivers on the map of Time.

This was the spring that with Joe, Myrtie, and Neal she took the long drive one Sunday to Nebraska City to visit Arbor Lodge, the beautiful old estate of J. Sterling Morton, now a state park.

All the buds were unfolding under the soft warmth of the sun. There was a smell of burning leaves. Tulips were pushing up through the warm ground. Odors from recently turned earth still lingered in the air. The old grounds were lovely in their new spring growth.

Not once had Amalia ever returned to Nebraska City since the day she stepped from the ferry and found Herman waiting. Sixty-one years.

They were to eat their lunch here under the trees so Myrtie said. Joe said they would drive down toward the town afterward so Grandma could try and find the place where she stood by the overland trail when she was married to Grandpa.

It was the first time Neal had ever been told about it.

He thought that was just about the darnedest thing he'd ever heard. "What do you know about that, Grandma? Married outdoors! And standing by the wagons on an overland trail! Well . . . I'll be . . . Say, you could have sung 'It's a Long, Long Trail A-Winding,' couldn't you?" And he rolled on the pine needles in one of his moments of mirth.

They spread their lunch on a cloth under the pine trees growing on a portion of the grounds. The mansion was visible through the trees, the snowy white pillars of one of its three great rounded porches glistening in the spring sunshine. Here, somewhere, perhaps even where the lunch cloth lay, was held the ceremony in which the Indians made the treaty with the whites, signing away all their rights to Nebraska Territory. Joe said there was a large oil painting of the ceremony in the house, on the landing of the great stairway,—that they could see it when they would go in later.

There were several other groups in the grove. Myrtie was hoping that it was no one she knew, for she was always a little fearful of meeting some of her friends when she was with Grandma who looked so queer these days.

Joe knew who one of the men was in the group nearest, —it was Carter Meier, the banker over at Cedar City. He had seen him the time he went there with Orval Black on that note. That must be his wife and young daughter with him. Myrtie was all interest,—they certainly looked well groomed and as though they *were* some one.

"And I suppose the gentleman with the white beard is old Mr. Matthias Meier, his father," Joe explained.

Amalia trembled a little with the sudden shock of the queer thing Joey had said.

"What did you say his name was, Joey?"

"Matthias Meier. He lived in Lincoln until a few years ago. Now he lives in Cedar City at his son's home."

"Joey, . . . I knew . . . I knew a man in Illinois vonce by de name of Meier."

"Sure you did . . . and you'd known one if you'd lived in Indiana or Michigan or Ohio. Pretty common, Grandma."

When the lunch was finished, Amalia walked over to a bench under the trees and sat down. She wanted to think. Matthias Meier! So often she had wondered about him. Old Amalia Holmsdorfer in her rusty black dress and her little black bonnet with the jet buckle sat and wondered if it could really be the same. After a life-time!

And then it happened. The tall white-haired and white-bearded old gentleman of the group came walking down the path. Old Amalia who could not see to read could yet see him coming. He was straight and tall and he swung a cane rather pompously. Amalia knew him,—by his walk and the set of his shoulders and the way he held his head,—by her heart and by remembrance.

The years turned back and he was swinging off his horse . . . coming toward her. . . . Yes, old Amalia knew him.

She was suddenly agitated, frightened. Her heart,—it pounded loudly. Should she call to him to stop? Get up and walk toward him? Should she let him know? Should she say something? Or nothing? She sat still and blinked up at him with faded eyes.

If Amalia saw a fine-looking, well-preserved old gentleman, highly groomed and prosperous appearing, Matthias Meier, sauntering down the path, saw a queer little old woman sitting on one of the park benches,—a brown gnome of a woman peering up at him with pale, watery eyes. She looked like one of the peasants of Bavaria he had seen abroad, he was thinking,—or a Breton painting, perhaps. She looked so tiny and ancient, so picturesque in her funny old clothes, so detached from the civilization of to-day, that he nodded courteously to her. Yes, she belonged there under the trees with the squirrels.

"Spring again," he said pleasantly to her.

Amalia twisted her knotted fingers together. "Yes," she said. She tried to wet her shrunken, dry lips over her toothless gums. It all sounded queer and strange,— but familiar, too, like a thing one has learned long ago and never forgotten. "Dey keep comin'."

"Even though we grow old," he added humorously, placing himself humbly in her class.

She clung tightly to the seat, pressing her hands against the wood,—trying to fit it all in,—the puzzle,—nodding acquiescence to the strange thing he had said.

He passed on, leaving the queer-looking little old lady sitting there nodding—nodding agreement that spring was here even though they were old.

For how could young Matthias Meier once have known he was to keep his rendezvous in such a way? And how could old Matthias Meier know that he had not broken his promise,—that he and Amalia had kept their tryst?

CHAPTER XXXIII

IN the fall of Neal's junior High School year, Joe and Myrtie moved to Westville.

Myrtie chose a house on the corner of Fifteenth and Oakland Streets,—a big brown brick and stucco. Joe tried to get her to be satisfied with a smaller one for he reminded her many times that Neal would be away at school in two years' time.

"High School was good enough for me, but Neal is to have college. Even if he goes back to the farm as I hope he will, he'll always have something you can't take away from him. Can't say I ever missed it, but I'd like Neal to go."

Prices were high and the house cost a pretty sum of money. Joe had to do a certain amount of juggling to arrange for its financing, as his lawful limit had been reached at the Westville bank.

He got a personal loan from Henry Kratz for a cash payment and gave a mortgage on the new house to the original owner. When he was going to put a mortgage on the home four hundred, he found it tied up yet in the original owners' names, his grandfather's and his great grandfather's homestead titles, as there had been no settlement of the estate. Not many direct descendants could boast of that, they told him at the courthouse,—there had been so much changing,—but the county recorder said he would bet his last year's hat and the one from the

year before, which was the same one, that there were
more families on farms which their ancestors homesteaded right there in that valley than in any other section of the state.

It was fairly complicated but not hard to straighten,—
Wilhelm Stoltz's one-hundred-sixty acres by the laws of
the state were divided equally between Amalia and Fritz.
Fritz's half at his death became Amalia's, one-half of
Herman's homestead went to Amalia and one-half to
Emil, the latter having gone *in toto* to Joe as did also the
eighty Emil had purchased later. To sum it all up to
Myrtie, Joe told her that after all, out of the land in the
farm, Grandma still owned two hundred and fòrty acres
of it and maybe she would have something to say about a
mortgage,—all of which seemed especially foolish to
Myrtie when Grandma was so old and didn't even care.

"She'd care if she'd lose it," he said grimly.

The town house was eventually financed and Myrtie
furnished it newly from top to bottom for she was leaving
the furniture in the stone house to the renters.

Whenever Joe grew blue about his finances, knowing
that he was going against all the teaching of his people,—
all the traditions of the thrifty midwestern pioneers,—
reminding himself and Myrtie that Indebtedness was an
animal which ate houses for breakfast, farms for dinner,
and lunched between times on stock sandwiched between
chattel mortgages,—Myrtie would laugh it off and call his
attention to the fact that four hundred and eighty acres
of the best Nebraska farm land was worth three hundred
dollars an acre any day, which according to *her* arithmetic
was one hundred and forty-four thousand dollars.

"We *think* it is," Joe would say, "but do we *know* it?"

Another change in Joe's life came now.

At a little bridge party one evening at Banker Meredith's, Myrtie, who was sitting on the davenport with Mr. Meredith before the games started, said in her pretty pouting way that she wished Joe could get in the banking business,—"Oh, maybe not *work* at it but own stock and meet with the directors and feel that he was one of the *business* men of the town."

Mr. Meredith looked at her a moment rather oddly, said she was a bright little woman and he thought maybe it could be arranged. So it came to be that Joe was allowed to buy fifty shares of stock at the bargain price of one-hundred-sixty dollars per share and was made fourth vice-president, which was really the very nicest thing that could have happened to the Holms family.

Myrtie said that it took a woman's ambitions and intuitions together to help a plodder like Joe get anywhere,—and it was not, in fact, until the moratorium of 1933 several years later, when the bank failed to reopen and Joe was assessed for twice the amount of his stock, that Myrtie's intuitions and ambitions appeared not to be puncture-proof.

But that situation had not yet arrived and these years were prosperous ones. Joe's crops brought good prices. They bought a larger car. Neal was to turn his old one in and get a new one the day he would graduate.

So now Mrs. Joseph Rhoden Holms could launch out on what she termed "real living." Neal went in for football and a general good time.

And Joe—?

Joe in his early forties, miserable and uncertain just what life was doing to him, would drive out to the farm nearly every day and look around, "overseeing the tenants," as Myrtie wanted.

But something was happening to the old home place. Spring rains had washed out part of the corn and the renter apologetically said he had thought there wasn't any use to replant when it was so late. Fences were broken here and there. The stucco was dropping off the house in large South-American-shaped chunks. Dandelions and burdock had taken over part of the lawn. A barn door hung by a roller. The old soap-kettle in the yard at the side of the drive hung dejectedly by one chain over the frozen geranium roots and with rotted snow-on-the-mountain spilling out of it.

Sometimes Joe worked all day at these defects, eating his noon meal with old Amalia. Nearly eighty she was, but fairly spry about her house-work and as neat as ever. Her kitchen shone like a child's scrubbed face. No one could make *kaffee kuchen* so well or fry chicken like Grandma.

It always made him feel better to talk to her. He told her many of the things that worried him, but he never complained about Myrtie. It did not seem square to Myrtie to discuss her even with Grandma. Once when he was there Amalia told him Rose Schaffer had been to see her. "In her own car . . . such a fine-looking voman . . . wit' a fur coat."

He started to say something, thought better of it evidently and did not finish.

Together they sat silent and embarrassed.

Sometimes he talked to Grandma about Neal. "Four hundred and eighty acres of the finest Nebraska farmland there is," he said sardonically, ". . . that's what he'll have some day and Myrtie wants him to be a lawyer."

"Vell," old Amalia said cheerfully, "any lawyer can alvays use a goot farm," and laughed at her own joke. Always she was wanting Joe and Myrtie to get along well.

"If there's anything left," Joe said grimly. "I don't like the way my debits and credits look in black and red figures."

Neal graduated from the Westville High School in 1929. One could scarcely contend that it was scholarship which sent him through with more or less flying colors. Football prowess plus a reputation for squareness and a personality that was most likable,—these rather were his assets. Amalia looking at him, sometimes wondered what he had of Myrtie's excepting the cleft in his chin and the gracious manner all the time which she showed only when things went her way. He had something of the noisiness of Emil, his grandfather,—the physical prowess of Herman, his great-grandfather,—perhaps even a little of the arrogance of Wilhelm Stoltz, his great-great-grandfather. From Amalia herself he had several of those traits she had given him when under her care, but that she did not see.

The night of the graduating exercises in the new auditorium Joe drove out to the farm to get Amalia, eighty-one now. She was dressed and waiting for him, and if they were both remembering that other graduating night, neither spoke of it.

She had on her black dress gathered full at the waist-line. Her hair was knotted in its tight little wad on the nape of her neck. She was as shrunken as a tiny brown mummy. There was not a tooth in her head.

Seeing her so, as with newly opened eyes, Joe said suddenly: "Grandma, I'm afraid you're getting along in years. Don't you think you better come to town and live with us?"

"Tsk! Tsk! *Nein.* Besser you come live wid me."

"That's no joke." Joe was solemn.

Myrtie had a new lavender crepe outfit for the occasion, and she loved people telling her it was unbelievable that she was the mother of that strapping big foot-ball player.

Amalia could plainly see that Neal was the finest looking boy in the class of thirty-four young people. And at that, even discounting for prejudice, Amalia was not far wrong, for Neal was big and well-knit and the happy-go-lucky glint in his eyes added something to his charm.

In truth it helped get him into the Pi Beta Chi fraternity at the University that fall, along with the excellent facts that he was a foot-ball player, had a high-powered roadster of his own and a dad well enough off to be retired. That no one inquired into his scholastic standing is not too astounding.

A fraternity bid being, as it is in most midwestern colleges, a ticket to Paradise, a fraternity pin, the receipt of the ticket's purchase, there was no question in Neal's mind but that he would "go frat."

Several of the fraternities looked upon Neal Holms of Westville with covetous eyes, so that there was rather a concerted and noisy fight over him on rush week. And rush week being largely a survival of the fightest, it was hard at one time to tell which of the steam-rolling methods would capture him.

Those methods were varied and telling. Although he did not see it himself, he was told of the fellow taken up in a plane by three Phi Psis, hearing that he was to be wearing a Phi Psi pin en route down or he wouldn't get down, deciding during the third loop to pin it on,—of the fellow who thought his dinner invitation was a bid and arrived with his baggage,—of the mortgage-holding uncle who threatened to foreclose on the house if his nephew didn't qualify.

As for himself and the methods employed to get him— there was the way the Alpha Sigs flashed the magic of Sam Towle in his eyes,—(gosh, *the* Sam Towle who was the All-American half-back). There was the way the Betas dazzled him with the luxury of their palatial house which they spoke of casually as "the dump." There were the Delts trailing across his vision, like a red flag of distress, the plea that he alone could bring back to them the pristine glory that had been theirs when the great Pat Smithson had bled and died for them on the gridiron. (Imagine *that*,—thinking *he* could take Pat Smithson's place.) With fine disregard of laws concerning "sweat shops," the Sig Alphs tried to wear him down in the shower room. The Pi Beta Chis trotted out a Phi Beta Kappa alum as nonchalantly as though he were not the only one of the species that had ever been coralled behind its wrought-iron doors, and who, they said, would be tickled to death to help Neal in any way he could.

"Might be handy to be in a frat with a few walking

encyclopedias dashing in every night or so—what, old boy?"

He attended smokers and dinners at the Cornhusker, was taken for shows and for walks and rides, was called "Pal" and "Buddy" and "Old Chap" and "Kingfish," was slapped on the back, shoulders, knees and in the pit of his stomach, was told he could room with the president of each frat, with every fraternity member of the football team that had licked Pittsburgh, and with every hit in the masculine dramatic Kosmet Klub. He was promised the absolute run of the Theta, Kappa, Delta Gamma and Pi Phi houses, dates with the Junior Prom girl, the Mortar Board president and Nebraska U's Sweetheart.

Small wonder that Neal Holms in tailored suit and high-powered roadster and collegiate spotlight seemed far removed from Herman Holmsdorfer in blue jeans cracking his blacksnake over the backs of oxen on the lonely prairie.

All this time each fraternity house was a womanless Eden,—your college men fight this thing out alone without feminine interference to complicate matters.

Suffice to say, Neal found himself at the end of the battle with five pledge buttons, which under existing conditions were several too many, so that he was compelled to think up four air-tight excuses.

He went Pi Beta Chi,—and sometimes after that the fellows in other fraternities who had nearly wept on his shoulder and tapped him lovingly in the stomach, took time out to speak to him on the campus, but more often they did not.

And life became a geographical thing bounded by a few city blocks and a campus,—a mental affair of no small

effort,—a physical one of hard freshman foot-ball practice,—and an emotional one of rather formidable dimen-
sions caused by the sight of more pulchritude running
around at large than he had been accustomed to see.

CHAPTER XXXIV

IN the last ten years Cedar City had grown accustomed to seeing old Matthias Meier walk up and down the streets of their elm-shaded town, swinging his cane pompously. From his son's home down Washington Street to the corner of Main, turning down Main to the bank, speaking to every one along the way: "Good morning, Miss Smith," "How are you, Boze?", nodding to those whose names he could not recall or did not know.

At the bank he would walk through the lobby into Carter's office. There they would discuss for a time the problems of the day,—to buy the Waterville bonds or not, —whether John Seliger's note could be renewed,—could Tessie Porter, the dressmaker, have a hundred-dollar loan on nothing much but an honest character. Back home toward noon, there to rest and read until about three when he would go down again for the last hour "to see how the day had gone."

Sometimes he went to Lincoln, grown to eighty thousand from the four log-cabins, visiting with old friends here and there for a few moments, always taking one stroll past the Pi Beta Chi house to see how it looked now,—"just as good as ever,—*there* was a house for you, built for the years,"—and always to the new capitol which rose like something of his own he had dreamed.

Uncompleted, but giving promise of perfection, it satisfied his very soul. American, that's what it was,—the

broad sweeping base was the fertile prairie,—the tower to
rise from this great white spread of stone was to symbolize
all the aspirations and dreams and ideals the old builders
of the state had held in their hearts but could not express.

No one knew it, but he would rather have been on the
capitol commission than anything he could choose. Too
old, of course. Lots of grief connected with it. Younger
men must serve on that. But he liked to talk with those
who had its building on their hearts,—men who were
giving it all the loyalty they bore the state. Stop in
and see them when he could catch them,—talk over the
old days with the State Historian who knew every phase
of its beginning and growth.

Once he and Charlie Briggs went up to the capitol together. Matthias, tall and well-tailored, snow-white hair
and beard,—Charlie Briggs, little and gnarled, shaggy-
whiskered, his navy blue suit hanging sack-like on his
thin body,—both in their eighties. Together they walked
through the main corridor and rotunda, looking at the tiles
and the mosaics. More than one person turned to glance
at the two old men, so different in appearance, apparently
so engrossed in their own conversation.

"Seems a thousand years ago you advised me to come
over here and locate in the prairie grass, Charlie."

"More like yistiddy to me, Matt."

"It's a great old state. Founded by substantial folks.
Given the world something, too, besides grain and hogs.
Given it artists and writers, singers and actors, big men
in educational and business lines, dean of the Harvard
law school, a general of all the armies. Something of

the strength of the prairie may have been built into her children."

"She was kind of a harsh old mother, Matt,—the prairie,—but sufferin' snakes, I liked her."

There was a long pause, and then:

"I want to live to see it completed, Charlie."

"Me, too, Matt."

But now the trips to Lincoln were all over. Over, too, were the trips down Washington to Main,—down Main to the bank.

Old Matthias was nearly done for. Every day this spring when it was sunshiny enough he sat in the yard for a few hours,—waiting. They didn't need to try to cover it. He knew. Ever since that sudden sick spell. Lucile and Carter in cheerful voices called this convalescing. All right, call it anything they wanted.

Sitting here to-day in the sunshine old Matthias' mind was delving into the past. Until lately he had never been guilty of doing much of that. "Too busy with the crowded hour to fear to live or die,"—Emerson he thought that was. No, he had not succumbed to the habit of retrospection to any great extent as did many men of his age. It was a vicious habit, belonging only to those old people whose mentality could not keep pace with the times.

He had always disliked those who did it too much, making bores of themselves with their ancient reminiscences. Charlie Briggs lived almost entirely in the past with his " 'Long about 1872," or "I recol'ect the winter of '89." But for some reason he had been doing some of it himself lately—going over old memories, suddenly finding how easy it was to recall happenings of years before.

This afternoon with the sun making flickering leaf shadows on the new grass at his feet, he tried to understand this tendency to return to the scenes of youth. Did one go halfway through life, as though to a hilltop, and then start this looking back? No, there was no definite time in which it happened. One seemed always to be looking hopefully and enthusiastically forward,—and then without realizing it, found one's self in these moods of looking back.

On a trip to California, he and Ida, in the Hancock Park section of Los Angeles, had once seen the old La Brea pits where the tar of a score of thousand years bubbles up to the surface of the ground. There had been found the skeleton remains of prehistoric animals,—the saber-tooth tiger and the lion and the sloth,—a bone at a time, the animal skeletons had been found and fitted together for museums.

This afternoon he dug in the past of his life as the workers had dug for bones in the La Brea pits. He took out single scenes, fitting them together with others as the bones were fitted,—a bit of this and a bit of that,—seeing now from his hilltop how events might have been. Some things could have been bettered,—some should have stayed the same. No matter, for good or ill, they had been fitted together, and it was too late now to figure out how productive of good any change would have been. Queer, how things he used to think important, seemed less so now. Little things of minute value at the time, now loomed large in retrospection. Wherein should life have been different? How much of it was Fate? How much his own decision?

Suddenly, with almost no warning thought, he remembered his first sweetheart. She stepped into view out of the past as clear as a picture. He had not thought of her for years, but she came now, white and pink and blue-eyed and lovely. She had been Romance. Ida had never been Romance. She had been steady undying Love. She had been wife, comrade, friend,—but never Romance. That belonged with Amalia. And though desire had long died within him, yet for a moment his blood stirred to the memory of the touch of the pink lips of Amalia and the supple warm body of her.

Yes, some of the things in life we decide for ourselves. In others it is Providence, Luck, or the Spinning Fates. He thought of his youthful hot-headed race to Nebraska City, smiled at the thought of those days on the sandbar,—of the way such a situation could be handled now. Cars, motor-boats, planes. What the outcome would have been if he had arrived in time, of course he could not know. But to have seen her and to have talked with her, she would no doubt have gone with him. Her father could scarcely have held her against her will.

How different girls were these days. One couldn't imagine a modern girl displaying the weakness with which Amalia must have succumbed to her father's authority and gone obediently with him. She would have been as ready to go with her lover if he could have appeared in time to influence her. But by the hair's breadth of a few hours the thing had been decided. When he arrived, the marriage had been consummated. Now they wouldn't even stop at the marriage vow but would hurdle that too. In those days it constituted a formidable barrier. Well, it was a good thing, perhaps, that some of these decisions did fall into the hands of Providence or Lady Luck or the Spinning Fates. Once he would have chosen Amalia. Probably Ida had made him a better wife,—but even without that in her favor, he could not imagine any one else in her place for the half-century.

Hazel was coming down the terrace toward him with her long athletic stride and her air of freedom from all restraints. She was nearly ready for the University, some of the rough edges toned down, her brace off for several years, the freckles miraculously disappearing into her creamy complexion.

Could one imagine two more opposite young women than Hazel and this little Amalia of whom he had just been thinking? He smiled at the thought, and when she had thrown herself in a chair opposite him, he said suddenly: "Hazel, did you ever stop to think how a person imagines he is carrying out his own decision, doing the thing he planned? But is he? How much is predestined? Except for our higher order of minds we are like the little moles under the earth carrying out blindly the work of digging, thinking our own dark passage-ways constitute all there is to the world. . . ."

Hazel was frankly bored. Restless, energetic, it seemed rather a waste of time to sit here and listen to grandfather's vague generalities. They sounded too much like his pal, the old Indian scout. No longer was old Charlie Briggs a hero to Miss Meier. She twisted about a bit in her chair, as though seeking a more comfortable position,

giving him credit in her mind, though, for one thing,—
he seldom emitted a lot of junk like this.

"A half-dozen people . . ." he went on, "out of all the
hundreds we've contacted stand out in the end as really
and recognizably influencing our lives. A few whom we
have loved or hated or emulated. Why, I've even been
thinking of my first sweetheart," he laughed deprecatingly.

Hazel sat up alertly. Here was no generality, nothing
boresome. Here was interest, concrete and definite. No
longer was she the little girl who had said she would have
none of Romance.

"Oh, I say, Grandad, that *is* something. You mean a
girl . . . *not* Grandmother?"

"Not your grandmother."

"Why, you old flirt . . . tell me about it. She didn't
die?"

"No, . . . much worse." He smiled across at her.
"She married some one else."

"Yes . . . yes . . . go on. Am *I* all *ears?* Tell me.
Tell me everything."

"There's not much to tell. I suppose spring had something to do with it . . . spring and youth and propinquity.
I was working in a foundry in Illinois. She came stepping
out of the sunlight one day into the dark foundry like
a little blue and white and pink figure stepping out of a
miniature,—or a little Dresden china figure."

"Not *really*, Grandpa! Why, you old poet."

"You're the only person in the world I've ever told this
to. She moved out here from Illinois . . . and married.
I came out here, too, to what was then called the new
west . . . following her in a blind sort of way, a young

blade thinking I could pick her up and carry her off, even though good sense told me how foolish it was. But . . . you follow your wild enthusiastic fancies when you're young."

"And you never saw her again?"

"I never saw her."

"Nor heard of her?"

"Nor heard of her specifically . . . but once. I knew in a general way . . . the farming section . . . where her group of people located, but I never saw her again."

"Grandpa . . . tell me this." Hazel leaned forward with wide, dark eyes. "Did you *ever* get over it?"

He laughed aloud. "Oh, yes . . . yes, indeed. The long journey on the boat, the docking at strange towns, the excitement of arriving in the new country, all had their place in the scheme of things. I was young and ambitious. I rather think I was beginning to recover very soon. After awhile there were other young people too . . . your grandmother. Life was very full. And yet. . . ."

"Yet what, Grandfather?"

"Oh, I think one never entirely forgets an emotional experience like that. But after awhile the thing was only half remembered . . . and then almost forgotten . . . then entirely . . . until now."

"Why *now*, Grandpa?"

"You'd laugh."

"No, I won't, Grandpa . . . honestly, I won't laugh."

"I heard a meadow-lark sing."

"It reminded you of her?"

"Yes."

"Oh, how *romantic*."

"And perhaps because I've had time recently to sit and think . . . and remember times of emotion. In business you have no emotion,—you have only a hard-boiled mental life."

"I think it's a lot sadder that you got over it, Grandpa, than if you hadn't."

"Perhaps it was."

"What was her name?"

"I haven't said it aloud for nearly sixty years. It was . . . Amalia." His voice lingered over it, drawing it out liquidly.

"Amalia. It's kind of musical, isn't it?"

"That's what I used to think."

Old Matthias Meier did not live to see the capitol finished. He died in a few months as he had felt he would. Toward the last he knew it was not going to be so hard to leave as he had always thought. Sometimes during that last month, in his exhaustion and weakness, when the nights were troubled and unnatural and the days no better, he looked forward longingly to that place in Lincoln called *Wyuka,* which is Indian for "a place to lie down and sleep."

Charlie Briggs came as soon as he heard, trudging up the sidewalk to Carter Meier's house, his blue suit hanging baggily on his thin little frame. "Matt knowed I wouldn't fail him."

When it was over,—Matthias' things put away out of

sight, and much of the necessary business attended to, Carter Meier settled down to life without his father.

On a rainy evening when Lucile and Hazel were both there, he brought out and opened his father's small, old-fashioned trunk,—a queer little calf-skin chest bound in brass. He had never seen one just like it anywhere else, with its few red hairs worn by the original animal owner still plainly visible along the sides.

"I wonder if the Historical Society wouldn't like it?" he said to Lucile and to Hazel sitting near.

Lucile had a book and merely said pleasantly but vaguely: "Maybe it would."

Hazel, intent on the opening of the trunk, made no comment for a moment. When she did it was to say: "Do you know, there's something sort of heathenish and unkind about it, Dad. After a death, delving into a dead person's things that way when they can't help it. Don't you feel as though you were trespassing?"

"Oh . . . I might with some people's things. But not Father's. I've had charge of his affairs so much this last year and his life was such an open book."

For a half-hour or more Carter Meier took out and examined the neatly folded papers and account books, a set of income and expense books,—all of ancient vintage and worthless. Anything important was in the lock-box at the bank. There were two or three pictures of his mother,—one in a tight silk dress with panels and enough buttons up and down its length and breadth to start a re-tail button shop.

There were pictures of himself, too, as a scared-looking baby in a dress cascading to the floor, and as a little boy.

At one he laughed long and loudly and called his family's attention to it. In a velvet suit and lace collar he stood heavily on one foot with the other leg neatly crossed over it, in his hand the end of a long ivy vine wandering down from a flower-pot above him.

"To this day I remember how I was pinching that vine, taking out of my murderous heart all the venom I felt for the photographer and putting it into the death of that innocent plant."

And after his laughter came something more serious,— it seemed such a very short time ago he was that little Fauntleroy-looking boy with an Apache heart,—and now he was fifty-six.

Everything was out now but a dingy, brown wallet. He had not seen it for nearly a half-century, but he could remember his father carrying it in that long gone time. There proved to be nothing in the old thing but a yellowed piece of paper which fell at his touch into six slim oblong sections. It was written in German and almost illegible at that.

"Hazel, how much German do you know?"

"Oh, I can *habe* and *heil* a little. Let me have a try."

She went to the library table and laid the six parts carefully together, bending her fresh loveliness over the musty broken pieces of the yellowed paper.

". . . *'ist es besser.'* That's duck's soup for a starter," she said aloud. *"It is better."*

Her father and mother were both listening, more impressed by their gay young daughter's smartness than with anything the old letter might say.

" *'Zu gedenken'* . . . let's see . . . *'zu gedenken,'* "

her voice slipped into a low murmur as she tried to think of it. "I know . . . *to remember.* How'm I doin', folks?"

They nodded approval. These modern girls!

" *'im frühyahr'* . . . that's 'in springtime.' Now . . . all together . . . pull! *'It is better to remember in springtime.'* "

Suddenly she saw for the first time the word *Amalia*. Something came into her mind,—stole in subtly,—something bringing a faint far-off breath of a long-gone year and the lilt of a meadow-lark singing. This was a note from Grandpa's first sweetheart.

"You're the only person I've ever told . . ." he had said.

She read the remainder of the legible sentence to herself. It was Grandpa's secret and because he was not here to guard the little message as he had evidently done all the years, she would do it for him,—would not drag it out into the open even for Dad and Mother.

Unsre liebe,—our love. Something about the forlorn little note touched her unaccountably. A swift mist came to her eyes and she had to clear her throat to say lightly, "Oh, that's all I can get out of it, folks."

All the rest of the evening it filled her with a vague sadness. She was glad he had married Grandmother, couldn't bear to think of it otherwise. But there was something pathetic about that one legible sentence,—the way life moved on and changed and love went with it, too.

. . . it is better to remember our love as it was in the springtime.

CHAPTER XXXV

IN the fall of 1930 Hazel Meier went up to the University too. Lucile had taken her to Omaha to outfit her,—she had purchased sports clothes and silk pajamas, dinner gowns, dresses for afternoon wear, and accessories for everything. Lucile had no trouble in pleasing Hazel with the sports clothes,—it took some effort to get her into long, slinky gowns in which she declared to all and sundry salesladies that she felt like kicking something with every step. But Lucile was firm. Hazel was a young lady now,—no more of this living in tennis outfits all day long. Everything ran to browns and tans and oranges for her,—cream or white or eggshell for evening with that hair and complexion.

When Carter saw the bills he whistled long and loudly. Bonds these days were anæmic,—he was worried. There were more griefs in the banking business now than in all his other years put together. He missed his father every day.

There was no exciting fight over Hazel by the sororities. Lucile had been a Theta. The Delta Gams gave her a half-hearted rush, knowing she had too much Theta blood in her to inoculate with any other virus. The Kappas told her Theta was so badly run down since her mother's time that of course she would put aside that old mother-daughter sentiment, to which she might have given ear if she had not heard a Theta hand out the same line to a Kappa daughter with a mere reversal of Greek letters.

After the usual three days of breakfasts, luncheons, teas, and dinners, with time out to look up her courses, she went Theta. No one was surprised,—it was in the cards. Followed registration,—consternation,—concentration,—amalgamation,—sophistication,—the metamorphosis of a Greek letter girl can be traced as readily as the growth of a tree, by rings of different fibers.

At first she was timid, afraid of the upper classmen, prone to say "Yes, indeed" to any comment from them, deferred to the house mother as to an oracle.

Gradually she began dating. She whose masculine attentions in Westville had consisted heretofore largely of neighbor boys draping themselves at intervals over the front steps and calling to her to get a move on, now learned what collegiate dates were, both of the open-eyed and blind varieties.

By her sophomore year, what with her good clothes and her reputation of being a snappy little number, she was credited at the House with one-hundred per cent dating ability. In her junior year she was sophisticated, svelte, unruffled under any situation, told the house mother in velvet-concealed words where to get off, removed the velvet shield on occasion when some good sister crossed her path in social territory.

It was getting toward spring of that year when she went into the old library, took a casual survey of empty chairs and with apparent superb indifference to her surroundings carefully chose one across from a junior law,—an awfully good-looking Pi Chi by the name of Neal Holms. She

gave him a slanting glance several times, but evidently
he was occupied with some ponderous volume. All right,
—he didn't have to deign to look her way,—suit himself.

In a few moments he was pushing a card toward her.
It contained his name engraved thereon, with a penciled
caption under it,—so that it now read:

Neal Holms

Pass the tomes.

She frowned,—shoved the two voluminous books near
her his way, scribbled underneath:

Hazel Meier

Don't rouse my ire.

Unsmiling, he found his reference, then turned the card
over, wrote on it, pushed it back. It questioned:

Why don't I dare?

And was sent back with the laconic answer:

Red hair.

A little later he handed it back. It said:

Date you?

Hazel wrote promptly:

Hate to.

This time he drew a picture,—two toothpick-looking
creatures hand in hand, and wrote underneath:

Aw, give in.

Hazel scribbled:

You win.

Neal Holms dated Hazel Meier for a fraternity formal.

From the first he liked her,—liked her tip-tilted nose
on which, if the light were right, you could see a freckle

or two,—liked her independence and her creamy complexion,—her hazel eyes and her snappy come-backs,—the cocky way she wore a beret on the side of her head.

Two more care-free young people financially and otherwise in the University it would have been hard to find.

He dated her again for another formal, other times for no reason but "a date,"—then for the Junior-Senior prom which ended the winter social season. And for that matter it almost ended everything else for them, too. There was an inauguration of a new president in Washington,—followed by a peculiar phenomenon in banking circles called a moratorium. Carter Meier's bank closed.

Even before this the echoes from the eastern coast financial marts had reverberated to the outskirts of the last little village, to every farm home in every state. But for a time in the small places of the midwestern states, they had been only voices heard afar off. Contrary to geometric equations, the shortest distance between the two given points of Wall Street and Carter Meier's bank was by no means a straight line. It took a multitude of directions, and arrived through various channels,— South American bonds being one of its routes of travel.

Carter Meier had seen the value of his various bonds slipping under par,—skidding, sliding with sickening pace. It was a condition shared in fraternal worry by his colleagues.

All were frightened, bewildered. Not one could share the anxiety with another for fear of giving away his own secret worry.

No, the ocean of catastrophe known as the Wall Street debacle did not sweep at once with full tide into some of the sections of the country. Where its waves crashed with devastating force in many places, in others the back-wash rippled in later. Cedar City seemed secure. It was bounded by agriculture,—its soil rich, its banks secure, its farmers honest. Even though prices were far too low, crops were almost always good these years. A poor wheat year usually found a good corn crop,—when the corn failed, the wheat crop had recompensed for the failure.

But now the back-wash came in,—bonds that had been purchased for one hundred went to eighty, sixty, forty,— defaulted. Two of Carter Meier's corresponding banks stayed closed. Farmers could not pay because they had nothing with which to pay. More, a strange and unbelievable attitude seized a portion of the population, a slipping of morale. "Try and get it" became the manner of some. Carter Meier in noting this insidious change thought often of his father, of old Charlie Briggs, of those others of the old school whose word had been all the legality one needed.

He worked, planned, collected, figured, fought. Sometimes he grew bitter with the injustice of it. Others no smarter or better than he were getting through. The difference of a bond purchase or two,—of a few less notes that had to be charged off,—and they were weathering the storm.

Time,—if he only could have time for things to stage a come-back, he would be all right. Time! That was what a man who was to be hung wanted. He had days of feeling he had won,—followed by days of realizing he had lost,—high moments of hope,—black ones of despair.

The depression won. The bank stayed closed. You could not do with life as you wished.

He paid twice the amount of his stock. It took the last of what his father had left him. The estate, too, had shrunk when Depression, that rough laundryman, had finished with it. Some of the investments had been left as a trust fund for Hazel,—that, of course, could not and should not be touched.

He sold the house for what he could get,—moved to a Lincoln apartment when a receiver job was given him. Lucile was sobered, hurt, still incredulous over what had happened, but game. "For better or for worse" spoken that day in the Lincoln church before an elaborate wedding party of eight bridesmaids attending her, with all the leading families looking on, had meant something to Lucile. The situation was a reversal of her own parents' experiences and that of Father and Mother Meier. The "worse," so far as hard work and getting established, had been their earlier portion, their easy life at the last. Her own was the other way around,—harder, too,—for she and Carter had none of the buoyant hope they had possessed a quarter of a century before.

Farther out in the state Joe Holms wondered every hour of the day and during sleepless nights how any one could get so heavily involved when much of the land had been given him.

Over and over in his mind he pondered the turn of his fortunes. He knew there were great economic forces at work over which he had no control. If things had been as Myrtie always said,—if the land had stayed worth the price they had so blithely put upon it,—if they had not bought so lavishly, had not gone so deeply into debt, had stayed on the first good old half-section without purchasing any more acres,—above all, had *worked* it themselves, earning their living there, content with what it would bring, as his father and grandfather had worked before him for their daily bread, this great indebtedness would not be looming always before him like some fearsome giant.

He went back often in his mind to the first of Myrtie's pleadings to change things. Pasting a cheap stucco over the good old stones of the house had been almost prophetic in its covering up the real issues of life, the things that were vital. Work? Why should he have lessened his activities because there had seemed enough to live on? Work was good. Work was every man's portion in life. He had grown soft,—under fifty yet, and he was flabby. Old Charlie Briggs in his eighties who came visiting through the neighborhood sometimes, wouldn't ride anywhere, wouldn't accept a lift on the highway for fear he'd grow soft.

Yes, that which he had labeled a kindness to Myrtie and which Myrtie had labeled a kindness to Neal had been no kindness at all. But he wouldn't hide behind Myrtie's skirts. He was the head of the house, or should have been. Now he could see he had been no better than the loafers sitting on the sidewalks spitting their contempt at a world which they thought owed them a living.

Other farmers were getting through. All had been

under the same general outside forces,—all under the same weather conditions. But not all had been caught as he was. Young Carl Schaffer was working out,—the Lawrences. But they had used better sense. They had lived on their own butter and eggs, chickens, and small produce. When they sold a crop, it had gone to pay off their principal. He and Myrtie, with their hands in the sack as though there were no end to the income,—they had been caught.

He sat now on the stone-house steps at the farm looking out at the old soap-kettle there in the yard with the dead stems of ancient flowers left in it. There was something symbolic about it, he suddenly decided. His grandmother had made soap in it every spring and fall,—enough to last for a half-year. His mother with her lessening activities had dispensed with it, letting the men take it for hog-feed and chicken-mash. His wife had planted flowers in it,— typical of the way they had grown to look at life,— flowers, no work, but plenty of income. Flowers over all the harsh facts of life. Flowers in the soap-kettle,—and a complacent feeling that the soap would arrive some way.

Well, the flowers in the soap-kettle were dead and rotted now. So were all the fancy notions of life.

He called Neal home from school that week-end for an interview.

He was a long time getting at what he wanted to say, so long that Neal with his more direct way of looking at life said: "What's the racket, Dad? Let's have it out."

"I mean . . . the way things are . . . the town house here is going back to the owner,—the eighty I bought, too,

—the eighty my father bought goes to the bank for notes . . . I have to pay my double indemnity on the Meredith bank. . . ."

"You mean we're sunk?"

"Something like that. Grandma's two hundred and forty is left unencumbered out of the wreckage."

"Here's where I stop school."

"No. Let's figure it out together. I've just one son and he has just one year more. We'll make it some way. You'd disappoint me now not to go that much longer. But for God's sake, don't spend any more than you have to."

"I promise you that."

"And don't tell Mother just yet. It would worry her."

"If you ask me, Dad, there's been an awful lot of that not-telling-mother stuff. I'm going out and tell her."

Joe followed Neal anxiously, protesting, out to the sunroom where Myrtie sat with a book, to hear him tell his mother the bold and bald facts.

Myrtie put her hand over her heart. "Oh . . . oh! I can stand anything but that."

Joe tried to stroke her hair, but she pushed his hand away.

"We'll go back to the stone house, Myrtie. We'll fix it up nice. I'll go into the field again. We'll get some comfort out of life now, not owing any one."

"Oh, Joe . . . how could you . . . how *could* you?"

"He's not done anything disgraceful, Mom. He's just caught like a thousand others. He'll go back and work out, and I'll help."

"Oh . . . oh . . . just the same old thing . . . just

corn and dirt and pigs and chickens." She was gasping, her hand at her throat.

Joe would have called a doctor, but Neal was unmoved. "That's just high-steericks, Mom." He laughed at her. "Tears and wailings and beating your head against the old wall aren't going to do any good." He touseled her hair as though she were a youngster. "You're going to move back to the farm *and like it*. And thank your lucky stars you've got one to go to."

Joe stood looking at him in astonishment, deep respect, and with no small degree of envy.

Joe and Myrtie went back to the big stone house where Myrtie said she just gave up, there was so little to live for.

CHAPTER XXXVI

MOISTURE was below normal all summer even where the lands like Joe's were rich and loamy. But farther west where the season was one of drouth, the powdered top soil was lifted into the air with every high prairie wind. It was as though Mother Nature in disturbed mood was beginning to clean her house, to set to right her disarranged plans. With a giant broom she whisked the dirt from those rooms in which she had intended only grazing lands to be.

But unheeding, the wheat farmers scratched again the pulverized soil and dropped their seed in the looseness of its powder.

Neal and Hazel both went back to school. Life had taken on a more serious aspect, but Youth is hard to keep down. Unless it is cold, hungry, ill, and discouraged, it can find an outlet in its own bubbling vitality,—and they were none of these. To be sure, Hazel, who had walked into the shops and chosen her apparel with little thought to expense, now planned every move with an eye to economy.

"Take a look-see at the dress," she said to Neal who had come for her on a date. "That which used to be the front is now the back, the inside is the outside, the top side is now the bottom side,—proving that all which goes up must come down."

"Huh—that's nothing. I've got a big-time job,—currying Doc Sanders' car. I went over to Prof. Morrison's to see if I could get his yard to mow,—would have gotten it, too, but Bud Merrill, the squirt, took the lawn-mower right out of my mouth, so to speak."

Neal drove home often. "Seems as though my dad has sort of lost his nerve or something. Goes over and over the same old hashing of what he did or didn't do. It isn't that he doesn't work. It isn't physical. He acts bewildered all the time about what's best to do,—all this corn-hog stuff,—anything with a decision to make. And I'll be darned if I know whether he'll ever make any money again or not—what with plowing under the piglets and not letting the big cornstalks have any little corn-stalks. He knows a lot more about the whole thing than I do but is always cornering me and asking my opinion. Makes me feel chesty."

"My poor Dad, too. Says he never wants to be responsible for anything again, content to work for some one else the rest of his life. Queer, isn't it, what a year can bring you?"

And it *was* queer what a year could bring you, for when school ended Neal and Hazel were engaged.

What matter when it was or where it was, or the words that were said. Youth is Youth and the words remain similar. As a matter of fact, perhaps it was at no special time or place. Perhaps too often Neal had said in the jaunty modern unromantic way: "I like your aristo-snooty-looking nose" or "You're some little trick, Red Head," or sung boldly at her in an atrociously frog-like voice: "Stay As Sweet As You Are," to make any proposal necessary.

Spring Came On Forever

Suffice to say Neal sent the candy to the Theta house, and broke the news to his Pi Beta Chis in the old Meier house where the neckties hung untidily through the grill-work of which Ida had once been so proud, and their owners tried with tragic success to imitate Fred Astaire's dancing on the inlaid mosaic of the great entrance hall.

Mr. and Mrs. Carter Meier announced the engagement of their daughter Hazel to Neal Holms by way of the Sunday papers. Ivy Day arrived. Examinations. Commencement,—in the setting of countless huge buildings with many thousand students swarming over the campus where once the cows snatched at the prairie grass. Hazel had her diploma from the Teachers College of the U,— Neal his law degree, and if "superior scholarship" and "cum laude" were strangely missing from these, the two young people were in the good company of many others of average intelligence.

Hazel was to teach one year at Irving, a small town in the Republican Valley,—Neal was to stay at home with his father for the same length of time, lending his young strength and his unflagging spirits to Joe's discouragement before hanging out his law shingle.

It was a bad summer. Drouth came on like a malignant sore on the breast of nature. Hot belching winds blew in from the southwest. Thin clouds, dry as feathers, slipped across the blue. The grass in the pastures burned as with a prairie-fire. Weeds, devoid of sap, rattled in the hot winds. Leaves, too lifeless to cling, dropped from the dry elms.

"Like in de old days," Amalia said often and shook her head dubiously. Tsk! Tsk!

There was a great deal of talk about legislation and regimentation. Joe snorted: "Legislate the hot winds and regimentate the clouds and we farmers'll get along all right by ourselves."

Neal took Hazel to Irving in September, stayed to cast his eye over her school and her boarding-house, got back to the farm in time to see the rain come. Leaves on the elms dripped clammily. Puddles stood on the graveled highways. Water ran off a hillside that was baked too hard to hold it. And it was not raining anything so sentimental or ornamental as daffodils. It was raining wheat for bread. It was raining forage crops,—sudan grass and rye and sweet clover. It was raining pasturage and wild hay and alfalfa,—next year's apple-buds and cherry-buds and vegetables in gardens. It was raining hope and courage and a renewed morale.

"Stars fell on Alabama," he said jubilantly when he went into the house, "and that's all right with me, but showers fell on Nebraska and that's much more to the point."

Joe worried a good deal now about Grandma down there alone at her little house, but old Amalia was cheerful. "I am goot company for myself," she said. "I vork ven I vish; I sleep ven I vish; I sew my qvilts ven I vish; I do not'ing ven I vish."

Joe and Neal were both good to her,—Myrtie not unkind, merely wrapped in her own troubles.

Toward spring she seemed much more feeble. So little did she walk out now that Neal decided to put in a radio for her. For a while she stood out against it. "For vat should I vant to have de singin' here at all times of de night, Neal?"

When he assured her that no quartette or jazz orchestra had any intention of presuming on her hospitality at times when they were not welcome, she let him put in one.

Her first manipulation of it was under his instruction.

"You snap this first. Then turn this until you find what you want, and then this one to get the sound just as you want it. Now try."

Old Amalia snapped the brass knob. Then she turned *this*. Columbus sailing westward, a Wright brother going up in the air,—and old Amalia turning the knob on a radio!

". . . headin' for the last round-up" it blared forth like semi-musical thunder.

"Now tune it down softer."

"Loud I like it," said old Amalia. And loud she kept it.

To the family's surprise it proved to be news that she liked the best. Old Amalia who had lived most of her long years on her Nebraska farm liked best the happenings from far places. She knew when every news period came on, settled herself with her latest quilt, rather appropriately doing the Around-the-World pattern, and listened to the latest happenings in places she had never been, and of whose existence she scarcely knew. Through the waves of the air, across the brown prairie, every day now the mountain came to Mahomet.

CHAPTER XXXVII

SPRING came to the midwest in a cloud of dust. To Carter and Lucile in their modest apartment in Lincoln it was a hazy, disagreeable one, the sunlight sifting through the yellow, dust-laden air from the black blizzard farther to the west.

They had never grown used to Hazel being away,—often in the evening they found themselves sitting idly, listening for the footsteps of a gay young crowd which no longer came. Once in one of these idle moods Lucile caught Carter's eye. "That way lies madness," she laughed, but not quite whole-heartedly. "Let's throw a wild party and go to a movie."

To Hazel in the little town of Irving in the Republican Valley the dust was more severe for she was nearer the source of the storms. It came in clouds, a scourge rolling eastward like reddish-yellow gas across no man's land. Too long in the country farther west had men torn at the earth's vitals,—too many times had the edge of the plow gone into the lands which were meant for grazing. There were sections out beyond Irving and in the neighboring states where schools were closed, traffic paralyzed, business suspended, street lights shining all day through the murky atmosphere.

To Neal and his father on the farm it was a season of worry and discouragement. To what extent were the dust storms affecting them? Were they bringing in enough sandy soil to damage the rich loamy Holms' lands? Was soil erosion to be serious?

Day after day the clouds of dust rolled in from the Panhandle district, northwestern Oklahoma, southeastern Colorado, part of Kansas.

To old Amalia there was no great discouragement,—no deep worry. Too many years had she lived with a Nature that was changeable, as coquettish as a girl.

Too often had she seen rains after drouth, green after the brown of burning, buds after dried stalks, stillness after the strife of storm, life after apparent death. "It vill come all right," she nodded with calm conviction. "It alvays comes right again."

And it came right again. The winds ceased. Snow fell like a white benediction over the wind-torn land. Rains followed,—prolonged soaking rains. The grass grew lush in the pastures. Cattle stood knee-deep in moisture-covered forage. Buds burst forth from the elms, the fruit trees and the lilac hedge. Crocuses bloomed in sheltered spots. The timber-land gave forth the rich, pungent smell of water-soaked undergrowth. Nature's face had the look of a freshly scrubbed child. It was the eighty-sixth miracle Amalia had witnessed.

Neal spent a certain Saturday and part of one Sunday with Hazel at her home in Lincoln, taking her back to her school at Irving in the afternoon.

Carter and Lucile were satisfied with Neal,—liked his energy and his gay humor, his steady blue eyes that looked clean and frank. Of the boys that had ever squired Hazel about, they liked him by far the best they agreed when the two had gone.

It was not until they were well out on the paved highway toward the valley that Neal broached the subject with which he was to confront Hazel to-day, for which he had chosen this very time.

He approached it with a bit of trepidation for he had no idea how she would take it, and because he felt that uncertainty, he was blunt in the telling. Now that his year of helping his father was nearly at an end he had decided to forget law and stay on to manage the farm.

Hazel, assuming for a time that he was joking, was later filled with sudden alarm to discover that he was in deadly earnest.

"I've kidded myself into thinking I was there for just the year. I'm staying. I like the independence of it. I've grown interested in our plans. Besides, I'd have had a heck of a time getting on in the other, what with the thousands of us turned loose and lining the sidewalks waiting for cases."

Because Hazel sat quietly, looking coldly down the highway, he went rambling on rather indefinitely: "You'll like it there . . . not a half bad old place . . . with a little care the lawn looks quite like a park . . . a lot of grand old trees my grandfather planted . . . the house is sturdy and big even if it's old . . . Father and Mother will turn it over to us and live in the small house with Grandma."

He glanced at her but she was stony-faced, so that he went on nervously with his explanations: "This is a business all ready and waiting for me,—not a dub job of looking up references for some older man or starving to death behind my own shingle. And if you don't think it calls for as much of a business head as any other, it's just because you don't know your onions or any of the other crops."

Hazel spoke for the first time. "I just can't *see* myself. That's all there is to it. Just don't speak about it again and kindly drop the whole idea."

"But I *am* speaking about it. And I'm not dropping the whole idea, kindly, benevolently, or otherwise."

"You can't mean that you're in earnest about this crazy notion?"

"I'm in earnest . . . and the notion is so sensible it should take the Pulitzer prize for wisdom. Three hundred and twenty acres of the best and richest land in Nebraska with my Dad ready and willing to turn the management of it to me. To be sure, one of the eighties has a big plaster on it, but we can soak that off. We lost two other eighties in the late lamented depression. I'd be a nut to stick out a shingle in some little burg or run errands for a law firm in a bigger town just as agriculture is going to pull out."

"I don't see it."

"And *I do*."

They were speaking with suppressed heat, firecrackers sputtering under ice.

"And you call this an ambitious idea?"

"About as ambitious a move as I've ever made in my life." His voice dropped to a pleading tone. "I'm terribly in earnest, Hazel. Give me credit for growing up and making my own decisions. You know every one who has any stamina . . . There's another word but not so pretty . . . Drop around some day and I'll tell you what it is . . . Any fellow who hasn't lard in his veins has to map out his own life and his own work. Well, mine's running that big farm and running it *right*. I know it now for sure. I feel energetic about it, enthusiastic, with a hundred plans of things to do. It's my best bet because I *want* to do it. There was a time when I wouldn't have said that I ever would. I know my own mind now."

"And apparently that broad mind of yours doesn't comprehend that I'd have anything to say about it,—that I should be the one to make the decision."

"You can put it that way, of course, to make me feel quite the villain. But I'll have to be more honest than gallant and admit that in this particular thing . . . you shouldn't."

"One could imagine . . . the casual observer maybe . . . that I *would* have the deciding vote."

"I've seen how that works out, Hazel. You don't need to get me wrong,—I think the world of my mother. But she just had her way with my dad in a lot of things he should have decided for them both. Well, it nearly got them."

"I'd make a *scalding*-hot farmer's wife, wouldn't I?"

"Sure you would. You'd . . ."

"I don't know a silo from a centipede . . ."

"A centipede has more legs than a silo, dearie. You can always tell them that way." Now that she was talking he felt easier.

". . . or oats from wheat."

"Wheat has a beard, honey,—whiskers like old man Briggs."

But Hazel would not meet his flippant conversation. "I

tell you, I don't know *anything* about it. I don't know a plow from a harron . . . harrall . . . harrow . . . whatever it is."

"For that matter, would you have known a rejoinder or a summons or a brief if I'd have gone into law?"

"I could learn."

"You can learn this other."

There were icicles in the air now. Hazel stared straight ahead into the diminishing point of the paved highway. Neal, face solemn and jaw set, leaned over and turned on the radio.

"Ah'll call you back in a few minutes, Kingfish. Amos 'n I has got a big business man in here . . ." He snapped it off petulantly.

For a mile they rode in frosty silence.

Hazel broke it with sarcasm. "So you really think I'd move on a farm . . . that I would give in to you about this wild thing?"

"Do I get it that you've not at any time cared for me, myself,—that you've merely liked the smug little idea of marrying a man who sat in a mahogany-furnished office in a downtown business block . . ."

"Maybe I have. Maybe I think that's the sort of environment I'd like to have my husband in."

". . . so that you could have a nice plate-glass window to sit in and see the Shriner's parade go by?"

The car had accelerated in speed with Neal's rising temper. They were passing through Niles Center, such a small village that the general store, the postoffice, and the filling-station flashed by like bits of colored posters. They were both silent, agitated and uncomfortable. It did not add anything, therefore, to the gayety of the nations when the Niles Center constable overtook them. When they stopped, he came over to the car, a big, red-faced man with a curiously small button-like nose set in the full moon of his face.

"Where you think you are—Indianapolis speedway or Ormond Beach or some place?"

"I didn't even see your sissy town," Neal retorted. And for the pleasure he derived from the saying donated unwillingly a five-dollar bill toward the erecting of a new village bandstand.

For the rest of the trip they were silent, excepting for an occasional remark that had neither interest nor entertainment for either one.

The long paved highway passed through fields and orchards of the peaceful Republican River Valley. Acres of green wheat on every side lay shrouded in the soft cool evening. From the alfalfa fields came the fragrance of the budding blossoms,—from the pastures the faint odor of meadow-grass lush with moisture. Only a few weeks before the great billows of dust had enveloped the valley. Wind had blown eerily out of the west. Dirty gray clouds had scudded across yellow skies. Then as though the Caretaker had said: "Thus far shalt thou go and no farther," the winds had ceased and like a benign benediction had come the rains. The Republican Valley was as peaceful now as a lovely lady with emerald pastures and wheatfields for jewels.

They drove into the town of Irving and turned to the street upon which Hazel's boarding-house stood. Neither one knew how the strained interview was to terminate,—both were uncomfortable.

Neal slid up to the curb where a low barberry hedge scraped across the running board. Because they were serious and angry and uncertain what the next move was to be, in the embarrassment of the moment they did nothing,—merely sat, each waiting for the other to speak.

At once three of Hazel's little girl pupils, arm in arm, passed along the street and giggled at the sight of their teacher sitting with a strange young man.

"Hello, Miss Meier."

"Hello, Miss Meier."

"Hello, Miss Meier."

"People all speak the same dialect here." Neal tried to assume his old light way. But because Hazel would not smile, he dropped it immediately. "Well, I guess there's nothing more to say, excepting where do we go from here?"

"I guess that's not going to be hard to interpret."

"You mean . . . ?"

"I most certainly do . . . under the circumstances . . . if they still exist . . . we're through."

"They exist all right. I'll say just one thing more. You've probably had a fond and kiddish notion you were about to marry a member of the United States Supreme Court. Well, you weren't. You were about to marry a young fellow who was going to have a long, slippery climb,—and if you won't do this with him now which is a wise move, you wouldn't have liked the monotony of the other, either,—so it's a good thing for us both you found it out in time. But you can rest assured he will get somewhere a darned sight faster doing the thing he wants to do.

"Become Secretary of Agriculture, maybe." Hazel hated her own sarcasm, even while she gave vent to it.

"Maybe . . . who knows? Stranger things have happened."

"Well . . ." he said again after a strained silence, ". . . let's don't prolong the death pangs."

At that, Hazel was out before he could get around to the door. But he walked along stubbornly by her side to the porch, carrying her small bag, and because he was bursting with hurt and disappointment, he said: "This is the way Emily Post says all engagements should be terminated,—politely and with subtle grace."

But at the door, he broke: "Hazel . . . we're just talking to hear ourselves say words. We're both that way . . . we just enjoy the ragging. Neither one of us meant anything but to bark our heads off. There's no one I could ever love but you,—no one in the world for me but *you*." And would have put his arms around her, but that she said with infinite sarcasm: "Oh, yes, there is. There's *you*." And was gone into the house, shutting the door with infinite pains.

CHAPTER XXXVIII

SPRING rains, heavy, drenching, filling the creek-beds and flooding the lowlands!

They beat upon the Holms' fields and pastures sending moisture down to the grateful sub-soil which had been so long without it, while Neal worked doggedly all day, tight-lipped and serious. So recently life had been such a gay and happy thing,—now so void of interest without funny flippant letters, so dull appearing in the future with no plans involving the constant presence of a merry red-headed girl.

They beat steadily and drowsily upon the little white-painted cottage of old Amalia, piecing her Around-the-World quilt and listening to news from places of which she had never heard. They beat upon the old German country church high on the knoll and the sodden grasses of all the old Kratz and Schaffer graves, and those of the Gebhardts and Rhodenbachs who had come into the prairie together over sixty years before.

They beat upon the apartment building in Lincoln, where Carter and Lucile Meier lived, trying to get along on an absurdly small amount so that they could begin saving again in their fifties for old age. And they beat upon the stone mausoleum covering Matthias Meier and his wife Ida in *Wyuka* which is the Indian word for a place to lie down and sleep.

Out in the Republican Valley in the little town of Irving

the rains beat on Hazel Meier going back and forth in her tan-colored raincoat and cap to school, trying to keep her mind on lesson plans, on hard work, on an interview with the superintendent in which she was to tell him she had changed her mind and was withdrawing her resignation if they would still consider her for next year.

Life was a strange thing now,—all the loveliness of it had vanished, leaving nothing but school work. Beyond the moment she would not look, merely putting her energies and thoughts into the day's teaching.

This morning she took time at recess to scribble a few lines to her parents, making them as gay as though life were still a pleasant thing. They had experienced enough trouble,—she would carry this break with Neal through with head high. She mailed her letter at noon and changed her dress to a fresher one, for she was going out to the Johnson's with Marie, one of her pupils, for supper. They lived out of town, so she was going to have the experience of riding in the school bus. Marie and Katie were both in her room,—Katie had been out sick, was convalescing and wanted "Teacher" to come out for supper. Mr. Johnson would bring her back in the Ford, or if it should rain too hard, she was to stay all night.

As a matter of fact, "Teacher" was going to be distinctly bored and would have preferred going to her own rooming-house where at least she knew what to expect. A pupil's home was always and distinctly X, the unknown quantity. But as she told Miss Evans of the fourth grade, "hers not to question why, hers but to do or die."

When evening came, the school bus occupants were thrilled to death that Miss Meier was entering their chariot for the time being, seven girls wanting to sit by her, and virtually all the boys taking part in voluntary exercises of standing on their heads, cat-calls, and baboon-like climbings up the side of the windows in order to display masculine prowess in front of feminine charm.

Arrived at her destination she found the Johnson's abode was just about what she would have expected from personal appearances made all year by Katie and Marie. The sitting-room had a cheap rug with eye-puncturing red roses which Mrs. Johnson told her Mr. Johnson surprised her with at Christmas, picking it from the catalogue, "hisself," to which the convalescing Katie added the information that to-day in honor of Teacher they took off the newspapers and rag rugs they always kept over it.

While Mrs. Johnson prepared her supper, the intervening time for Hazel was occupied by a protracted sitting on the couch with a girl on either side and the little brother in a state of doubtful stickiness leaning on her knees, all enjoying a never-ending entertainment of stereoscopic views of such titles as "Niagara by Moonlight," "Lake Erie in a Storm" and a side-splitting one of "We Three Donkeys," the big joke being that whoever looked at the picture was *one* of them. "That caught you, didn't it, Teacher?"

Supper was ready. Mrs. Johnson was hot and flurried, forgetting to bring on her biscuits for a time. Mr. Johnson was there, just in from the milking, scrubbed and combed. The hired man was there, a queer crooked-nosed individual with one eye slightly turned.

"Mr. Nils Jensen, Miss Meier."

"Pleased to meetcha."

There was some delay caused by the little boy's insistent demand that he sit by Teacher, too, but the girls were adamant over their personal ownership, and Nils with rare diplomacy put a quietus on the disturbance by reaching for a hot sparerib and bestowing it upon the trouble-maker.

It rained most of the evening. Hazel stayed all night, for which Katie and Marie gave evidence they would eventually lord it over the other girls in their room, for not once had Teacher stayed all night at any of their homes.

Mrs. Johnson loaned Hazel her wedding nightgown,—a high-necked lace-yoked affair with blue ribbons pulled through the holes. Teacher was to have the spare room downstairs,—all the others were to sleep on the second floor. The bed had starched pillow-cases with brown cat-tails and yellow water-lilies embroidered on the ends. Some of the mercury behind the mirror on the dresser was off so one could see the wall-paper through it. The last thing Mrs. Johnson said was: "I do hope you sleep good, Miss Meier. They ain't nobody slep' in here since Grandpa died in this bed."

Hazel got into the erstwhile deathbed, in the ruffled wedding nightgown, laughed a little, thinking of all the funny things she would tell Neal when she saw him,—remembered, and watered the starched cat-tails with a few tears. It did not seem possible that Life could be so miserable and so uninteresting.

She must have been asleep a long time for it seemed near daylight when she heard noises.

"Miss Meier." It resolved itself into her name and some one pounding on her door.

"Yes?" She was sitting up, alarmed: not so much at the disturbance itself as at what it might portend.

"Get up and dress quick." It was Mr. Johnson. "There's water comin' in through the kitchen door,—the whole yard looks under water."

She sprang out of bed in a daze of sleepiness and uncertainty.

Water! Well, what of it? The first of the spring had been dry and dusty. Every one had wanted water. And now they had it. Never satisfied. What was the big commotion about? Water never hurt you,—when you were in a house, it didn't.

She realized her mind was not quite lucid, that her very fear of this unknown thing which had given Mr. Johnson's voice its anxious tone was making her a bit panicky.

She got out of the beribboned wedding nightgown and dressed in a fumbling sort of way, as though in one of those dreams where you couldn't get your clothes on. Her step-ins were wrong side out,—well, no matter. What a ghastly time of morning to get up,—scarcely light.

She could hear a queer swish, swish, a liquid gurgling sound that was not quite right. Some way it just did not seem to belong in a house. There were voices,—Mr. Johnson's,—Mrs. Johnson's. Children crying,—Marie and Katie and the little boy. The hired man was calling, —the hired man with the crossed eye and the crooked nose. A door was banging, too. And through all the other noises that constant swish—swish—swish!

Hose next, never mind the seams. What was the matter with every one? Pumps next. Her brown one-piece dress over her head. Did Mr. Johnson mean they were going away,—going to get out of the house on account of some water? Then she had better put on her beret and jacket, for it was chilly.

She pulled her gay orange beret over her hair, and with scarcely any volition of her own looked at her dim image in the dresser glass from which part of the mercury was missing, gave the beret a pert slant, and reached for her jacket.

Swish, swish—

No! No! Water couldn't do that,—couldn't come slithering under your bedroom door in long creeping lines.

Voices again. Mr. Johnson's. Mrs. Johnson's, this time, calling excitedly: "Miss Meier, are you dressed?" They were anxious for her to come. The children were crying again.

She stared at the long creeping lines under the door—coming—coming—

"Yes, I'm dressed."

Something fearful which ought not to be happening—was happening anyway. Water slipping that way, snake-like, over your bedroom floor.

She tiptoed over the long ribbon-like lines and opened the door. Mr. Johnson had the convalescing Katie in his arms. Mrs. Johnson had Marie and the little boy by the hands. The water snaked and slipped all over the sitting-room, over the fat red and green Axminster roses and under the cheap upright piano. It oozed around the basket of stereopticon views under the center table, and

287

Mrs. Johnson tiptoed through it and set them up on the stand.

The stair door stood open. Mr. Johnson was pushing his wife ahead of him toward it and telling the children to hurry along.

The water ran everywhere now,—bolder and more of it. Tiptoeing didn't do much good,—the red roses were almost obliterated. Some one was pounding or sawing upstairs.

"Shan't we get in the car?" She didn't know whether she whispered or shouted it. "And drive away from this?"

"There's no way," Mr. Johnson said shortly. "It's a regular river . . . everywhere."

"Down the highway?"

"Can't see the highway."

They went up the narrow stairs, the children thumping loudly in their heavy, unlaced shoes.

It seemed good to be up here where everything was dry. It was queer, though, to be in these strange upstairs rooms with a Mr. and Mrs. Johnson whom you did not know well,—the beds not made,—clothes scattered about, —a teddy-bear hanging over the side of a crib.

She knew now what had been making the noise up here. The hired man was cutting a hole in the ceiling of the smallest bedroom. For heaven's sake . . . he didn't think . . . ?

"I'm so sorry . . ." Mrs. Johnson said through her tightly closed teeth. There was a frozen sort of attitude about her, trying to be polite as on the evening before, but frightened to death. "So sorry . . . for this . . .

when you come, Miss Meier. So good to see about Katie
. . . You could be . . . in the dry . . . there in Irving."

Yes, why had she picked to-day . . . no, yesterday, to
come out here? Why do people do queer things . . . on
certain dates? Grandpa used to say no one knew whether
it was Providence or Lady Luck or the Spinning Fates.

Any other previous night on which she might have
chosen to come out here to see her pupil, this water-in-
the-house accident never would have occurred.

But that was always the way,—no matter what happened, people never knew it was *going* to happen, and
so they were always caught doing just the ordinary things
of life. That was why they had found the people of the
Pompeiian ruins in front of ovens and at the bath and
asleep. Heavens, that was a cheerful thought to drag in
just now,—the ruins of Pompeii. Lots of catastrophes in
the world. You read about them in the papers. People
trapped in queer ways. It always seemed so senseless
and stupid when you were reading it. "What were they
doing there?" you always said. Perhaps they couldn't
help it. Perhaps they were sometimes caught. But
nothing could happen here a mile out of Irving, Nebraska,
in the peaceful Republican Valley, in this day and age,
with electricity and radios and telephones and automobiles and . . .

Mr. Johnson came back from the stairway. His eyes
looked frightened and his face above the sandy mustache
was ashy white. "It's a lot higher," he said quietly.

Hazel slipped back to look down the well of the stairway and felt a definite illness at the sight. The dark
water lapped and slapped against the third or fourth stair,

—a chair floated, lightly hitting the door jamb back and forth with little insistent taps, and a fat red pin-cushion bobbed about like a bright-colored floater on an invisible fish-line.

She went back to the Johnsons and the hired man with the cross-eyes and the crooked nose.

"Don't stand, Miss Meier. Sit down." Even yet Mrs. Johnson's hospitality had not forsaken her.

It was queer how quiet every one was. Even the children, sensing something beyond them, stopped crying and only clung to their parents. The little boy wanted his teddy, and Hazel slipped into the tumbled bedroom and brought it to him. She pulled Marie onto her lap, keeping her arms around her. She felt close to these strange Johnsons, closer to them than to most of her friends. When we get out of here, I'll always be their friend, she thought,—I'll come out often to see them.

It was gray daylight now. One could see out of the small bedroom windows,—if one had the temerity to look.

Water! Water rushing through the barnyard. She could tell it was the barnyard for the big barn still stood there, even though a hayrack and a lumber-wagon floated with the current.

The high foundation was stone or cement and the upper part was frame, probably painted the usual barn red. In the gray dawn only a little of the white stone was still showing so that it looked like a fat old lady holding up her skirts from the wet. As she looked, a horse floundered through the water, head up, swimming, thrashing about for solid ground. A chicken-coop whirled crazily about with an old hen and chickens squatted precariously on top.

And now the water seemed rushing harder. There was more of a current. Mr. Johnson went back to the stairway. "My God!" They all heard him. "On the roof!" he called as he ran back.

He helped his wife up on a chair which he placed on the flat-topped bureau. She looked funny trying to squeeze her heavy bulk through the hole that Nils had sawed out. That is, she *would* have looked so if the world hadn't suddenly lost all its fun.

When she was through, Mr. Johnson helped the sick Katie up the same way. Then the little boy. Then Marie. "Hang to Mamma tight," he said each time.

"Now, you . . . Miss Meier." Mr. Johnson took hold of her, and the cross-eyed Nils steadied the chair on the bureau. No one said anything. One couldn't believe that people would stay so quiet under stress.

Hazel pulled herself through the hole and worked her way close to Mrs. Johnson and the children. The roof was wet and sloping and she had to be very careful to keep her footing.

It was frightening out here,—much more so than in the house. The height of the roof, the great puffy clouds billowing so close overhead, the dark rushing water below! It made her feel a distinct nausea, and very chilly. She was shaking uncontrollably. It was noisier here, too. One couldn't know that water would make so much noise, —whirling, sucking, rushing.

Much of the time she felt dazed, as though she were an onlooker at something of which she was not a part. It was a movie on the screen and the suspense would soon be over. Or a bad dream and after awhile she would awaken. But the nightmare persisted. The movie went on, reel after reel.

Mr. Johnson came up through the hole and then Nils, his cross-eyes appearing grotesquely above the aperture, then his crooked nose.

"If it once on its foundation stays yet a'ready," he volunteered.

If it stays . . . ! The house? Whatever put that silly notion in his head? Houses always stayed where they were built. Of course it would stay.

Pigs went by, tumbling along right side up or upside down,—anyway. Chicken-coops. A wagon-box with a dog standing shiveringly in it. A hayrack still partly loaded. And then . . . "Oh, don't look, Mrs. Johnson" —a woman on a house roof, clinging, crying, calling out to them. A woman on a house *that had not stayed on its foundation.*

Helpless, they watched her whirled on through the flood waters.

And now Hazel knew. They, too, might be whirled away with the current.

"Daddy, I'm cold," little Marie was saying. Without a word Mr. Johnson slipped off his coat to put around her.

"How about you, Katie?" Nils wanted to know. "Mebbe you have Nils' coat, huh?" And that came off, too.

Hazel was thinking about people,—homely, uninteresting people, people to whom she had never given a second thought. How different they seemed when you knew them,—when you were on a wet roof with them and the whole world had turned to water.

And now rain fell. The water below whirled by with that peculiar rushing, sucking noise. Water from the skies beat upon them. They cowered under its pommeling force. Mrs. Johnson, clinging to the wetness of the roof, bent her body low over Katie who had been sick, shielding her as best she could from the onslaught. Mr. Johnson held Marie in his arms.

"Don't let go of Jimmie a minute, Nils."

"I won't."

They clung to the roof over which the water ran, while water from the sky pounded them, and water below rushed darkly past. There was no solidity in anything. The world had gone mad, for everything in it was liquid. There was no world at all,—nothing but water.

Then the rain ceased. They could move their stiffened bodies slightly, pull the soaked clothing away from cold beaten flesh, push sodden hair from their eyes, change the position of aching bones.

Mr. Johnson broke the long silence.

"You all right, Mama?" cheerfully.

"Yes, I'm all right?" quietly.

"You all right, Miss Meier?"

"Yes, thank you."

"Too bad . . . by golly . . . when you come to see us so good."

"I want to go back in our house" from the little boy. The girls were crying.

Nils cracked a joke for them. "Don't make more water

wid tears, girls. We got enough water already yet,—huh?"

And now there was some conversation,—all with one import. Some one would get them. There would be people out in boats. Not for long would the neighbors let them stay here.

Neighbors! Mr. Johnson looked up and down the valley. The waters ran darkly as far as he could see. A wagon-box went by,—a horse swimming with the current. Small objects bobbed up and down here and there, —a chicken-coop, boxes, boards.

And then it happened,—the sickening thing which made of Hazel a mad young woman whose eyes would not believe their seeing, nor her ears their hearing, nor any sense function sanely. It all came quickly with crashing, horrible sounds and wrenching movements of the only solid thing in the world. Under them somewhere, solidity moved and dipped and whirled in circular fashion. Mrs. Johnson screamed and clutched the air. Katie was thrown into the gray space. Then Mr. Johnson holding to Marie and grabbing for Katie. Bodies hurtled off the turning building. Staring, uncomprehending, she saw Marie's pink dress for a moment before it sank. Mr. Johnson, his face in the water a dead white mask, came up, swam a way,—and she looked no more.

The roof to which she clung was moving down the current. Nils, too, was clinging near her, his arm still around the little boy who was crying loudly.

"Where did Daddy and Mamma go? I want to go in my house."

"Sh, darling. You're all right. Nils and I will take care of you."

And now the roof under the three went on down the stream, sometimes dipping a little, sometimes whirling in a cross-current. Hazel knew there was no further fear to which she could be subjected than this. She had reached the depths of terror. This was the end of fear, for it was the end of life itself.

But there was one more dread. Nils told her about it, —cautioned her about what to do. The house was making for the top of a grove of trees, or apparently so,—one couldn't tell, for it was subject to so many cross-currents. If it caught in the trees, it might be their salvation. On the other hand, if it struck with force, tree branches could sweep them off into the water. If the house approached it, she was to use all her wits about avoiding that,—was to lie flat, face downward. He would hold Jimmie tightly down by him.

Now, all of life consisted of knowing whether this was to happen or not. They moved, dipped fearfully, swayed, whirled sickeningly. The grove was to the right, no, straight ahead of them,—to the right again. Now it loomed up in front of them. Green dripping foliage and gnarled brown branches were there straight ahead. She pulled her beret down tightly over her ears and lay flat down, face concealed in an arm, clung tightly with one hand, and crooked the other elbow over the roof ridge. The branches swept her, tore at her skirt and jacket and hose. Heavy rain-drops shaken from them pelted her.

When all motion had ceased, she raised her head into the twigs and leaves of a tree top. Protecting her face, she peered through. Nils and Jimmie had withstood the impact, too. Jimmie was beyond the crying stage now, lay supinely on the wet roof, tired out, his teddy-bear in his arms.

"If once it holds together and don't go to crackin' up already yet," Nils volunteered.

Sometimes he climbed carefully from branch to branch trying to see out better, sighting their location. Sometimes he crawled stealthily about the roof top looking over into the dark waters. Often he shouted, his voice, used to hog-calling, echoing across the waters.

She marveled at his patience with Jimmie. There was a place where a stout branch had wedged itself across the roof. Against this he placed the child who slept now on his hard, wet bed.

Time wore on and she did not know whether it was minutes or hours that went by. Whatever it was it had no end. It was eternity. There was no sight but green branches and water,—no human sounds but their own.

Jimmie woke and cried with hunger.

Perhaps it was early afternoon,—they could not tell for the sun was hidden in the gray of the clouds,— that Nils came to his decision to swim,—he would go downstream with the current working gradually toward the right. He knew the gamble of it, but he was assuming it stoically.

"If I get there, I bring help. If I don't, we ain't no worse off anyway, huh?"

"Oh, Nils . . . are you going to? I don't think I can look after Jimmie and hang on, too."

"Yah . . . you can all right. You're a strong girl. Betcha you play that there tennis."

He stripped to underwear, felt his way carefully from branch to branch, looked back: "If . . . I don't make it . . . and you're found all right . . . would you get word to my ma on the Missouri mud flats just below Omaha . . . Mrs. Christine Jensen?"

"I would, Nils . . . oh, I *would*. But you'll get there."

"Yah . . . I'll get there . . . maybe."

"Good luck, Nils."

Nils was gone into the dark waters. She could hear the steady splash of his strokes and then the sound ceased.

And now there was no such thing as time,—nothing but pain in one's wrists and fingers, and a wet numb body that would soon fail to function.

Now there was nothing but a clinging to the wet roof wedged in the branches that still swayed sickeningly with the current,—watching the orphaned child sleeping there against the heavy limb, ready to grab for him if, as Nils had suggested, the roof might break up with the pounding. Nothing to do but cling and pray,—watch and think.

CHAPTER XXXIX

NEAL was having the experience of a puncture a half-mile from home with the exasperating knowledge that he had taken the jack out to use for his father's car and failed to put it back. With a few choice epithets directed exclusively toward himself, he started down the highway toward home,—a paved highway now. And although he gave no thought to that fact, so used was he to it, if he had done so, he could have called the roll of the various periods through which that highway had progressed. Pathless prairie grass. Grassy road. Dirt road from which all sign of green had vanished. Graveled highway. Pavement. In the valley, the evolution of that road was the history of the people who lived beside it.

He had not gone but a few paces until a roadster drew up and a woman called to him. "Hello, hitch-hiker."

"Oh, hello, Miss Schaffer." The trained nurse from Omaha who came sometimes to the valley to visit her brother.

He rode to the gate with her. She was immaculate, well groomed, exuded freshness.

"So you're going to marry a University girl, Neal?"

" 'So you *were* going to' is a little more appropriate now."

"Oh, Neal . . . I'm sorry I bungled."

"That's all right. You can't keep news like that in cold storage,—not in this neck of the woods anyway."

It took such a moment for a half-mile's drive. Rose Schaffer wished that it might have been longer. "Believe me, Neal, I hope . . . with all my heart whatever happens to you, it will be for the best."

"Thanks—for the interest."

He might have shown his surprise at her words more than he intended, for she laughed, then said quickly: "You know how old maids are, incorrigibly romantic. And besides, they say I helped save your life once when you were a small codger, so I've a right to be interested in your welfare."

As he turned into the graveled driveway, old Amalia came to the door of her little house and peered out.

"Evidently laying for me," Neal said to himself.

She looked so tiny standing there just at the stoop's edge, her hands holding to the door jamb to steady herself.

"Joey!" She was calling to him and motioning.

Neal walked up the path toward her cottage to see what she wanted. It made no difference which name she used,—Joe or Neal,—whichever one was nearer to her responded. Sometimes she called them "Emil" or "Fritz," too. No one ever corrected her.

"Der iss news," she called.

She was at it again. Well, he would have to humor her.

Ships in trouble far out at sea and Omaha shoe sales, talk of foreign wars, and the local grain elevator's receipts, deaths of people of whom she had never heard, and the five babies all at one time in Canada,—they were all exciting to her, one of as much consequence as another. It gave her a sense of importance to tell it and have them listen as though interested.

Always when a news period was ended she came to her door to see if there was some one to whom she could call out what she had just heard. Two or three items out of the whole list were all she could remember. Sometimes she garbled those until they were no news at all. Usually she was a bit of a nuisance with any of it. But they tried to be patient,—she was so palpably pleased at the telling.

Neal had to laugh to himself now as he walked toward her. The little news-hound, he thought, her own radio certainly had given her a new lease on life.

"Well, did a man bite a dog, Grandma?"

"No. . . . So long as I am living, Joey, a man biting a dog I never knew. But do not get me off . . . or already I forget. Neal, dere iss trouble by de big rains. Rivers go over. Towns iss swept away. People iss in trees hanging. Railroads iss gone. All iss water where vas de farms."

"Where, Grandma? In Hong-Kong, Czechoslovakia, or Tasmania?"

"No. Close by . . . I remember. It was in de Valley of de Republican River. Some folks ve know in pioneer days by name Weitzal stayed at our house and vent on to de Valley of de Republican. Dey had to sleep on de floor. I remember, dey had dere own bedding . . ."

Neal was not laughing at Grandma now, nor listening to her prattle of a family by the name of Weitzal in pioneer days who had to sleep on the floor on their own bedding.

He was standing in the path and scowling at her. "What towns, Grandma? What towns are swept away?"

"I forget vich, Joey. Alvays I forget . . ."

"Was Irving one? Try hard to remember."

"It sounds so, Neal. Irwing? . . . Yes . . . I tink . . ."

Neal turned and went into the big house, still scowling. He felt a curious fright that he could not shake off. It was silly, too, for Grandma was so unreliable. Probably the catastrophe was in Oregon instead of Nebraska,—maybe it was fire instead of water,—and a few other points of misinformation. Maybe she had heard part of a play. Several times she had mistaken one for a real happening. One morning she had come all the way over to the house in her slow way to tell them about a group of people being lost in the desert and it proved to have been one of the Death Valley plays.

But he went to the 'phone and called for information. Yes, it was true. There was a flood of gigantic proportions over a large area of the Republican Valley . . . probably several hundred lives lost . . . millions of property damage.

"How about the town . . ." his throat was dry, ". . . the town of Irving?"

News was meager, but that was one of the places reported in a bad way.

He hung up the receiver, ran to the garage for the jack, went back to fix his car, drove home, had a hurried bath and change of clothes, and came down to tell his mother he was driving to Lincoln and possibly would go on to the flood district.

Myrtie was worried and fearful for him, but he paid no attention to her complaints, went out to see his father for a minute, and was gone down the gravel driveway in his roadster.

In Lincoln he went directly to the Meier apartment. Carter was home with Lucile,—both worried to distraction. All morning they had been trying to get in communication with Irving or some point near there. The town was as isolated as a foreign planet.

A plane carrying a newspaper man had gone over and was not back yet, Carter told Neal.

"A plane,—that's the idea," Neal said. "I'll see if I can go over that way."

Lucile told Neal about a letter from Hazel that had come in that morning. It had been scribbled at the morning recess the day before, mailed at noon, had arrived on the evening train and been delivered that morning. In it she had mentioned going out to one of her pupils in the country.

"That probably took her farther away from the river," Neal said cheerfully. "Or closer," he was thinking.

In the midst of the conversation Hazel's mother suddenly said: "I've just remembered, Neal . . . I thought you and Hazel . . . ? She wrote me . . ."

For the first time during these anxious moments Neal gave his old boyish grin. "I guess I'd forgotten it, too. Officially our engagement wasn't just what it had been previously. This interest on my part is off the record."

It relieved them both immensely to laugh. It seemed to assure each one that Hazel could not help but be all right now.

But they came back to the letter several times. Neal had Hazel's mother read the part again carefully in which she told of her movements—a careless little note written with no thought that a few hours later her family would hang on every word.

> Am going out to a Johnson family's home this afternoon in the school bus with my little Marie. (I always think of Booth Tarkington's Little Marie of Kansas City.) Katie Johnson, also my professional property, has been sick for several days,—nothing catching, so don't worry,—and now she's sitting up and Dear Teacher is invited out to supper,—not dinner,—supper, for which I have been informed we are having *spare*-ribs. Papa Johnson will bring me home afterward, or pending another hard rain of which we are having no end, I can stay all night in the *spare* bedroom. Woodman, *spare* that tree.

It was so like her, gay and flippant, that it brought her clearly before them all. The three who had been so worried about her, stood there together, each thinking: "She's all right. Nothing could have happened to her. To other people out there, maybe, but not to Hazel."

When he left them, Neal said: "I'll get to her some way. And I'll get in touch with you as soon as I can. If you don't hear, don't worry. I'll be driving, walking, flying, or swimming."

They followed him out to the lobby door,—anxious, wanting to go with him, sending their hearts along.

"Oh, she's all right."

"Yes, as safe as she can be."

"Of course. But I rather think I'll go see for myself. Good-by."

"Good-by, Neal." It was just a little spat they had, Lucile was thinking.

"Good-by, Neal." Twenty-four, thought Carter, what wouldn't I give to be twenty-four again.

CHAPTER XL

CLINGING—watching—thinking,—life had resolved itself into these three functions for Hazel. Sometimes it seemed the easiest thing in the world just to relax and let go. There would be a few moments of dread, a few moments of swimming with the current, then oblivion, for she could see nothing within her own swimming distances to which to go. Clumps of trees, emerging from the rushing water, another marooned building far in the distance,—nothing better than the roof to which she must still cling.

And there was the child, thrown so strangely in her care, sleeping his troubled, sighing sleep against the wet branch. No matter how painful the clinging nor how dulled her mind she must not forsake him.

There was no sound nor sight of help. Nils, then, had failed. Poor Nils,—so nervy about it all.

In the stillness and the vastness of the flood, then, she grew deathly frightened, panic-stricken.

Up to now something had sustained her in all the horrible experience,—that it would soon be over, that some one would come. But now hope was giving away,—maybe her sanity with it. She cried out, and the little boy cried too at the sound, so that she forgot her own fright and comforted him.

His helplessness steadied her, and under her soothing words he fell again into his troubled slumber.

It seemed late afternoon. Night would soon be coming on. That would mean death, for she could not cling through the night. Her thoughts centered on life as she had known it, as though the thinking could give it back to her. What a glorious thing it was at its very poorest! The hours she had most disliked,—how she would welcome them now! The simplest things would give her pleasure,—the gifts of life we accepted so casually, how beautiful they were.

Three people centered her life,—Mother, Dad, Neal. She saw them all as through a long vista. They were standing there at the end of it waiting for her to come,— were holding out their arms to her, but she couldn't go because she had to cling to this wet roof. They held her,—the wet rotting shingles and the green branches over them, and would not allow her to go where Dad and Mother and Neal were waiting.

Suddenly she remembered a queer thing her grandfather had said the last week of his life. He had been asleep, and half waking, had called out sharply: "Sands! The sucking sands! They hold you back and will not let you go."

She, too, knew the agony of being held back and not allowed to go.

And now she felt only an unselfish sympathy for the three she loved most. She pictured their sorrow until in the torture of it her mind could no longer stand the thought and turned in anguish from it.

She and Neal had quarreled about something, so trivial now she scarcely gave it space in her mind. Dad.

Mother. Neal. She said the names over as a nun says her beads.

She had but those three thoughts, and the thoughts were prayers. Dad. Mother. Neal. Those, and "God, but give me back my everyday living and I will use it to the full."

All the extraneous matters of life were swept away with the flood waters. All the foolish unnecessary things which surrounded it were vanished from her mind as the fields were vanished from the landscape. Life was a simple thing of love and work and courage. Nothing else mattered. To have those, one had everything.

She dropped her head into her arm, tried to still the throbbing and the aching of it with a cramped numb hand. But the pain was sharper,—the throbbing grew loud and louder until it filled—

She jerked her head from her stiff arm, sat up suddenly.

The throbbing was a plane flying low, circling over the flood waters,—a great wide-winged bird throbbing its message of hope. She pulled the now wakened Jimmie to her. She waved, called, cried out. Jimmie added his three-year-old voice to it. They must have seen her for they went around her in one complete circumference of flight, then disappeared rapidly in the distance.

She could not tell how long the time,—it only seemed interminable,—until she saw the two boats. They bobbed about sickeningly at times in the cross-currents. Once it appeared that one would be swamped. Those who were managing them certainly knew their business.

"See, Jimmie, the boats are coming for us."

"I know, it's my Daddy."

Hazel hugged him tightly. "No, Jimmie, it isn't Daddy. Jimmie, have you . . . have you anybody besides Daddy and Mother? Have you any grandma or aunties?"

"I've got my Grandma Johnson and my Grandma Snell and my Aunt Callie and my Aunt . . ."

Wet-eyed, she kissed him.

"I'm glad, Jimmie,—more glad than you can ever know."

The first boat came up, bumping against the trees and the submerged part of a house that had once been a home with a rug of red roses and stereopticon views and a wedding nightgown.

"Oh, Nils, you did make it . . . and you got some dry clothes on and came back. How good you are."

Very soon she was to learn of a hundred incidents like that one, of the reactions of various types of humans under pressure, of the resourcefulness of the rescued and the rescuers, of evidences everywhere of the Nebraska pioneer spirit which had not died out in the third and fourth generations.

She was to know of the rescue of the men marooned for twenty-four hours on a light plant, and of the big gravel-pumping raft floating down the river to them as though Providence had taken a hand in the situation, of the groups clinging to the roofs of houses and trees saved by heroic deeds, and of others which vanished into the boiling current. She was to hear of men rescued from their perilous positions of sixteen hours changing into dry clothing that they in turn might help, of doctors braving the torrents to get to isolated districts to bring new babies into the harassed territory, and of tired women serving coffee until too worn out to go on.

She was to see the shambles of town homes and farms, the washed-out paved highway and the twisted railroad tracks with ties standing as upright as so many fence posts.

It was only later that she was to see the valley peaceful again and new farm homes go up, villages rebuilt and Nature begin to cover her ugly scars with verdure.

It took planning and care to get Jimmie safely down into the first boat. Nils and the man with him pulled away. The second boat came up then.

"*Neal.*"

"Hello, Pink-Hair."

"*Neal* . . . where did you come from? Was it you in the plane?"

"Yes. What do you mean, Woman, by getting stranded on a desert isle with a cross-eyed man and appearing later with a child?"

And now Hazel was down, too, in a swaying boat which a strange man was helping Neal handle. And absurdly enough, Hazel was crying,—sobbing and crying in the reaction of their coming.

Neal comforted her as best he could with the boat unsteady in the current. She clung to him, a little girl who had looked upon Death and found it awful.

"Neal,—Katie said she hoped I'd finish reading 'Black Beauty' when she got back . . ." and she burst again into loud sobbing.

Hazel snapping come-backs at him as with a rubber sling-shot was nothing new. Hazel a little emotional under a full moon or the spell of an orchestra,—Hazel matter of fact and managerial, giving decided opinions on any subject, ancient or modern,—Hazel as a peppy little tongue-lasher or a gracious social partner,—any and all of these moods were familiar to him. But not this sobbing reaction to a vital experience, nor the anguished tears. It made of her a girl he had never known. She seemed closer to him, tender, more human. He loved her for it.

The two boats navigated the rushing stream back,—in one Neal who had handled oars ever since he could remember, and in the other the cross-eyed Nils Jensen who had spent his boyhood years on the bottoms of the Missouri. It was well for them that they had been water-bugs or they might have been swamped more than once where the ugly water poured heavily around a submerged building or a clump of trees.

As they were coming into the land where people were waiting with blankets and coffee, Hazel said: "Neal, there's one thing I wish you'd promise me,—that if he wants to come, we'll hire this Nils Jensen."

"*We'll* . . . ?" He grinned. "You mean as a law partner?"

And now, life given back to her, Hazel was her old self.

"No,—Muscle-neck,—on our farm."

CHAPTER XLI

IN the early summer Neal took Hazel to his home to meet his people and to see the place where she was to live. She saw the long graveled driveway, the wide sweep of yard under the big trees, the solid old house which Fritz and Emil had built so many years before and which had been modernized with sun-room and furnace and lights in Myrtie's time, and felt a distinct surprise at the lovely old place set so far back from the paved highway.

"In England they'd call it an ancestral home," she admitted when they were circling up the driveway.

A rabbit, bounding across the grass at that moment, Neal said in his light way to cover the emotion he felt: "Ah, the hare! Higgins,—the hounds. We ride at once."

She met Neal's father and mother, warming immediately to his father with his natural dignity and quiet manner. She was not so sure about the mother,—a fluttery little woman whose conversation ran largely to speaking of things she wished she could have or do. She was glad the two were to live over in the small house beyond the lilac hedge.

In the late afternoon Neal took her over to the cottage to meet his great-grandmother.

Hand in hand they sauntered down the old path which led through the bluegrass and the white clover, thick and luxurious again since the great rains.

Neal was a little perturbed as they approached the old house. He wanted in some way to prepare Hazel,—to explain old Amalia to this girl he loved, wished boyishly that he knew how to put her in the best light to this lovely, modern Hazel whose own grandmother had been so different.

"Hazel, you know Grannie is awfully old—eighty-something—I've even lost track of her exact age," he began diffidently. "I guess she's pretty funny looking to strangers,—sort of weather-beaten and toothless and wrinkled as an old walnut. But gosh, she's been awfully good to me . . . you know, cookies in jars, and kiss the bumps and taking care of me when Mother was nervous or away. My dad feels the same way about her. I suppose I can't ever see her the way she must seem to others."

Hazel slipped her arm through Neal's in a sudden tender gesture. For the first time she thought of him as a little boy, felt for a moment much, much older than he. It is eternal Motherhood forever compassionate toward eternal boyhood. "I'll like her, Neal."

To the boy it brought a swift renewed rush of love for her,—he could not have told why. It made him stop in the pathway, suddenly kiss her forehead and her cheek tenderly,—not the kiss of passionate young manhood but a tribute to her friendship and sympathy,—engendered at that moment by a feeling which would be deeper and more lasting than the other.

They went on up the curving path between the petunias toward the little house in which old Amalia had lived for so many years.

They passed the sloping cellar door with the stone crocks in a row, the clump of gooseberries over which the dish-towels dried, and the thick bushes on each side of the steps with their fat cabbage-roses in blossom now.

Old Amalia was just inside the screen door in the sitting-room in which there was all the accumulation of the years,—old blue plates on a shelf and gilded milk-weed pods, a little mirror with blue brush and comb in a tin tray underneath, the sale carpet with its scroll figures tacked tautly over thick oat straw.

Hazel had a feeling that the whole thing was a stage setting or a movie scene,—on the wall the *Guten Morgen* and *Gute Nacht* pictures of the chunky half-nude child with the daisies on her head, the couch with its bright pieced quilt cover, the oval walnut stand on which there were the Bible and some star fish and a blue plush album. There were odors, too, peculiarly fitting to the place,—old clean odors,—soap-suds and mothballs and cinnamon. Whether the latter came from the roses beside the door or the kitchen beyond, she could not tell.

Old Amalia was patching, putting a neat little square in the corner of a table-cloth with small, even stitches. Hazel saw that Neal had described her quite definitely. Her hair, plastered down tightly over the pink spots of her head, was wound in a little hard knob at the nape of her neck. In the big chair she looked as tiny and wrinkled as a little brown gnome.

As the screen door opened she looked at the young people from pale old eyes that had to adjust themselves slowly to the new focus.

"Hello, Grandma. Do you know me to-day?"

313

"Yes. It's Joey," she said with apparent delight at her quickness.

"No . . . guess again. It's Neal . . ."

"Tsk . . . tsk . . . Neal! So big a boy you're gettin' to be."

"No . . . you're fooling, Grannie. I'm only six-feet-one, and one hundred and ninety is all that I weigh."

"And who iss dis?" Old Amalia wanted to know.

"Now this," said Neal, and he slipped an arm around Hazel, and drew her forward, ". . . this needs explaining. *This* . . . is Hazel."

"Hachel?"

"Yes . . . like the other nuts, you know." He grinned, but when he saw old Amalia was not appreciating his little joke, he explained: "She's *my girl*, Grannie. You know I told you about her. We're going to be married."

Old Amalia put out a brown little hand as shrunken as a mummy's. "Excoose me," she said to Hazel with a toothless smile. "Alvays I forget." She spoke apologetically. "Of de long ago I remember . . . but of only yesterday already I forget."

Hazel felt a sudden tenderness toward the little, brown doll of a woman, so shy and so gentle in her broken speech. "Neal has told me about you."

"Neal iss a goot boy. You vill be a goot vife, I hope?" she questioned.

"I hope I'll be."

Old Amalia scanned her closely. "You vill be," she nodded. "A *schön* . . . nice face you have. And your name it is Hachel?"

Neal answered for her. "Yes, Grannie. Hazel Meier,
—but not for long."

"Meier?" old Amalia repeated.

"Hazel Meier," he said it louder and more plainly.
"Her father, Carter Meier, was a banker at Cedar City.
And the old gentleman, Matthias Meier, was Hazel's
grandfather."

"Matthias Meier?" Amalia was confused,—was grasping for something,—some queer puzzle which she could
not piece together. "Has he come, too? To Nebraska
City has he come?"

"He's dead, Grandma. Why, you wanted to go to the
services for him yourself. Don't you remember? When
we read it in the paper? You wanted to go but Dad
thought it was too hot and too far."

"Yes . . . I remember. Alvays I am forgetting . . .
and remembering."

"What, Grandma?" Hazel asked. "What are you
remembering?"

"Just that . . . *immer* . . . alvays . . . spring . . . comes
on . . ."

"That's like a poem I know:

> " 'One thing, I remember:
>   Spring came on forever,
>   Spring came on forever,'
> Said the Chinese nightingale."

"It is so." Old Amalia nodded as though she knew all
things, as though her life had embraced all wisdom.

"Perhaps it makes you remember when you were
young."

315

"*Vielleicht* . . . perhaps . . . it does."

But Neal was impatient now.

"Well, how do you like her, Grannie?"

The old woman's eyes still peered up at Hazel's. She reached out a tiny brown hand and stroked the firm white one of the girl. "*Kleine taube*," she murmured.

"Talk United States, Grandma. What's that?"

"Little dove."

"Little dove . . . my eye! Snapping-turtle you mean."

"Hachel Meier," the old woman nodded as though she understood a very wise and very ancient thing. "So it vill be."

"Can't you get up a little more enthusiasm, Grandma? Say something a little more exciting and strong. You surely like her."

"In German I say it, to her, Neal. '*Ich liebe dich.*' "

"That's better. Well, we'll go now, Hazel,—now that Grannie has leeby-dicked you."

They said good-by to the old lady sitting there in her big rocking-chair like a little brown Buddha, and went happily down the path between the fat cabbage roses and the petunias.

Amalia watched them go,—tall, strong, young. For a time she sat there quietly, saying something over to herself as one learns a lesson by rote.

She must think this thing out very carefully and be sure she had it right. She knew she was apt to imagine things that were not true and forget those that were real. It was very hard to know always which ones had happened and which were but dreams.

This was different. This must never get mixed with

the fancies. It belonged here and now among the things that were true. She must not allow it to slip away from her into the shadows,—must hold it as steadily in her mind as she was holding to the chair.

There was something she wanted to do,—something she would do at once while she remembered.

She pulled herself out of her rocker and picking her way carefully from table to chair, went into her bedroom. All the time she held steadily to this queer new thing so that she would not forget any part of it. Sometimes that happened, too,—recalling only a portion of a thing, so that the half-memories worried and distressed her. But this one was still wholly clear.

She opened the bottom drawer of her dresser and removed an unwieldly-looking bundle wrapped in very old muslin, yellowed and worn. This she unwound layer by layer until she had uncovered a long box. It was ornamented with sea shells, angel-wings and moon shells, Roman snails and other fragile, fan-like shells of a sea she had never seen. They were broken and nicked and unglued in places so that ugly brown patches of the wooden frame showed through. Almost were they symbolic of things that had never been,—journeys to far-off seas, hearing the sound of wind in whipping sails and the call of the gulls on the sand.

With hands that trembled with their eighty-six years, she lifted a tray and took out two quilt blocks. Strangely enough in the dark of its shelter, the pink had not faded, —only the white was yellowed. A needle in one of the blocks was brown with rust so that it crumbled to the touch. This she removed and replaced with a bright one from the cushion on her bureau. Then from the box she took a darkly tarnished thimble and fitted it to her tiny finger.

Still holding carefully to the thought in her mind as one might hold lovely fragile china lest it drop, she made her way cautiously back to her rocker and sat down to finish the *Baum des Lebens*—Tree of Life—quilt.

CHAPTER XLII

NEAL and Hazel were married in August with the wheat harvested and the corn maturing for its October husking,—a simple wedding in the rented apartment of the Meiers.

Joe and Myrtie with old Amalia drove down to Lincoln in the big car,—Neal in his own roadster. Myrtie had not been any too gracious about taking Grandma, but when Joe said definitely: "Grandma is going if she is able to take the long ride," Myrtie made no further excuses, but merely went about with a martyred air of having more responsibility on her shoulders than any human could quite bear.

She had a new outfit, too, one of the first of the fall suits with a matching hat of beige and her fox furs: "for no telling what elaborate sort of thing Mrs. Meier will wear" she had said to Joe. So she was somewhat astounded now to be met at the door by Hazel's mother in a simple printed silk.

There were only a few present at the ceremony, three of Hazel's sorority sisters, an old family friend, two of Neal's fraternity brothers, the minister and his wife, Carter and Lucile, Joe and Myrtie, and old Grandma Holmsdorfer who stubbornly would not change her name to Holms.

Carter Meier, looking at Hazel in the traveling dress in which she was to be married, wondered how she felt about this simple affair, whether she was missing the pomp of a big church wedding such as her mother had,—as she might have had if things were different. If she were doing so, she was game about it, giving no intimation of her thoughts.

They were all there now, and some one was whispering that it was time. Neal and Hazel were walking over to the mantel with its garden flowers as informally as though they were playing charades and the members of the little group were to guess what they were portraying. The minister took his place. No ushers, no pipe-organ, no "Promise Me," no bridal-veil,—not a hot-house flower, excepting the bridal bouquet. Hazel, in her soft brown going-away suit with egg-shell blouse, golden-yellow roses in her arms,—Neal, well-tailored, a fine-looking, upstanding figure of a chap with keen, honest eyes. University graduates. And there were people in the world who thought all farmers were bewhiskered gents forever chewing on a succession of straws, and their wives drab creatures always standing forlornly at the doorways of shanties.

The minister was speaking: "Dearly beloved . . ." his voice a mere accompaniment to Carter Meier's thoughts. His little girl was being married. What a short while ago they had watched her first baby step,— she had made one little tottering forward movement, and overcome by her own accomplishment let forth a jubilant crow of delight that lost her the equilibrium she had so recently gained.

And now something was getting in Carter Meier's way so he could not see the bride at all: a little girl skipping up and down the lawn of the Cedar City house in the early morning, arms outstretched like a bird's wings,—

on a single roller-skate propelling herself wildly up and down the sidewalk,—riding her Shetland pony around the streets, her dark red mop of curls blowing in the wind . . . his active, happy little daughter! What would her life be? Hard? He would save her from all the blows it would deal her, if he only could,—from all the hard work of it, if it were possible. But who knew, at that, she might be happier than young women to whom work was a foreign thing. In what direction lay happiness anyway?

Joe Holms was thinking: "That's my boy taking the big step. You won't make mistakes all the time, Neal . . . you're different . . . you'll always be different . . ."

Lucile was thinking: "I mustn't cry . . . if I start I couldn't stop. I left my mother without thinking much about it. I must look straight at Hazel and smile so that when she looks at me she can see how happy I am. I *am* happy . . . I *am*. . . . Oh, no, I'm not, I'm miserable and I want to be young again and have my little girl back."

Myrtie was thinking: "He won't care for me any more. He'll take her places and bring gifts to her and give her all the attention."

Old Amalia Holmsdorfer was not thinking about either Hazel or Neal. She was peering with pale watery eyes across the room at Carter Meier, her thoughts in queer confusion: "So that's your boy, Matthias. He isn't as tall as you, and of course he's gray, and you're not. But he holds his shoulders like you, and you would have looked like that if you had lived to be over twenty-one."

CHAPTER XLIII

THERE are those who would call it the end of the story when Hazel Meier married Neal Holms. To say the story is finished is not true, for no mere story can ever be complete, no family history contain a beginning or an end. One may only cut out a bit from life, trimming away all that went before and all that will come after.

It was early September when Hazel returned from her wedding-trip with Neal and went to live in the old house set in the elms and the maples far back from the paved highway.

Strangely enough, then, she was beginning her married life on the same land where old Amalia had homesteaded so many years before but with two great differences— all the wonderful modern surroundings in contrast to the primitive ones of the pioneer days,—and the fact that where Hazel carried the flame of love burning deep in her heart for her young husband, Amalia had known only gray ashes.

Peculiarly, in spite of the difference in the generations, Hazel approached her task much as the young Amalia had once done, vigorously and with responsibility. With her resourcefulness and her power of accomplishment she put her young shoulder to the wheel, mapping out her day's work just as she had planned her University schedule. She allowed no waste about her. Nothing thrown away. Every potato peeling had its use, every bone its nutritive value. "So don't try to get up any debate with *me*," she would laugh, "that higher education unfits woman for the home."

It was characteristic of her that one of the first things she did was to ask Neal's parents if the half-hearted pink stucco could be pulled off the honest old gray stones underneath.

"I'm sure I don't care what you do, Hazel," Myrtie said with tired resignation. "There's so little money to do anything with. I wonder how you have the heart to plan a single change."

Joe and Myrtie were living in the small house with Grandma. But on a morning of that September Myrtie came over, stepping daintily through the bluegrass.

Hazel, finishing the last of her dishes, said: "Come on in the living-room, Mother Holms, where you will be more comfortable." Every one always saw to it that Neal's mother was comfortable.

She washed her hands, followed Myrtie into the living-room where she picked up the braided rug she was making. It was apple green and egg-shell. "How do you like it?" she asked. "I'm using all the old green drapes that were worn out. Grandma showed me how and I'm perfectly fascinated with it. I think it tickled her pink to show me. Isn't it funny—this returning to all the old ways? Ever since I knit my dress I'm crazy about the old hand-craft. I've even gone so far as to think I'd like a loom set up in the vacant bedroom. Maybe I'll weave Neal's clothes yet." And she laughed gaily.

Myrtie did not laugh. "I don't see how you can do such homely things cheerfully, Hazel. Well . . ." she broke off abruptly, "I came over to see you about something rather important. Hazel, you know me well enough by this time to realize that I never beat around bushes. I go straight to the point with sincerity and honesty. You know that, don't you, Hazel?"

"Why . . . yes . . . Mother Holms." She was not sure whether it was complimentary to agree or otherwise.

"Hazel . . . my life has been very difficult." Myrtie pressed her little white hands together, as though she must keep herself well under control before this inexperienced girl. Hazel watched their delicate softness, the narrow gold circlet and the flashing of the big diamond solitaire. As always they fascinated her in their fluttering. Katherine Cornell hands they were, she told herself,— they ran the gamut of all her emotions.

"What I have been through . . . no one of your youth, of course, can realize. Childbirth . . . loss of property . . . disappointments . . . nervousness. Oh, well," she sighed, "we won't go into all that. It would only worry you and needlessly torture myself. When one gets cornered in life—in a trap as it were—all one's ambitions frustrated . . . life all inhibitions . . ."

Hazel could have laughed aloud if this had not been Neal's mother. How little like her he was. She was really very sweet and attractive, too, excepting when she mourned and whined.

"But what can one do . . . or say?" Tears came to Myrtie's eyes, but she threw Hazel a brave little smile. "My husband doesn't understand a woman's aspirations . . . her scope of mental vision . . . her emotional reactions. With all your youth and inexperience, Hazel, you are a woman . . . and you can understand . . . this constant beating of your wings against life . . ."

"Oh, I don't know, Mother Holms." Hazel had a swift memory of black water rushing, of bodies hurled into gray space, of the whirling and dipping of wet, rotten shingles. "I guess I'm just too fond of life as it is to do much beating."

"All my life, Hazel, I've been doing things for people . . . and now . . . that I'm in my middle forties . . ."

"Well, life begins at . . ."

"Hazel," Myrtie leaned forward. There were tears on her lashes. "You spoke just now of the vacant bedroom. What I came to see you about is this: Will you take Grandma back here to live with you?"

"You mean for all the time?" It did not seem right. She and Neal were so young . . . so filled with life and energy. Grandma was so old . . . so very old and childish.

"Yes . . . if you will, Hazel, without Neal or his father knowing anything about my speaking to you. Men can misunderstand motives so easily." Her sensitive lip quivered. "I have spoken to Grandma about it . . . sounding her out before I said anything to you."

"What did Grandma say?"

"She said in her broken dialect: 'When you're as old as I am, Myrtie, it won't make much difference what happens.' So you see,—it's immaterial to her."

All noontime and for several hours later Hazel thought about this new thing, how cleverly Neal's mother was manipulating it, pondered on a half-dozen other times in which she had seemed to attain her ends. Sweet, pleasant, babyish,—how she must have wound Neal's father around her finger all these years. Now she was manipulating this about Grandma as sweetly, as adroitly. "And when Grandma dies before long," thought Hazel, "it will be Mother Holms we all must comfort."

By afternoon Hazel was ready to give her answer. The little Grandmother was not to be hurt or made uncomfortable by it, that was sure. So she went down through the grassy path to the small house. "Wouldn't you like to move over to the big house with us for awhile, Grannie?"

Old Amalia looked up, her faded blue eyes filling. "It's not so goot, Hachel, to live too long."

"*You* haven't lived too long, Grannie. Neal and I want you to come. We've been asking Mother Holms for you. We don't like the vacant bedroom shut up. It just needs a little old German grandma and all her things in there to make it look home-like."

The old woman nodded. "I see. To old German grandmas second sight sometimes Gott gives. You're a goot girl, Hachel."

So old Amalia, always shuttled back and forth, went again to the stone house,—a little old lady who had lived too long, clinging to the flotsam left by the tides of life,— old quilts and scrap-books, albums and tintypes, and a work-box from which the shells were broken.

There is one other thing you will want to know,—did Hazel ever discover that the old grandmother over whom she watched for the short time remaining was the girl of her grandfather's youth? And the answer is yes, she and Neal found it out. Else how could they have pieced together the broken fragments of this story and the strange crossing of paths by their two families?

A certain morning dawned with velvet-pink and lace-lavender and satin-yellow lights in the eastern sky, like so many gay bridesmaids stretching gauzy ribbons for the sun down the aisle of the world. Hazel had been up in time to see this bridal procession of the dawn for there was much work to do.

There was the first feeling of fall in the air. The elms, tawny as lions, lazily dropped a leaf or two. The maples held high their ruby-crowned heads. Over by the creek-bed scarlet-flamed sumac shouldered the silver-green of the willows, and orange-colored bittersweet crept through the tangle of wild plums. Winter wheat was faintly green against the brown of newly plowed earth and the tan of the cornfields. Over all was that haze which clings to the midwest landscape in the autumn,—the soft blue far-away haze which dissipates as one rides into it. It seems always to lie softly over the low rolling hills and the valleys in the fall of the year, this faint ghostly smoke from the Indian camp-fires of long ago.

Hazel, on her way out to the mailbox at the roadside, stopped to look at the picture which lay before her,—the low rolling hills swelled and dipped, black with newly turned earth from the fall plowing, tawny brown with their cornfields, green with the faint shoots of winter wheat.

There was something about the new crispness of the air that was energy-creating. She felt a capacity for

327

turning off work this morning that made her think of a dozen tasks she wanted to do,—clean house, bake, sew. However did some people enjoy being idle? She placed her letters in the box and returned to the house, regretting the fact that she could not stay out here in the open in the crisp early fall air.

Mother Holms was out on the porch of the other house sitting in the morning sun, a knitted lavender jacket around her shoulders. Hazel waved to her and called out some little foolish greeting. At that moment she passed the iron kettle hanging on its two chains and stopped abruptly. Why not try her hand at soap? She had promised herself to experiment with it sometime and what better day than the present one which was so enticing in its call to the out-of-doors?

In anticipation of tackling the job before her, she went into the house and put on an old green turtle-necked sweater, a short brown skirt, and a brown beret which with feminine concern she arranged over her dark red hair as jauntily as though she were to be in the pep chorus on the bleachers. Then she was back in the yard bending over the old iron soap-kettle hanging tipsily on two of its three chains with dirt spilling out from its slanting side, unloosing the snaps, and scraping out the hard clods.

Grandma came to the dining-room door and peered out under a gnarled hand,—old Amalia, short and shrunken and toothless, her little knot of colorless hair twisted as hard as a walnut.

"What be doin', Hachel?" she called in her high, cracked voice.

"I'm going to make soap, Grandma," Hazel said loudly,

and when first the old woman did not understand, repeated it patiently.

"Soap?" old Amalia called back tremulously. "Iss spring comin'?"

"No, Grandma, it's fall."

The old woman came out on the porch then, stepping cautiously, taking careful hold of the pillar to assist herself.   For a few moments she stood blinking, adjusting her old eyes to the brightness of the day, the pools of light on the meadow, and the hills beyond.   Then her face became all wrinkled eagerness.   "I smell spring," she said in her high-pitched voice.

"Do you, Grandma?"

Old Amalia standing there with her head thrown back looked at that moment like a painting by an old master,— as though the girl in Breton's *Song of The Lark* had grown wrinkled and feeble after eighty-six years of listening.

"Iss meadow-larks singin'?" she quavered.

"No, Grandma.   It's too late for meadow-larks."

Old Amalia cupped her ear with knotted, trembling fingers, then broke into a toothless smile.   "I *hear* meadow-larks singin'."

"Oh, all right, have it your own way," Hazel said to herself.   But she knew that old Amalia was hearing only the songs of long-silenced meadow-larks.

At that moment Neal came bounding up from the lower lots, chasing a hog that had worked its grunting way through a broken fence.   The young man's strong legs, encased in their puttees, covered the ground with such twinkling speed that Hazel's laughter rang out.   "Still after the pig-skin?" she called gaily.

Neal tossed her a grin over his shoulder and shouted back: "Score at the end of the hind quarter is nothing to nothing in favor of the pig." And they both laughed at the foolishness, young untroubled laughter.

"What's he say?" Amalia quavered.

"He says he'll get it all right," Hazel called up to the old woman. It took so little to make her cheerful, such small effort to bring childish joy to her.

The hard clods with their decayed flower roots loosened from the kettle's sides now, Hazel went into the kitchen, emerging in a moment with hot water and a short mopstick. As she passed Grandma, the old woman piped: "No soap iss made here for many's de long year."

Hazel, who was saying to herself: "I can believe *that*," smiled back at Grandma when she questioned: "Hachel, iss you knowin' the soap-kettle come across country from Illinois wid me?"

"Yes, I know."

As a matter of fact, she knew nothing about it, for it was the first time the old kettle had ever been mentioned since her marriage, but the answer would keep Grandma from prattling on indefinitely. In that hope Hazel was mistaken, however, for old Amalia was not to be squelched with such ease. "Dere's more about de kettle dan you know," she called childishly, nodding her head.

Unheeding, Hazel went on with her preparations. Never having made any soap in her life she went into the venture with gay energy.

And so there was to be soap again in old Amalia's kettle that so many years before had rocked tipsily on its rounded bottom in the covered wagon crossing the creek-beds and the hummocky prairie lands. But how could Hazel know this about the old iron kettle? How could she comprehend the fact that in its varied uses . . . soap . . . hog mash . . . geraniums . . . and soap again . . . it had gone through the whole cycle of the changing economic problems of the midwest? And how could she understand that the fate of both,—the humans in two families and the ugly inanimate black thing at her feet,— had been so inextricably bound together for several generations? That the story, perforce, of the old iron kettle was the story of the people themselves?

So she only scrubbed away at the blackness of the old thing with its dangling chain, knowing that she could make good use of the grease from past butcherings. And old Amalia stood on the porch shading her watery eyes from the hazy fall sunshine, and because she was confused in her mind, kept calling out odd, inconsequential things.

Neal, having performed the difficult task of getting his animated pig-skin across the goal line of the hog-lot, came around the corner of the house then, a hammer in his hand from the task of mending the fence.

A little hammer began to tap in Hazel's heart, too,—a happy little trip-hammer as she watched him come up the path in the morning sunshine. She and Neal, together . . . night and day . . . day and night! A bridal procession across the sky in the morning dawn,—and a bridal procession in Hazel's heart!

"What're you doing, Red-top?" He came up to the scene of activities.

"Making soap, Pig-chaser."

"Well, s'ope springs eternal in the human breast," was his cheerful rejoinder.

And then, suddenly, old Amalia, who lately could never recall a thing that occurred the day before, but who would clutch at and grasp the happenings of long ago, like small bits of floatage from the past, said loudly: "Matthias Meier! Matthias Meier was his name."

Hazel raised her head. "What was that you said, Grandma?"

"Matthias Meier. My kettle for me in Illinois he made." And now Amalia was not old and toothless and wrinkled but young and pink-cheeked with hair the color of cornsilk before the summer sun has seared it. "Come here, Hachel. You want I should tell you somet'ing? Sunday afternoons I slip out and by de soap-kettle in de voods I meet him." She chuckled slyly. "Vile my fader sleeps."

Hazel, standing motionless, stared at the ancient woman. "Neal," she said in so queer a tone of voice that startled, he, too, turned and gazed questioningly at the old woman. "Do you hear what she's saying?"

"Yes . . . but don't pay any attention . . . she's like that a lot lately."

"Neal . . . my grandfather came from Illinois. He worked there in a foundry. He made kettles. And he told me once . . ." her voice was low, tense, every statement crisp with fact, ". . . that he came west because of a broken romance . . . that his first sweetheart married some one else. He said that she was a beautiful girl . . ." she finished in a whisper, ". . . named *Amalia*."

She reached out her hand gropingly to Neal so that he

took it quickly. Without moving, the two stared across at the little old woman, brown as a mummy, clutching the porch pillar and shading her eyes with a bird-claw hand.

Then, although Neal had not the slightest idea what his young wife meant when she said brokenly: "It is better to remember our love as it was in the springtime," he saw the mist of tears in her eyes,—something vaguely sad, too, and infinitely tender in her sensitive face,—so that he slipped his arm about her and drew her close, as though by so doing he could forever keep Love from growing old and shrunken and bleary-eyed.

For a time they were all poised there motionless in one of those unusual moments when ordinary life is brushed by the wings of drama,—the young lovers, an old, old woman and a rusted iron kettle whose history was the history of them all.

But already old Amalia was moving and speaking,— already she had forgotten that which so recently she had remembered.

"Meadow-larks iss singin'," she called out in her high cracked voice, "and I smell spring."